STRONG HEAT

The door opened and Lisha looked over her shoulder. Her eyes widened a bit at the man who stepped inside the room. He was tall and broad shouldered with narrow hips. His body was lean but obviously strong and he wore form-fitting jeans with a printed shirt. His face was simply handsome with strong cheekbones, chin and brows. He had long lashes around his slanted eyes and full lips. The silver flecks in his closely cropped soft hair didn't detract from his looks. Oddly, they enhanced them.

The brother was all the way fine. *All* the way.

Lisha was surprised at how fast her pulse raced and the way she literally felt breathless and alive, like the energy in the room kicked up a notch from his presence. She blinked rapidly to break the spell and looked away from him as she licked her suddenly parched lips.

Also by Niobia Bryant

Strong Family Series

Heated

Hot Like Fire

Give Me Fever

The Hot Spot

Red Hot

Friends & Sins Series

Live and Learn

Show and Tell

Never Keeping Secrets

Mistress Series

Message from a Mistress

Mistress No More

Mistress, Inc.

Make You Mine

Reckless (with Cydney Rax and Grace Octavia)

Heat Wave (with Donna Hill and Zuri Day)

Published by Dafina Books

STRONG HEAT

NIOBIA BRYANT

Kensington Publishing Corp.
http://www.kensingtonbooks.com

DAFINA BOOKS are published by

Kensington Publishing Corp.
119 West 40th Street
New York, NY 10018

All Kensington Titles, Imprints, and Distributed Lines are available at special quantity discounts for bulk purchases for sales promotions, premiums, fund-raising, and educational or institutional use. Special book excerpts or customized printings can also be created to fit specific needs. For details, write or phone the office of the Kensington special sales manager: Kensington Publishing Corp., 119 West 40th Street, New York, NY 10018, attn: Special Sales Department, Phone: 1-800-221-2647.

Dafina and the Dafina logo Reg. U.S. Pat. & TM Off.

ISBN-13: 978-0-7582-8716-8
ISBN-10: 0-7582-8716-X
First Kensington Mass Market Edition: December 2013

eISBN-13: 978-0-7582-8717-5
eISBN-10: 0-7582-8717-8
First Kensington Electronic Edition: December 2013

10 9 8 7 6 5 4 3 2 1

Printed in the United States of America

"As we grow older together, as we continue to change with age, there is one thing that will never change. I will always keep falling in love with you."

—Karen Clodfelder

Prologue

"How does that look, Kael?" Lisha Strong asked as she stepped back from the fireplace to study the large lit wreath she'd just hung above it.

At the continued silence of her husband of over forty years, she looked over her shoulder and then arched a brow to see his eyes resting on the curve of her bottom and not on the Christmas decorations. She cleared her throat and crossed her arms over her ample chest.

His deep-set hazel eyes slowly traveled up her body, not missing one bit of her curvy form in the deep green jersey dress she wore. "I've only got eyes for you, darlin'," he said, with clear appreciation of the V-neck top and full skirt floating above the thick legs he loved.

Lisha licked her lips and eyed him with a coquettish smile. It was her turn to take him all in. How good his caramel complexion looked in the chocolate sweater and matching cords he wore. His handsome square face was all the more distinguished by his silver ha ir. His towering height and broad shoulders were still solid and toned from decades of farming. His smile was still the one to make her heart swell just like it did all those years ago. "Our family will be here any minute, Kael," she said, crossing the floor of their living room to massage his shoulders in an obvious consoling gesture before turning away from him.

"Oh, hell, no," he said, wrapping a strong arm around her waist and pulling her body closely up against his. "Lock the door. Let's spend Christmas in bed."

She smiled as he pressed kisses to the base of her neck. "You still sprung after all these years," she teased, rubbing large circles across his back.

Kael leaned back and looked down at her. "And don't you forget that Big Daddy taught you everything you know," he boasted, his voice low and deep and only *slightly* playful.

Lisha moaned in the back of her throat as she let him taste her lips. "Yes, you did," she agreed with enthusiasm.

They both laughed until Kael shifted his large calloused hands down to massage her ample buttocks. Lisha felt her resistance ease away as she kissed her husband, bringing her hand up to press to the back of his head with a moan.

"Aw, man. Viagra is the devil."

At the sound of their son Kahron's drawl, they both opened their eyes and shared a brief look before breaking their kiss and turning to see their entire brood standing in the doorway looking at them. Kahron and Bianca with their six-year-old son, KJ. Kade and Garcelle with teenaged daughter Kadina and toddler son Karlos. Kaeden and Jade. Kaleb, his wife, Zaria, his adult stepdaughters, Meena and Neema, and his son, Kasi Dean, every bit the cutie at close to two years old. And their daughter, Kaitlyn, with her fiancé, Quint, and his fifteen-year-old daughter, Lei.

All of them. Their family.

"Viagra my ass," Kael mumbled for his wife's ears only, mindful of his grandchildren. He moved away from Lisha with obvious regret. "Come on in, you crumb snatchers."

Everyone removed their outer clothing and moved forward to shares hugs, kisses and Yuletide greetings. The house was now filled with not just Christmas décor galore that filled the house with the smell of pine, but also family. Lisha and Kael truly could not regret that as everyone gathered in the living room. Soon they were retelling stories of Christmas morning surprises as they got right to exchanging the brightly wrapped presents surrounding the elaborately decorated tree like a fort.

Lisha smiled her thanks to Jade as her daughter-in-law turned on the television to a station playing soulful Christmas songs. Soon the sound of the

Temptations singing "Silent Night" filled the air, mingling with the comfortable chatter of family gathered together for the holidays.

As Lisha pressed kisses to Kasi's cheek she caught Kael watching her from his spot in his favorite leather recliner. They shared a long heated look.

"Uh-oh," Kadina said from her spot on the floor by the ten-foot Christmas tree.

"Oh, leave them alone," Bianca said, down on all fours as she inspected the wrapped gifts under the tree. "I hope Kahron and I are like that when we are old—"

"Old!" Lisha and Kael snapped in unison, their eyes now on their daughter-in-law.

"Der," she finished with emphasis. "I was going to say old-*er*."

Everyone laughed.

"It was Christmas Day when I first told your momma I loved her," Kael said, rocking back and forth in his recliner as he kept his eyes leveled on his wife.

Lisha's face softened. "Yes, it was, Kael Strong. Yes, it was," she agreed, her eyes glowing from the memory.

"Awwww," the majority of the women sighed in unison.

"Best. Christmas. Ever," she told him.

Kael nodded. "Damn straight. And it needed to be after everything we went through to be together," he said.

They fell silent, lost in the memory as everyone but the children looked on at them as Donny Hathaway's rendition of "This Christmas" filled the air.

"Well?" Kaeden asked, walking over to tap his father's boot with his own.

Kael frowned a bit, looking up at his second eldest child. "Well, what?"

"You're not going to leave us hanging like that, old man," he said, accepting the mug of hot chocolate Garcelle was handing out from a large tray she carried in from the kitchen.

"We're waiting," Kade agreed, taking a cup from his wife as well.

"What are we waiting for?" she asked, her Spanish accent heavy.

"Kael and Lisha were just about to tell us all how they met and fell in love," Zaria filled her in.

Kael and Lisha shared a look.

"Leave out the . . . *warm* moments *please*," Kaleb drawled.

His siblings all agreed.

"Was it love at first sight?" Jade asked.

"Did Kael sweep you off your feet?" Bianca chimed in.

"What was the first date?" Garcelle asked.

Lisha held up her hands from the barrage of questions.

"Did Pop-Pop have any game?" Kadina asked, already sounding like she couldn't fathom that.

Kael pretended to look offended before tossing a pillow softly and hitting her full in the face.

"All right, children, gather up all your Christmas gifts and head up to the playroom," Lisha said, standing up and herding them toward the wide entrance of the living room. "Dinner in an hour or so."

"That is so wack," Kadina mumbled, accepting her squirming little brother from her father as she was guided out of the room as well.

Once the room was cleared of children, the adults all settled in comfortably and turned their eyes to the elders of their family.

Lisha glanced at her husband with love. "I was working as a physical therapist—"

"And dating a bunch of losers," Kael added with a playful smirk.

Lisha shook her head. "The shame of it is . . . he's right. . . ."

Chapter 1

Way back in the day

"*This* one will be different. This *one* will be different. This one *will be* different."

Alisha Rockmon leaned in closer to her reflection in the mirror as she used her pinky finger to remove any of the red lipstick outside of her full lips. She then used her hands to pull the soft ends of her shoulder-length jet black hair forward, liking how the new soft waves framed her round face, emphasized her high cheekbones and the pug little nose she'd inherited from her grandmother. After one last look she turned in the chair and slid on the black wedge heels that matched the wide-leg pants and blouse with sheer sleeves that she wore.

She looked—and most importantly felt—beautiful. She was in good spirits. She'd had a light snack so that she didn't eat like a starving man. Her breath was fresh. Her skin smelled of her floral soap. Her manners were in place. She even said a little prayer for God to send her the man meant just for her. She was absolutely date ready and optimistic about the night.

Just like every other time.

Lisha released a heavy sigh as she sprayed her pulse points with her Charlie perfume. The last year had been made up of a long line of men coming in and out of her life. Some for a few months or a few weeks. Some for just one night. Regardless, they all had made the choice to move on or gave her no choice but to ask them to be gone.

Leaving the bedroom of her one-bedroom apartment in Walterboro, South Carolina, Lisha was just sliding her wallet and keys into her clutch when the doorbell rang. The familiar nerves and anxiety of a first date hit her stomach. She forced herself to take a deep breath as she made her way to the front door.

"This one will be *different*," she mouthed before forcing a smile and opening the door.

"Damn, you look different out of those uniforms, Lisha," Byron Long said, his eyes taking her in from head to toe before he bent down just a bit to press a kiss to her cheek.

Lisha closed her eyes and paused with her face still close to his as she enjoyed the crisp scent of his cologne and the nice wave of awareness she felt for him.

Byron was a surgical resident at the Medical University of South Carolina where she worked as a physical therapist assistant in the outpatient clinic. Their flirtations over the last few weeks had led to him finally asking her out—something Lisha would never have the inclination to do. She didn't think she could ever be that forward with a man.

"You clean up nicely too, Dr. Long," she said, stepping back from him to retrieve her wool overcoat.

He gently took it from her to help her into it. His hands remained on her shoulders and squeezed them gently. She looked over her shoulder at him and smiled softly. "Thanks."

His eyes dipped down to her mouth and moments later he pressed his lips against hers before turning her body to face him and then going in for another kiss.

Lisha froze at the first feel of his tongue pressing against her closed lips. She fought the urge to frown as she backed out of his grasp. A small smack of the lips that took her by surprise? Fine. A deep tonguing down on the first date . . . *before* the first date even truly began? Never.

Byron looked apologetic. "I'm sorry. I couldn't resist. You look so damn fine, Lisha. Shit," he stressed, purposefully looking down at his crotch and then looking back up at her.

Lisha's mouth fell open at the sight of his penis hard against the zipper of his pants. *Lawd* . . .

"Maybe we could skip dinner, deliver in some food and chill right here," he offered, his black eyes darting over to her floral-covered sofa.

And with that Lisha's face became incredulous. "Maybe *not*," she stressed, rolling her eyes as she removed her coat and let the waves of disappointment settle on her.

Byron shrugged. "Okay, we can go eat first," he said, reaching for her coat.

"First?" she asked, moving the coat out of his reach to toss over the back of her sofa.

Byron's eyes shifted to take in the coat and then shifted back to take in her face. He looked confused. "So are we going out for dinner or not?" he asked, stepping forward to rub and then squeeze her rounded shoulders again. "I don't mind skipping right to dessert."

Lisha brushed her hair behind her ears as she licked her full lips and looked up at the man. "I'm a virgin," she said bluntly, loving the myriad of emotions that flitted across his face.

Everything from appearing shocked to looking wary.

"Not a do-again virgin or a play-play virgin," she said, actually enjoying when his hands fell from her shoulders. "My eyes have not seen the glory of the coming of a penis."

It was crass and she knew it. She wanted to shake him up in his shoes.

Byron opened his mouth and then closed it.

"I have made the choice to not have sex until I am married," she said, placing her hands on her ample hips. "I am more than ready to put on my coat and accompany you to a nice dinner where we can talk and get to know each other better . . . but that is *all* I have to offer you tonight or any other night."

Byron frowned. "So I misdiagnosed the vibe you was putting out?" he asked, sliding his hands into the front pocket of his slacks.

Lisha smiled at him. "Yes, if you thought the vibe was sexual."

He grunted and then turned his head to look out her window.

Lisha forced herself not to count the seconds that passed as she watched his inner debate. "Are you having a dilemma right in front of me?" she asked dryly in disbelief, already stepping past him to open the front door.

"Are you sure?" he asked, looking down at her.

Lisha nodded vigorously as she pressed her hands to his lower back to guide him out onto her doorstep. "Check you later, Byron," she said with saccharine sweetness before stepping back to swing the door closed in his face.

BAM!

"So not different at all," she said, kicking off her

heels and letting them tumble across the rust-colored carpet.

Lisha wondered why she even hoped for more. Be it one night or several months, she had yet to date a man who was okay with her holding on to her virginity until she was married. In fact, the real perverts wanted to bed her even more to stake claim on bedding a virgin or because they proclaimed their dick was made to "pop a cherry"—to pop *her* cherry.

Dream on.

Lisha made a face as she walked into her kitchen and picked up the headset of her bright yellow phone. She used her pinky to dial the phone number before turning to press her back against the wall as she waited for the line to be answered.

"Hi, this is Junie. I'm out living life. Leave me a message and I'll call you back . . . if I get home."

Lisha smiled at the animated tone of her cousin's voice and just hung up the phone, not bothering to leave a message. Being first cousins and next-door neighbors all their lives, Lisha thought of her more as a sister than as a cousin. Junie was the pop of color in a world sometimes filled with shades of gray, and Lisha could use some of her wildness to distract her thoughts.

She hung up the phone and walked over to the fridge to pour a glass of white wine. "The Lonely

Virgin rides again," she muttered into the goblet before taking a deep sip.

She arched a brow just as her front door opened and closed. Lisha felt a very quick moment of apprehension because the apartments lacked an interior hall and the front door was accessible to anyone who climbed the stairs to the second floor. But then she relaxed. It could only be one person—no one else had a key to her apartment. "Junie?" she called out, setting the goblet on the counter.

"The one and only," she called back, before strolling into the kitchen wearing nothing but an oversized tie-dye T-shirt that barely hit midthigh of her petite but curvy frame. Her shoulder-length hair was a tangled bird's nest around her head and her lipstick was smeared across her mouth.

"Screening your calls, huh?" Lisha asked, waving her hand at the bottle of wine as an offer for a glass.

"No thanks, cuz," Junie said, stretching her arms high above her head and causing the hem of the T-shirt to rise . . . exposing that she was sans underwear and quite bushy below.

Lisha closed her eyes and held up a hand. "*Hey,* put the lid back on the cookie jar," she snapped.

Junie laughed. "I left quite a few hard inches back in my apartment to come check on you."

Lisha opened her eyes and took another sip of her wine. "My date was over before it even began," she said, her grip on the goblet tight as she made her way past Junie and into the living room to plop down on the sofa.

Junie started to sit down beside her. She paused with her uncovered ass poised above the cushion as Lisha's eyes widened in horror. She rolled her eyes and remained standing. "Look, I just wanted you to know that if I didn't have company I would be over drinking wine and making sure you had company to your pity party."

Lisha sighed. "I just want to meet someone who feels like I'm worth the wait. As soon as sex is off the table they are out the door."

Junie pouted. "Then to hell with 'em because you are worth it," she said.

Lisha eyed her over the rim of her glass before she laughed into it. "You're really trying to get back to those inches tonight, huh? You're not trying to convince me to take the lid off the jar anymore?"

Junie shrugged a little. "Listen, I know that you want to remain pure until you're married. I don't agree with it for me, but I understand it's your choice. But that's the thing. It's up to you to give it up freely because you are ready to finally enjoy the wonders of a dick . . . but not just to get or keep a man."

Lisha handed Junie the rest of her wine to swallow down quickly. She rose to her feet. "Go on back to the wonders awaiting you and call me in the morning when you kick him out," she said, gently guiding yet another individual to her front door.

"Trust me, I'm getting enough for the both of us," she joked before turning in the open doorway to hand the goblet back to Lisha before giving her a soft smile and a wink.

Lisha leaned her head out the door to watch Junie's petite frame until she disappeared into her own studio apartment down. She shook her head at a brief vision of Junie whipping that T-shirt over her head and then climbing her naked body onto her futon to join her waiting lover.

Lisha was a virgin but far from a prude. She understood just what happened between a man and a woman when they were between the sheets. She was ready for it all. The heat. The chemistry. The kisses. The licks. The strokes. The fast and deep strokes. The climaxing. Over and over again.

Lisha made a little noise in the back of her throat as she crossed her legs and fanned herself. Oh, she wanted it. She was just saving it all up for her husband.

What's wrong with that?

Plenty according to Julian, Marc, Keenan, Josh, Harris . . .

I've been called everything from a tease to a blue ball specialist, she thought, snorting in derision and shedding her clothes as she made her way back to her bedroom.

She was in nothing but her red lace bra, matching high-waist panties, garters and thigh-high fishnet stockings when she stepped over the threshold. She moved over to the mirror above the eight-drawer dresser and tilted her head to the side as she eyed her reflection. With her high and full breasts pressing against the lace of her bra, the deep curves of her waist and the wide breadth of her hips and thighs, Lisha knew she shattered the myth of the docile, asexual virgin afraid of her own shadow and her own sexuality.

She twisted and turned her pin-up girl body a bit in the mirror as she traced her finger along the edge of her bra and gently tickled the full swell of her breasts. Her nipples hardened against the lace and her mouth opened a bit as she licked her bottom lip.

Celibacy wasn't always easy. The flesh could be *very* weak. Temptation was strong.

But her will was stronger.

The end of relationships was a hard enough blow to a woman's heart and Lisha refused the added heartache of adding another notch to her belt. Her last relationship ended four months ago and lasted just three months. Lisha shook her head remembering how she'd gotten lulled into thinking Jase could be the man she would love, marry and bed . . . until his true fiancée walked up to their table where they were having dinner and introduced herself.

That embarrassing-ass moment would have only been topped by having her body—as well as her trust and her heart—used up by him and his deceit. Her choice was more about her own set of beliefs than her strict Christian background. And it had been strict in rules but abundant in love and family. No doubt about it. Her father was every bit the clichéd fire and brimstone preacher, but he left all of that in the pulpit when it came time for his family. Although she loved her parents, Lisha hadn't found her first bit of freedom until she left home for college to obtain her associate's degree in physical therapy.

But her feelings were less about the purity ring she received at thirteen when she swore to remain a virgin until marriage and more about her own choice to save herself for the man who felt they were worthy of each other to wed.

But how will I ever get married if I can't even find a boyfriend willing to abstain?

The catch-22 was frustrating as hell.

Closing her eyes, Lisha released a long stream of breath through pursed lips as she let her hand ease down her body to the warm seat of her panties. She pressed her fingers against her intimacy and purred like the kitty she stroked.

She bit deeper into her full bottom lip as she side-eyed the top drawer of her nightstand. Turning, she eased her panties over her hips and let them fall to the floor to step out of before moving over toward her queen-sized bed. Her heart beat a little faster in anticipation as she opened the drawer and pulled out her vibrator.

She climbed under the covers onto her back and spread her legs wide. "Hell, I'm a virgin, but I ain't dead," she muttered dryly, before reaching to pull the covers above her head.

Soon the *bzzzzzz* of the vibrator and the *hmmmmm* of her moans floated up through the covers and blended in the air.

Chapter 2

"Home sweet home."

Kael Duncan Strong briefly looked over at his Realtor, Frieda Young, before casting his deep-set brown eyes back on the property before him. The six-bedroom, three-bathroom two-story plantation-style home was being sold "as-is," and with boarded windows, dilapidated stairs and peeling paint it was clear that it was badly in need of renovations to bring it back to its former beauty.

"Let's walk through it. Trust me, Mr. Strong," Frieda said, stepping a little closer to him to comfortably grasp his wrist with a friendly smile. "Come on."

His eye looked down at her shortbread-colored hand before shifting back up to her slender and pretty face surrounded by a short pixie cut that emphasized her large green and hazel eyes. Eyes that softened as her smile deepened and took on a new flirtatious intent.

Kael waved his hand toward the steps, accepting her offer to look inside the home and ignoring her subtle offer for things that had nothing to do with purchasing of the property. "After you," he said.

She moved ahead of him to climb the stairs. Kael did allow his eyes to dip down and take in her buttocks in the close-fitting flare-leg pants of her suit. He smiled a bit at the extra sway of her hips as she crossed the wide expanse of the porch and unlocked the front door.

Kael shifted his eyes and instead focused on the home as she led him from room to room on both levels. Although the home needed work, he liked the hardwood floor, oak mantels of the fireplaces and the large light fixtures. There were plenty of windows to draw in the sunlight and allow a 360-degree view of the surrounding lands.

He saw past the things needing repair and instead focused on the potential. The home could be restored to its former beauty with lots of elbow grease, paint, polishing and a few major construction repairs that he figured he could do himself.

"It's a lot of home for a . . . *single* man," Frieda said as they came down the stairs, careful to avoid clutching the weakened and loose banister.

Kael moved past her to stand at one of the windows flanking the large fireplace of the den. It was definitely a home meant for a large family with a wife to decorate and kids to enjoy being able to get into mischief inside. A home filled with lots of loyalty, love and laughter.

That was something he foolishly believed he had been working toward for the last five years of his life with Donna . . . until he discovered the rumors of her infidelity over the years were confirmed.

Kael's gut clenched and he winced, wishing he could forget . . .

Kael was bone-weary from nearly a month working on a ranch farm in North Carolina. The short-term work as a ranch hand had included long strenuous hours of physical work but paid well, and he couldn't turn down the opportunity to increase his savings as he focused on his goal of owning and operating his own cattle ranch one day.

But just as ready as he had been to leave his hometown of Holtsville, South Carolina, to make money and gain even more experience in cattle ranching, he was even happier to steer his battered blue and white Ford F-100 pickup past the large sign welcoming him to Holtsville.

Welcoming him back home.

It felt good. Damn good.

And getting into the arms, the bed and between the thick thighs of his woman would feel even better.

Kael felt his dick stir as he pictured the look on her face when he walked through the door of the mobile home they shared. They'd finished the cattle roundup a week early and Kael had tore up the road back to Holtsville with his bonus check in his pocket. Rushing home. To hold her. To kiss her. To love her. To make love to her. To feel his dick pressed between her lips—both of them.

He sped up.

A light rain began to fall just as he was turning down the unpaved dirt road leading to the half an acre of land where their singlewide mobile home sat. He sang along with the music on the radio as he drummed his fingertips against the steering wheel and surveyed the homes of his neighbors, taking note of anything new and surprising in the neighborhood.

Kael turned into the yard, passing Donna's powder blue Volkswagen Beetle. The sight of her little car made him smile. It was over ten years old and the paint was peeling in spots, but she refused to let the little Bug go and kept him busy under the hood making sure it still ran.

"What the—"

Kael pressed down on his brake pedal at the sight of a motorcycle parked behind the mobile home. He frowned deeply. Donna didn't ride motorcycles . . . and neither did he. Still, there had to be a reason.

Forcing himself to relax, he pulled up next to her Beetle and hopped out into the rain that was now a quiet but steady downpour that dampened the denim shirt he wore. He moved up the stairs with his keys ready in hand, but he paused just before he unlocked the door.

As the rain soaked his clothing to the hard contours of his body, all of the rumors of her infidelities over the years flooded him.

"Kael, I heard Donna was fooling around with some dude in Summerville."

"Kael, I saw Donna at the drive-in with some dude."

"Donna's messing around on you, man."

So many times over the last five years, rumors had floated to him about Donna. Whether he held his peace, questioned her gently about her whereabouts or just flat-out asked her, each time he walked away believing that Donna was faithful and loved him—and his dick—too much to betray him.

"What the fuck am I about to walk in on?" he wondered aloud, unlocking the door and finally stepping out of the rain and inside the foyer of their home.

As soon as he closed the door behind him the sound of the rain lessened and the sounds of mingled moans of pleasure echoed through the house. His heart pounded furiously before it felt like it stopped in his chest. Twelve steps down the short hall and he walked right into the scene of his woman being sexed by another man against the wall of the den.

There was no denying her cheating now.

Kael stormed across the room and the couple jumped apart in shock just as he grabbed the unknown man by the throat and literally shoved him across the room where he stumbled into the fireplace. Not finished with him, Kael moved quickly and grabbed the man by the throat again. In just seconds he took those same twelve steps and threw the man out the door with ease before slamming the door closed and locking it.

"Kael," Donna screamed, running up to reach out to him.

He glared at her as he swiped away her touch roughly. "Get out," he roared, as his anger swirled like a tornado inside his chest along with his shock and his hurt.

"I'm sorry, Kael. Please," she begged, her eyes filled with tears.

Kael ignored the beauty of her face and the supposed anguish in her eyes. He loved this woman and she was everything people had warned him about. Everything. "You're damn right, you're sorry as hell," he told her, his voice as cold as the freeze he felt enclosing his injured heart.

He reached behind him and unlocked the door, pushing it open before he put her out of the house as well.

"Kael." She gasped in shock as she fought to cover her nakedness with her hands.

He closed the door and locked it again as he spotted her lover riding away in the rain, butt naked on his motorcycle.

Donna knocked loudly on the door.

Kael closed his eyes and shook his head to clear it of the image of the woman he loved betraying him in the home he worked hard to provide. He had to fight the urge to punch the wall where her lover had pressed her body as he screwed her.

"No good—"

BAM-BAM-BAM-BAM.

"Kael," she cried out.

He jerked the door open as she squeezed past him, soaking wet and shivering.

"Kael, let me explain, baby," she began.

His eyes raked over her body before he locked intense eyes on her. "You have one hour to pack your shit and get out," he said.

Donna swiped away the hair plastered to her face. "Kael—"

"One hour," he repeated, holding his hand to stop her from coming close to him. "Don't be here when I get back."

He slammed out of the house and rushed down the stairs to climb into his truck. His heart hammered so hard in his chest that he might have an attack. Biting his bottom lip, he pounded his fist against the steering wheel before letting his head drop onto it.

The pain of it had him captured.

In that moment he wondered if he would ever fully recover.

He loved that woman, devoted himself to that woman, remained loyal—even in the face of temptation—to that woman, trusted that woman, looked like a fool for that woman . . . only to discover that she was unworthy. Just how many men had been between her thighs . . . in their bed . . . in their home?

It was fucked up. Period.

"Kael, please."

He looked up as Donna, now dressed in her robe, pulled on the door handle of the truck. For a moment he allowed himself to look at her, but the pain of her betrayal caused all of his emotions to tighten his throat. Fuck love and fuck her.

With a growl of pure pain and frustration, Kael accelerated forward even as he used his left hand to roll down the driver's side window with jerking motions. "One hour," he yelled to her before speeding away from a life he wondered if he'd ever been clear about.

"Mr. Strong . . . Mr. Strong. Everything okay?"

He felt his thoughts focus on the present as he briefly looked down at the pretty Realtor standing closely by his side. Forcing a smile, he pushed away thoughts of Donna's betrayal and the pain he still felt at times. Four months wasn't long enough to get over a five-year relationship that ended in explosive flames.

And that day had been the end for sure. Kael could forgive, accept or deal with many things, but infidelity—especially an infidelity that had been so disrespectful—wasn't one of them. There was no coming back from that.

He changed the locks and phone number that day, packed up anything Donna left behind—inadvertently or not—placed the house up for sale the week after that and moved back into his childhood home with his father when it sold three months after that.

Kael definitely felt like he was starting all over again.

Frieda lightly touched his arm again. "Kael," she said softly, using his first name for the first time.

His male instincts honed in to her attraction for him. He wasn't quite sure whether it was good for a quickie on the dusty floor where they stood or something she hoped would blossom into love and commitment. He was game for one but not the other. And since he wasn't sure, he stepped away from her and moved to the window on the opposite side of the fireplace. "I was just thinking through some things," he finally said, taking in the line of pear trees on the property before shifting his gaze to the acres of land beyond them.

"It is the condition of the house that makes the price of the home so competitive, but the amount of remodeling is enough to not make it worth your while," Frieda said, her tone now crisp and professional with the slight twang of her Southern accent. "I really think the property suits everything you requested and could easily become worth more than its current asking price."

Kael nodded in agreement even though his thoughts and plans for the property had already moved beyond the house to the ten acres of land surrounding it. The house was in tatters and the land needed a big overhaul. For him the value was in the land and in his plans to create his own cattle ranch. Kael had every intention to use every bit of the blood, sweat and tears he had to build a ranching legacy that he could one day pass on to a son.

He turned away from the window to face her. "Can we ride over the lands?" he asked.

She nodded and headed toward the peeling front door. "As you know, there are ten acres that are excellent for hunting, including a small hunting cabin on the rear of the property," she said.

Kael followed her toward the door, giving the house one last long look before stepping out onto the wide wraparound porch and closing the door behind him.

Chapter 3

One month later

Lisha genuinely smiled as she watched her client, Mrs. Anderson, take the final step to reach her. "Excellent," she said, moving the walker from beside where she stood in the rehabilitation clinic to stand in front of the elderly woman recovering from a hip injury after a fall two months ago.

Mrs. Anderson begrudgingly smiled. "Thanks to you."

Lisha was particularly skilled in dealing with the elderly community. She was well-known for her patience and her ability to decrease the recovery time from their injuries because of her gentle persistence. Her clients went above and beyond for her and in the end it worked out in their favor.

Lisha made notes on Mrs. Anderson's progress on her chart. "Once you stopped hating me," she reminded her with a playful wink.

"I don't know what you're talking about," the older woman said, leaning her weight onto the bars of her walker as one of the physical therapy aides stepped close to her to guide her back to the waiting room where her niece awaited her.

Lisha checked her watch as she placed her file in the holder on the door of the physical therapist supervising Mrs. Anderson's treatment plan. She was done for the day and her body was happy. Working in physical therapy meant being on her feet for the majority of the day as she worked to implement the treatment plan put in place by the physical therapist she worked under. Helping patients perform exercises—especially passive range of motion where she took over moving the limbs, giving massages or supervising gait and balance training—she had to have her own stamina.

She was headed to the employee lounge when she spotted two of her male co-workers looking in her direction from across the room. Her steps faltered before she lifted her hand and purposefully waved at them. They waved back even as they continued to talk.

Her eyes widened as she thought she read the lips of one of them saying "virgin."

The word seemed to reach inside her head like it mocked her as she watched them both laugh. *Vir-gin, vir-gin, vir-gin, vir-gin, virrrrrr-giiiiin.*

Lisha shook her head as she made her way

down to the end of the hall where the employee lockers were located. The warmth of her embarrassment flooded her but she forced herself to stiffen her spine and notch up her chin. *I don't have shit to be ashamed of.*

Still, as she opened her locker and removed her handbag, she couldn't help but wonder if she'd read his lips right and just what else they had to say. "I hate men," she muttered, slamming the locker closed before she swiftly left the room.

The outpatient clinic where she worked was adjoined to the hospital but had a direct exit onto the streets of downtown Charleston or a well-directed path connecting the building to the main hospital. Lisha headed in that direction, but once she stepped in front of the elevator that would take her to the glass bridge connecting the buildings, she reconsidered her plan to hunt down Byron and . . . and . . . and . . .

And what, Lisha?

She stepped back as others pushed forward to climb into the elevator. She couldn't go and pick a fight where she worked when she wasn't even sure the man said anything or if she read lips properly—a skill she didn't know she possessed.

She could find Byron to question him, insult him or threaten him, but what would that serve? Who would that serve?

Releasing a heavy breath, she turned and

retraced her steps until she walked out of the
glass doors of the clinic. The tree-lined street in
downtown Charleston, South Carolina, was beautiful as the summer sun broke through the branches
and cast shadows of the leaves on the brick-paved
streets. She took a moment to inhale deeply of
the air before crossing the street to the small
gated parking lot where her bright red Chevy
Nova awaited her.

She spoke to and waved to the hospital employ-
ees she knew as she walked up to the trunk of her
car and quickly swapped out the shoes she wore
to work in for the shoes she kept in her trunk.
Hospitals were infamous for germs—sometimes
antibiotic-resistant germs—and Lisha never wanted
to track something into her home. Junie thought
she was crazy for doing that. Lisha didn't really
care what she thought.

She climbed inside the coupe and rolled down
the driver's side window, feeling the muscle
strain in her arm from a hard day's work. Pushing her Earth Wind & Fire cassette into the
player, she steered the compact out of the parking
lot and turned left and then made a right to navi-
gate away from one of the many one-way streets of
Charleston.

Singing along to "Shining Star" she made another right and accelerated forward to the light.
She closed her eyes as she stretched her arms and
pressed her head toward her shoulders to relieve

the tension. Just as she opened her eye she spotted Byron's black Jeep Wrangler in her rearview mirror pulling up behind her.

"Well, look at God working," she said, quickly checking that the traffic light was red before putting the car in park.

That had to be a sign.

Lisha grasped the handle to open the door, with her eyes still on Byron in the rearview mirror. In the end she eased her foot from the brake to the accelerator and put her car in drive just as the light turned green.

He's spreading my business because I didn't spread my legs to him. A dry dick and hurt feelings are hard for a man to deal with. He ain't even worth it.

As she left him behind and steered onto Highway 17 headed toward home, she enjoyed the feel of the summer air blowing against her face as she drove. She barely took in the beauty of the Carolinas. Her thoughts were on whether she should go back to school for her bachelor's and then master's to become a physical therapist. She loved what she did and would truly love being the one to come up with the treatment plans for patients and having assistants and aides reporting to her. She could even see herself one day starting a business centered on physical therapy provided in her patients' homes.

But she honestly didn't know if she wanted to dedicate more years of her life to being back in school. She would have to work and that meant part-time classes. She could be facing another five years or more. That made Lisha frown, but sometimes you had to work hard toward your dreams and not just pray for them.

Still wrangling with her thoughts, Lisha finished the rest of the forty-five-minute commute back to Walterboro, but instead of driving to her apartment building, she decided to go and check on her parents. Their three-bedroom brick home was on a corner lot in a small but growing subdivision of the city where a lot of African-Americans were purchasing homes through a government program created to offer loans to low-income families with an interest in home ownership. With every passing year the neighborhood was growing and developing.

Turning onto the concrete driveway, she parked behind her father's royal blue Buick Electra that Lisha thought looked almost as long as the house. She entered the house through the side door under the carport that opened directly into the kitchen. The bright yellow and orange wallpaper with silver highlights looked nothing like what she thought her parents would want. But the older Lisha got, and the more their relationship had changed in her adulthood, Lisha was beginning to wonder if she even really knew her parents at all.

Their dinner of lima beans and ham hocks was

still on the stove, but Lisha knew her parents had eaten at exactly six. She grabbed a bowl and scooped white rice into it before topping it with beans and a small piece of meat. It was still warm enough to enjoy without reheating the entire pot.

She looked out the window over the sink as she got a fork from the orange dish rack and chuckled at the sight of her mother leaning against the back of their shed in the backyard savoring one of her beloved Pall Mall cigarettes. The preacher's wife had one weakness and she tried to keep that secret from her husband of the last thirty years.

Continuing out the kitchen and down the narrow hall to her father's den she found him in his plaid La-Z-Boy recliner, kicked back, watching *Hogan's Heroes* on his floor-model television.

"Hey, Daddy," she said, leaning against the doorframe.

Reverend Charles Rockmon turned his body in his recliner to look over his shoulder at her. His face filled with surprise. "Hi, Alisha," he said. "We weren't looking to see you until church Sunday."

She came farther into the room and bent down to kiss his cheek, the prickly stubble of his beard lightly scratching her lips. Her father didn't shave until the night before Sunday service. "I wanted some home-cooked food," she said, sitting down on the arm of his recliner and forcing him to move over a little to make room for her.

Rev sucked air between his false teeth. "You cook just as good as your mama," he said.

"True," she agreed. "She raised me up at that stove."

"Your husband will thank you for it," he said, focusing his eyes back on the television.

"I guess," she said, feeling her appetite wane a bit.

"If he's not thankful for you then you don't need him," Rev said, his eyes leveled on her.

That's if I ever find him, she thought, not voicing her concerns to her father. She looked down into the bowl as she pushed her food around with her fork.

"Trust in God," Rev said.

Lisha nodded solemnly in agreement.

"Your mama still behind that shed smoking?" her father asked, his eyes now locked on the antics of the TV show.

Lisha's eyes filled with surprise.

Her father chuckled.

She wasn't going to lie for her mama, but she wasn't going to tell on her either. Lisha didn't say another word.

Kael pulled the reins on his bay-colored quarter horse, Sampson, to ease him from a full gallop to a trot as he looked around at the perimeters of his property. For the last two weeks he had spent long work-filled days making sure the fencing was secure so that the cattle he planned to purchase at an auction next month would not be able to roam beyond his property to the wooded acreage beyond.

Acreage I will own one day.

But first he had to get the ranch up and running to hopefully make the profits to one day expand it. Kael was cash strapped and using every bit of help from his father and friends that they would offer to get the land and the house ready for him. Every cent and every available moment spent not working his job as a ranch hand was dedicated to his own ranch. He barely had any hours in the night left to sleep but his desire to succeed fueled him when exhaustion tried to win.

Bringing Sampson to a halt on a slope overlooking a stream, he sat back in his saddle and enjoyed the sight of the sun setting in the distance. He had a million other things he could be doing, but he allowed himself a brief moment to enjoy the serene beauty of the skies beginning to darken to an inky blue with streaks of orange.

He inhaled deeply of the scent of the Bahia hay mingling with the pine from the towering trees as he enjoyed the last rays of the sun warming his face.

Life is good.

Kael shifted the Stetson he wore to keep the sun from burning his face as he worked. His shirt was soaked to his back with sweat—the summer heat was still stifling even as the sun faded—and the contoured muscles of his entire body ached, but he had never felt better than at that moment. Allowing himself one last deep inhale of the country air, he steered his horse around to head back toward the house.

He rode at a trot across the flat cleared land, now anxious to get back to the house before darkness completely reigned. He was just coming up on the first couple acres of land he'd cleared to graze the cattle, when he spotted his father's white Chevy C-10 diesel pickup truck parked at the newly installed paddock. He frowned when the driver's side door opened and his father's friend Monte began waving frantically.

Kael picked up the horse's pace to a gallop, coming around the wooden fencing of the paddock and pulling him to a stop at the door of his father's truck.

"Your father's been hurt," Monte said, the tobacco packed in his mouth slightly muffling his words before he spat out the brown juice that matched his matted and oily shoulder-length hair. "He fell off the horse back at the house. Looks like he broke his hip."

Kael felt sucker punched as he sharply pressed his booted heel against his horse's flank and loosened the reins. Sampson took off at full speed and he lowered his upper body closer to the saddle to maintain his balance and not hinder the horse's stability as his hooves ate up the dirt. He maintained control of the strong beast while still allowing it the freedom to fully stretch out to his max speed.

"Whoa. Whoa," he called out rapidly, sitting up in the saddle and tightening the reins as the sight of his house came into view. "Whoa, Sampson, whoa."

His eyes searched the grounds as he patted Sampson's neck to help calm him down as he steered him in a circle. His father's white Arabian horse, Ghost, was already secured in the double horse trailer they used to transport them from his father's home.

The loud rumble of the diesel truck sounded behind him as the muscles of both his and Sampson's chest heaved from the exertion. "Where is he?" he hollered to Monte.

"You took off like you was in the Derby before I could tell you the ambulance already took him to County. I stayed behind to find you," he said, just before another brown stream was released from his mouth like a bullet.

Kael rushed to dismount and led Sampson into the horse trailer. "Monte, please take the horses back—"

"Already on it, son," he said, driving the truck around to hook the trailer to it.

Kael rushed to his own truck and took off,

sending dirt and pebbles flying as he raced across the land and down the unpaved drive lined with trees that shaded the path to the main highway. His heart raced like crazy as he drove up Highway 17 toward Walterboro.

His father was in his mid-fifties but he was active, strong and could probably easily whip a man twenty years his junior. Still, a hip injury was serious and would most likely require surgery.

"Shit," he swore as traffic on the two-lane road came to a stop.

His patience was short because he was pissed at himself for sitting his ass up on a hill staring at the sunset while his father was being transported to the hospital.

Pounding his fist on the steering wheel, he leaned over to look to the right of the road before steering his truck alongside the car ahead of him. With half his tires off the road he passed the cars ahead of him and made the right onto the belt-line and then a series of lefts to bypass the traffic and head back down the beltline in the opposite direction.

Kael didn't slow down until he took the final turns to pull into the parking lot of the Colleton County Hospital. He nabbed the first parking spot and raced inside the entrance to the emergency department. "Logan Strong?" he asked the clerk standing behind the station.

The petite white woman's green eyes went from

bored to interested as she leaned back to take in all of his six-foot-five frame and broad stature.

He frowned a little when she licked her lips. "Logan Strong?" he repeated, hating the need to check his annoyance when she was the one being unprofessional.

But a black in the South in the seventies knew the littlest incident between someone black and someone white could quickly turn volatile—especially between a black man and a white woman. Times had not moved that far beyond the death of Emmett Till twenty years ago or the deaths of civil rights volunteers Herbert Lee and Louis Allen just ten years ago. And would anyone ever forget the murders of Medgar Evers or Martin Luther King, Jr.? The stench of Jim Crow segregation still clung to the air even after nearly a decade of its official end.

And so Kael took a deep breath and patiently stood there with nothing for her but the same question. "Logan Strong?"

She finally shifted her eyes to a chart sitting on the edge of the desk. She shook her head. "I don't see that he was admitted," she said, her eyes squinting as she read through the list of names again.

"An ambulance picked him up from my home. He broke his hip," Kael explained.

"Let me call dispatch," she said, picking up the phone.

He felt a whole new level of concern wash over

him. His mother died from a heart attack in his teens and his sister, Kelli, lived nearly three hours away with her husband. Logan Strong was Kael's father, his confidant, his teacher, his advice giver and his friend.

"Okay, thank you. Hold on," she said, moving the telephone headset down to press to her chest. "Your father put up such a stink about not wanting to come here. They rerouted him to MUSC."

Kael felt relief that his father was located and that he was feisty enough to make demands on his care. He smiled a little. "Thank you, ma'am," he said kindly, turning to exit the emergency department.

"Oh, no, sweetie, thank *you*," she called behind him.

Kael hopped into his truck and headed for Charleston. He shaved ten minutes off the forty-five-minute drive and a few minutes after that he was directed upstairs to the surgical unit to await the end of his father's surgery. Kael started to dig all of the change he could from his pockets to use the pay phone in the waiting room to call his sister, but he decided to wait until the surgery was over.

He finally settled into one of the uncomfortable puke green chairs pushed against the wall, crossing his arms over his chest and spreading his legs wide as his exhaustion settled on his shoulders so heavily that he doubted he could raise his arms. He let his head drift down until his square chin almost sat on his chest. His eyelids closed as if tiny weights pulled them down. His breathing became slow and even.

"Mr. Strong . . . Mr. Strong."

Kael's body jerked as he was startled awake. He looked around wildly as he wiped the slight bit of drool from the corner of his mouth. Everyone in the waiting room stared openly at him. He didn't even know when he fell asleep.

"Your father is out of surgery and post-op."

Kael turned his head to look up at the tall white man standing over him, still in his surgical scrubs. He rose to his feet.

"He'll be moved to his own room. Someone will come to get you when you can see him."

Kael extended his hand. "Thank you, Doctor."

"Dr. Taylor," he offered as he pressed his hand against Kael's. "Your father did well and with some physical therapy he should recover fully. The muscles around his hips are in great shape for his age and that will decrease his recovery time."

"Again, thanks."

"After you see your dad you really should get some sleep," Dr. Taylor said, his blue eyes filled with amusement.

"Humph. He already got *plenty* of that. Snores and all. Humph."

Kael frowned as he looked over his shoulder at a chubby black woman with a blond Afro and pale pink lipstick on her mouth. She gave him a sarcastic grin, flashing a gap in her teeth big enough for him to slide his thumb into.

Ignoring her, Kael followed the doctor out of the waiting room. He paced the hall, loosening his joints as he waited to lay eyes on his father.

"Mr. Strong."

He turned. A pretty nurse with a short curly Afro smiled at him. "Your father's asking for you," she said.

Kael nodded, enjoying the view of her curvy frame in her uniform as she led him to his father's room. "Bye," he said, pausing in the open doorway.

"Bye, Mr. Strong," she said flirtatiously.

"Kael," he insisted.

She smiled. "Bye, *Kael*," she said before walking away.

"You gonna burn a hole in her ass, son."

Kael's smile broadened as he turned and entered the room. His father was in bed and looked slightly pale beneath his medium brown complexion. His silver hair was disheveled. His eyes were still slightly glassy from his medication. But all in all he was alive and well enough to crack jokes.

Love for the man swelled in Kael's broad chest as he came to stand by his bed. "Since when do you allow a horse to beat you, old man?" he asked, swallowing the emotions tightening his throat.

Logan smiled. "Man, shit. I don't know what the

hell happened," he said, his voice still weak and tired. "Fuck that horse. His ass is glue."

Kael knew his father didn't mean it. Sometimes he and his sister joked that Ghost was the third Strong sibling.

"You call your sister?" he asked, closing his eyes as he winced a bit in pain.

"Not yet, but I will," Kael promised.

"You know she's coming."

"Yeah, I know." Kael looked down at his father's lower half. He could tell from the positioning on the pillows that it was his left hip that was injured.

"They want me to get right into physical therapy, but I ain't coming back and forth to Charleston three times a week, son," Logan said, his voice stronger.

"If we have to, we just have to do it, Daddy," he said.

Logan shook his head on the pillow, opening his eyes just enough to look up at his son. "I ain't doing it."

"I'll figure something out," Kael assured him.

Logan closed his eyes as he nodded. "I know."

That made Kael proud that his father knew he could trust and believe in him. He smoothed the white blanket covering him and allowed his hand to lightly rest against his father's before he lightly gripped it. His father had never been a touchy-feely person. Hugs and kisses were rare even if the love was in abundance.

Logan surprised him by tightening his hold on Kael's hand.

"I'm gonna ride again, son," he said, already drifting back to sleep.

"I know," he assured him with just as much trust and belief.

The next morning Alisha double-checked the chart before entering the hospital room. She was surprised to see her immediate supervisor, Nigel, still in the room. According to the chart he'd already met with Mr. Strong and set up his treatment plan.

She smiled politely at the middle-aged gentleman in the bed. "I'm Alisha. I'll be working with you, Mr. Strong, during your physical therapy at the outpatient clinic here," she said, not quite sure if Nigel was there just to observe her interaction with the patient.

Logan extended his hand to her and she moved closer to the bed to shake it. "You aren't hard on the eyes at all, are you?" he teased.

She smiled at him. "I hope not," she said, used to the harmless flirtation of older men.

"Actually, Alisha, Mr. Strong is being set up for his physical therapy at home," Nigel said.

She couldn't hide her confusion. "Oh, okay then. Uhm, well good luck with your recovery,

Mr. Strong," she said, handing the file across the bed to Nigel.

He didn't take it. "Mr. Strong's son spoke with me about who was best suited to handle his father's therapy and I recommended you."

The door opened and Lisha looked over her shoulder. Her eyes widened a bit at the man who stepped inside the room. He was tall and broad-shouldered with narrow hips. His body was lean but obviously strong and he wore form-fitting jeans with a printed shirt. His face was simply handsome with strong cheekbones, chin and brows. He had long lashes around his slanted eyes and full lips. The silver flecks in his closely cropped soft hair didn't detract from his looks. Oddly, they enhanced them.

The brother was all the way fine. *All* the way.

Lisha was surprised at how fast her pulse raced and the way she literally felt breathless and alive, like the energy in the room kicked up a notch from his presence. She blinked rapidly to break the spell and looked away from him as she licked her suddenly parched lips.

Kael paused as he stepped inside his father's hospital room. He was surprised by the presence of the woman who looked over her shoulder at him. Surprised and pleased.

Her shoulder-length hair was pulled back from

her face into a ponytail. The soft wisps of her ebony hair made her caramel-tinted skin gleam. She was pretty with her round face and high cheekbones. Her eyes were bright and round, framed by lush lashes that he wasn't quite sure were real, although he was quite sure it didn't matter. Her pug little nose and full mouth above her dimpled chin gave her even more appeal.

He didn't miss the way her eyes skimmed up and down his body. He allowed himself to do the same of her. Even in her printed scrubs he could tell she was curvy and soft where she needed to be.

Damn.

She looked away from him and he forced his eyes over to his father whose expression revealed that he'd seen his son's reaction to the woman. Even as he walked over to stand at the foot of the bed, he still felt that awareness of her in every fiber of his being. He had to force himself not to stare at her, but it was like there was a magnetic field around her and he couldn't resist.

"Mr. Strong, this is Alisha Rockmon, the physical therapist assistant I told you about," Nigel said. "Alisha, Mr. Strong's son, Kael."

Kael couldn't believe he felt nervous as he extended his hand to her. "Thank you for taking the position to help my father with his therapy," he said.

She slid her hand into his. "I'm not really sure that I am or I can," she said.

The feel of her fingertips lightly grazing his

inner wrist made him shiver. Kael quickly released her hand.

"We'll work around your schedule at the clinic and Mr. Strong is willing to pay for any of your services not covered by his father's insurance," Nigel said. "And you live right in Walterboro."

Kael saw the indecision on her face. "Take some time and think about it and get back to me," he offered, seeing she was put on the spot.

She rested her eyes on him. "No, no. I'll do it," she told him with a soft smile.

Kael nodded and said nothing else as he ignored the look of pure satisfaction on his father's face.

"Love must be as much a light, as it is a flame."
—Henry David Thoreau

Interlude

"So it was love at first sight?" Bianca asked, easing up on the edge of her chair as the sounds of soulful Christmas music continued to play in the background.

"Well, we wouldn't say that," Lisha said, reaching over to stroke the back of Kael's large hand where it rested on the arm of her recliner.

"Not then anyway," Kael added.

"But I knew he was *lov-ing* every bit of what he was seeing," Lisha teased, taking a sip of her hot chocolate.

"I saw your eyes on the cut of my jeans too," he shot back.

"Foul on the play," Kahron said, moving to sit down on the floor by Bianca's feet. "That was TMI."

"Definite TMI," Kade agreed from the sofa where Garcelle lounged back against his chest.

Bianca raised her legs to bring over Kahron's shoulders. She loved that he slid off her booties and began rubbing her feet. She looked down at the diamond charm bracelet he'd secured on her wrist early that Christmas morning as they lay in bed and watched the sun rise.

Every one of the seven custom-made diamond-encrusted charms represented each of their years together and a memorable moment in their lives. A heart for their love. A miniature truck for the first time she saw him driving ahead of her on the road into Holtsville. A triple X for their fiery sex life. A globe for their wedding vows promising to give each other the world. A lucky charm for the goodness of their seven years of marriage. A baby carriage for the birth of their son KJ. A horse for their mutual love and work with animals.

She could hardly believe she once thought he wanted her father's land badly enough to sabotage her attempts to revive Hank's business. They went from enemies to lovers. She had been so wrong and now knew Kahron was her biggest protector.

What they had was good. Damn good.

Bianca shifted her eyes down to take in her husband's profile as he laughed at something one of his brothers said as he continued to rub her feet. She stroked the back of his head, her fingers enjoying the softness of his low cut, prematurely gray hair and he looked up over his shoulder at her. "I love you," she mouthed, bringing her hand up to press against the side of his square and handsome face.

"Love you back," he said, his voice a husky whisper that she barely heard above the loud chatter of their boisterous family.

She didn't need the words because she saw the love in his eyes.

"Yes," she told him.

His face filled with confusion. "Huh?"

"Our *convo* last night," she reminded him with a meaningful stare.

A smile replaced the confusion and it was large enough to show every single tooth. His hand covered the one she still had pressed to his face and then he lowered it, causing her to need to lean forward, as he pressed it against his pounding heart.

Bianca laughed. There were only a few things in life that could make Kahron Strong so mushy and her agreeing to have another baby just made the list. *KJ's gonna have a baby brother or sister.*

Her veterinary practice was so busy that she actually hired another vet to help out. That made three vets total and an additional staff of five—more than enough to free her up to slow down a bit.

Kahron purchased twenty heads of cattle, thirty new acres of land and five more ranch hands.

Sometimes they barely made it home in time to cook dinner and put KJ to bed.

Over the last few years their love had grown, their family had grown and both of their businesses had grown. But they would find a way.

As Boyz II Men sang "Let it Snow," Bianca spotted Kade and Garcelle's teenaged daughter Kadina sitting on the bottom step just outside the den. She had on her pink Beats by Dre headphones but Bianca knew there wasn't a bit of music playing in her ears because Kadina was eavesdropping hard.

Easing her feet from Kahron's shoulder, Bianca stood up and walked out of the spacious den, already giving the snooping teen a disapproving stare.

Kadina gave a big glossy smile as she held one of the headphones from her ear. "Auntie B, I just want to hear the story too," she said, pouting and pressing her fingertips together like she was praying.

"No, ma'am, you will not have your parents mad at me," Bianca said, pointing her arm up the staircase only to spot Lei sitting on the top step snooping as well. "Young ladies, speak when you're spoken to and—"

"Come when you're called," they finished dejectedly.

Lei disappeared into the playroom and Kadina

rose up on her slender legs to slowly ascend the stairs.

"There you go," she said, smiling at the girl's obvious disappointment.

Bianca squealed in surprise as arms surrounded her waist. She knew from the instant thrill that it was her husband. No one kept her heated in the special way that he did. She turned in his embrace. "Another baby, huh?" she asked softly.

"Or two," he said, tasting her lips.

"Or two?" she protested. "I don't know about that."

Kahron just chuckled as he led her back into the den. He sat in the comfy leather chair and pulled his wife down onto his lap.

Bianca was lost in the holiday spirit. She felt just a little regretful that she couldn't share even a piece of the season with her dad and her stepmom/friend, Mimi. Ever since her ultimatum, her father had cleaned up his drinking and never wavered from his sobriety since. She knew his love for her wacky and unique older friend, Mimi, had a lot to do with that. The ex-TV star turned rancher's wife from Atlanta, Georgia, had a unique perspective on life and Hank loved it. Even now they were on a cruise around the Caribbean for the holidays.

She couldn't be mad at them for that.

Walking in on them enjoying "naked day" around their house . . . she was *still* mad about.

"Tell us about Grandpa Logan," someone said.

"He was a trip and half," Lisha said.

"That he was, that he was," Kael added.

Bianca settled into a comfortable spot on Kahron's lap. As Lisha and Kael continued reminiscing on their love story, Bianca was grateful to have one of her own.

Chapter 4

Way back in the day

"What's on your mind?"

Lisha turned her head from looking out the kitchen window of her apartment to look over at her cousin Junie. "Huh?" she asked, her face blank.

Junie eyed her cousin over the rim of her coffee cup with a picture of her favorite actor and obsession Richard Roundtree from *Shaft* on the side.

"Girl, nothing," she lied, looking down into her own cup with a huge smiley face. An image of Kael Strong's handsome face floated in the steam.

The caramel complexion and close-cropped silver-flecked hair. Long lashes above slanted eyes that were the brown of brandy. Square jaw. Strong chin. High cheekbones.

Just fine. Too damn fine.

Lisha picked up her spoon and spun it vigorously in her coffee until the image disappeared. She looked up to find her cousin's eyes still on her over that rim. "I have my first at-home patient today," she said, considering her words more of a shift in conversation than an outright lie. The truth was in there somewhere.

Since she first laid eyes on Kael last week the thought of him gave her the anxious, jittery nerves all too familiar with a silly high school crush. Although the pure excitement and charge she received when he walked into his father's hospital room that day was far more adult. Just being in his presence for that short time had made her alive and aware and so clearly tuned in to the shift of energy in the room.

She had found her eyes going back to him and then flitting away when she would find that he was already looking at her. It was like something she had never experienced before. Just a huge mix of nerves, anxiety, excitement and self-consciousness as she wondered how she appeared to him. Did she catch his eye the same way that he had caught hers?

Hoping she would see him again during her sessions with his father made the awareness all the more intense.

"You were thinking about going back to school for your PT license and eventually opening your own at-home clinic, right?" Junie asked, putting her foot up on the chair and wrapping one arm around her bent leg to press it close to her chest.

Lisha held up her hand to block the view her cousin was giving off in her pink shorts she wore with a lime green GOOD TIMES tank. "I could really do without your camel toe," she said, waving her hand.

Junie raised her other foot onto the edge of the white vinyl-covered kitchen chair and then spread her knees wide. "BAM!" she said sharply. "Don't be scared of the cooch."

Lisha laughed and closed her eyes, making a cross with her two index fingers.

"You are missing out on a prime sex position," Junie said. "You scoot that thing right to the edge like this—"

Curious, Lisha opened one eye and dared to learn for future use with her husband.

"And your man gets on his knees to line that dick up right. And whoo!"

Lisha closed her eyes again after Junie began to make tiny thrusts with her hips.

"Shit, that's a winner right there," she said. "You can have that one, I got plenty more."

"I bet you do," Lisha said, leaning over to snatch the dish towel that hung on the door of the oven to toss between Junie's legs.

She laughed and lowered her legs, tossing the towel back at Lisha. "When you do give up them cookies—"

"To my husband," Lisha inserted.

"Or whomever else," Junie insisted, "just remember there is more to life than missionary."

Junie was wild, fun and completely uninhibited. That's why Lisha loved hanging with her. "You're a trip," she told her, glancing at the oversized white Starburst clock in the center of the wall covered with horizontal stripes in primary colors.

7:03 A.M.

"Let me get ready for work," she said, rising from the square Formica table to scrape the remnants of her egg and bacon breakfast into the trash can before setting the plate into the sink. "I have a half a day at the clinic and then a couple hours in Holtsville."

Junie made a face. "Holtsville! You going in dem woods?"

With a population of over six thousand, Walterboro was a small town compared to other South Carolina cities like Columbia and Charleston, but in comparison to the neighboring rural small town of Holtsville it was more developed with businesses, more paved roads and more heavily populated subdivisions.

But Holtsville was far from the archaic living standards of *Little House on the Prairie*. Far from it. Still, that was the viewpoint of the people who never visited the town.

"It's not that bad, Junie," she said, making hot and sudsy dishwater in the sink.

"Girl, there is nothing in Holtsville to make me travel to those backwoods."

Humph, one sight of Kael Strong and you'd move to Holtsville.

"Kael who?" Junie asked, standing next to her as she slid her scraped plate in the sink.

Lisha shifted her eyes to her cousin. "Did I say that out loud?" she asked.

"Yup. So who is he?"

"The son of my client in Holtsville and he is some kind of fine."

Junie reached for the sponge to sink into the water and wring out before she began cleaning the grease splatter from the stovetop. "How fine?"

"You'd give Shaft the shaft," she answered without hesitation.

"Yeah, right," Junie said, rinsing the sponge under the running water and going over the stovetop again. "Horniness messes with your visuals."

Lisha shook her head slowly. "Oh, hell, no, I ain't," she insisted. "And he has silver hair."

"Now I know you're horny, talking 'bout some old dude," Junie said with a frown.

"He's not even thirty."

Junie turned and walked out of the apartment. Lisha thought she had gone to prepare for her day's work in the kitchen of Colleton's County Hospital.

Lisha was in the bathroom brushing her teeth when Junie suddenly reappeared with a Polaroid camera in hand. She set it on the edge of the sink. "Photo proof. Pretend you're taking a picture of your client's injury or something. Running late. Gotta split."

And with that she was gone again.

"Breakfast on you tomorrow, and I don't want cereal," she hollered out the door.

"It's Friday night and I have a date so you'll be lucky to see me in the morning," Junie hollered back just before the front door soundly closed.

Lisha barely had time to close her mouth in surprise. She rinsed the toothpaste from her mouth and picked up the instant camera—already knowing that as photo worthy as Kael Strong was, she would never sneak a snapshot of him.

She examined the camera, turning it over, and noticed a photo jammed in it. She grabbed her pair of tweezers and worked to pull it out.

Because the photo never fully injected, a piece of it never developed properly. She turned it this way and that. "What is . . ."

Lisha gasped in shock as she recognized the tip of a large penis resting on a hairy thigh. She dropped the photo into the wastepaper basket between the commode and the sink. It was far too shiny not to be wet.

Thinking on the last time the camera was obviously used, she frowned and damn near tossed it like a hot potato onto the closed lid of the commode before rushing to scrub her hands with hot water and soap.

Lisha rushed to get ready for work and tried not to feel any excitement about seeing Kael again. She tried and failed. She did know that Kael's sister, Kelli, was listed as the primary caregiver, but that didn't mean he wouldn't stop by to assist.

Throughout her half-day shift and then all during her drive back to Colleton County, Lisha was well aware of a slight tremble of nervousness in her hands. Feeling like she should get herself together before reaching the Strongs' home she stopped at the lone gas station on the small town's main street.

She pulled up to the lone pump and grabbed her wallet from her pocketbook just as the attendant walked up to the driver's side window. She read the name on his uniform overall. "Good afternoon, Cyrus," she said, climbing from her Nova as he held the door.

"It is now," he said, flashing a bright smile as he looked up at her.

They looked about the same age even though he was shorter than her by at least four inches.

"Fill her up please," she said, after checking to make sure the price per gallon was about the same as Walterboro. *Forty-four cents.*

"Yes, ma'am."

Lisha fanned herself, trying to keep some of the sweltering heat and humidity from pressing so cloyingly against her skin. She looked around, recalling Junie's earlier disdain for the small town. There was a secondhand store across the street and a brightly painted blue store with a sign proclaiming they sold the coldest pop in South Carolina. On the next corner were a small mechanic shop and an empty lot. The rest of the street was brick homes with elaborate fencing.

"What's coming over there?" she asked Cyrus, holding her hand over her eyes as she watched a concrete truck backing up to the empty dirt lot.

"A diner," he said.

She looked over her shoulder to see him leaning against her car and whittling away at a piece of wood. It seemed something very odd for a young man to be doing, but she could tell by the smooth movement of his knife against the wood that he was well practiced at it.

Her eyes squinted as she eyed him. As she did with people who intrigued her or caught her eye, she wondered what his story was. Single? Married?

No kids? Or ten? Was he as happy and content as he appeared to be?

"It's good to see a new business coming," she said, walking over to him.

"Yup," he agreed, looking up at her briefly before returning his focus to his project. "Just as long as this stays the only gas station, though. I'm gonna own it one day."

"My father always taught me that anything you believe in and work hard for is possible," she told him, patting his shoulder before passing him to enter the store and pay for her fuel.

She added a bottle of Crush soda to her purchase, paying the teenaged boy sitting behind the crowded counter like he'd rather be anywhere else.

"Who's your father?" Cyrus asked when she got back to her car.

"Reverend Rockmon," she said, noticing he'd cleaned her windshield while she was in the store.

Cyrus nodded, his bright eyes gleaming from his smooth dark complexion of his round boyish face. "Good man," he said.

"Thank you. I'll tell him I saw you, Cyrus," she said, climbing back behind the wheel of her car.

Lisha was used to hearing people praise her father. He was a man who spoke *and* lived the word of God.

She directed the air conditioning vents to blow directly against her face and neck as she remembered Kael's directions to his father's home and followed them. She had to slow down as she took the large dirt road directly off the main street and counted the homes until she eventually turned onto a paved road lined with small brick homes that reminded her of a more spread-out version of the subdivision where her parents lived in Walterboro.

She slowed down and turned onto the drive of the Strong home behind a cute VW Beetle. She instantly loved the charm of the small house with its trees and flower bushes. She felt the now-familiar anxiousness shimmy over her as she exited the vehicle and retrieved her tote bag from the passenger seat.

The door opened before she even had time to ring the doorbell. She stepped back a bit as a fair-skinned woman in her early thirties swung the screen door open. "Hi, I'm Lisha Rockmon. I'm here for Mr. Strong's physical therapy," she said.

"Come on in. He's waiting on you," she said with a friendly smile. "I'm his daughter, Kelli."

"Nice to meet you," she said, extending her hand. "You'll be the primary caregiver . . . besides the home health aide, right?"

Kelli nodded. "Yes . . . well, just until we get Daddy stabilized and my brother finishes up working on starting his ranch. I live up near Greenville."

Lisha's heart jolted at the mention of Kael. "Is he here? I have some restrictions that I like to review with the family just to help make sure your dad doesn't hurt his recovery."

Kelli nodded her head. "No, Kael's not home yet, but I'll go over them with him."

Lisha blinked away her disappointment. "So he lives here with your father?"

"For now," Kelli said, guiding Lisha through the living room and down a short hall. "He just purchased another home and a ranch that he is renovating, but I know he won't move out until Daddy is feeling like one hundred percent."

"Okay. Good," Lisha said, feeling a thrill again that she would see him again . . . eventually.

Kael grunted as he brought the ax down onto the center of the log to split it in half. The logs fell off the tree stump and he gave the ax one last swing to lodge it into the stump. The summer sun glared down on his bare back and he felt the sweat leave his pores and race down his body to soak the rim of his jeans. His chest heaved from the exertion of cutting logs from the trees he cleared around the hunting cabin.

Using the back of his arm, he swiped away some of the sweat on his face before quickly stacking the logs alongside the side of the small one-room cabin. When winter came the logs would be ready for use in the fireplace for much-needed heat.

Surveying his work one last time, he grabbed his

sleeveless T-shirt from where he'd flung it over a bush and made his way over to his pickup at a leisurely pace. His stomach grumbled and he remembered he hadn't eaten since he left the house early that morning once his sister, Kelli, had arrived. He was in no rush to get back there because he knew it was the first day of the pretty physical therapist, Alisha, arriving to work with his father.

A memory of his first look at her flashed as he climbed into the driver's seat of his truck. In the past few days since then he found himself thinking about her. He was a man who could appreciate the beauty of a fine woman, but his intense attraction to her, plus his distraction with her days later, didn't bode well for him. These days he was more about a woman who was convenient than one who would draw him in.

Kael didn't know if he could take another dose of Alisha Rockmon quite so soon.

Pulling up to park in front of his home, he surveyed the bright white paint and brand-new red shutters he had installed. The house seemed to gleam under the sunlight and he loved it, but one day when his money was right he planned on facing the entire house in brick.

When his stomach grumbled again he glanced at his watch. It was well after six. *She has to be gone by now.*

Kael steered the truck off his property and drove toward his father's home. His sister was supposed to get in town earlier that day and he knew she had food cooked. His hunger for food trumped his desire to fight off his hunger for the sexy physical therapist. He was willing to risk it.

It took him less than five minutes to reach the three-bedroom one-bathroom brick home where he was raised. It was set nearly 300 feet back from the road and was shaded over by moss-covered oak trees. The crepe myrtle bushes his mother planted during the first years of their marriage still bloomed brightly in shades of pink, purple, reds and whites.

As he pulled up the cemented drive he noticed a bright red Nova parked next to his father's diesel pickup and his sister's yellow Volkswagen Beetle. He hated that the sight of it reminded him entirely too much of his ex, Donna.

"To hell with her," he mumbled, climbing from his truck to walk across the lawn and up onto the stoop.

The front door was open wide but the screen door was closed, allowing fresh air to float in while keeping the flies and mosquitos out. The scent of something frying wafted to him as he entered the house. It stirred up another raucous grumble.

"Didn't Daddy teach you not to slam the screen door, little brother?"

Kael smiled at his older but much shorter sister as she came across the living room to open her arms wide. He picked her up easily for a bear hug before setting her back down on her feet. She was the spitting image of their mother. Tall and slender with angular features and a light complexion that hinted at their mother's mixed heritage of Black and Cherokee.

They were close and had always been. After their mother's death, Kelli had taken on the role of homemaker at the young age of seventeen. And she was prone to dishing out advice like she was his mother as well, but Kael loved her.

"Good to see you, Smelly Kelli," he teased her, mussing her hair and receiving the swat she always gave him.

"The interstate to Greer goes in both directions, you know," she said.

She was constantly getting on him and his father because they had only been to visit her and her husband's, Willie's, home in Greer twice. He didn't bother to explain that her husband, an attorney and local politician, never made them feel comfortable—or sometimes even wanted—in their home. Kael didn't particularly care for his brother-in-law and all of his showboating and grandstanding, but he never let on to his sister. It was her life, her love and her choice to make. He did a good job of letting the words, "Man, shut the hell up," not escape from his lips when he was in Willie's presence.

"How'd Daddy do today?" he asked, easing past her and her chastising look to enter the kitchen.

He headed for the stove and raised his hand to

lift the lid to the pot. His sister beat him to it and swatted his hand away.

"Wash your hands," she reprimanded him.

He moved to the sink.

"In the bathroom."

Kael chuckled as he left the kitchen and headed down the hall past two of the bedrooms to the lone bathroom of the house. He paused at the sound of his father's laughter. It was decidedly mischievous. Devilish.

Frowning in curiosity, he quickly washed his hands in the white porcelain pedestal sink that was clearly a part of the 1930s when the house was built. As were the white and black subway tiles.

Kael left the bathroom and headed left down the hall to the master bedroom. Alisha was holding both of his father's large hands as he gently sat down on the bed.

"Careful, remember to keep that ninety-degree angle like you're in a chair with a back," she said.

His eyes went to her profile and he instantly noticed she was as pretty from an angle.

"Like I'm on the john," Logan said.

Alisha laughed and shook her head as she stepped back from him and picked up her clipboard to make notations. "Yes, Mr. Strong. Straight up and down like you're on the john."

His father looked up and spotted him. "How's the ranch coming along?"

Kael stepped into the room next to the dresser

as Alisha glanced up at him. His heart pounded. "I worked on the hunting cabin today," he said. "How are you?"

Logan shrugged in his plaid pajamas. "Same."

"If you do the exercises you will not be the same by the time I come back Monday," Alisha said, sliding her clipboard into a bright orange tote bag.

Logan snorted in derision. "You want a horse, 'cause I got one I'm selling for a penny," he grumbled.

"You have offered me that horse ten times since I've been here and the answer is still no," she told him with a playful wink.

Kael shifted his eyes back to her. They traveled down the length of her body in the dull green scrubs she wore. She bent over to pick up her tote. He could see the outline of her panties slightly pressing into the thin cotton and he looked away from the delicious curve of her bottom.

Damn.

She turned and stepped toward him to reach the door. "Mr. Strong—"

"Kael," he corrected her.

Her eyes fell to his lips when he spoke and shifted back up to his eyes when he stopped. She cleared her throat. "Uhm, Kael. I already went over some restrictions for your father with your sister. I could go over them with you or—"

"No," he said abruptly.

Her face filled with surprise.

His father glared at him over her shoulder from his spot on the edge of the bed.

Kael softened his stance, knowing he was being rude even if he didn't intend to. "Thanks."

Alisha squinted her eyes just a bit as she studied him. The top of her head reached his chin, causing her to have to look up at him as she did. She opened her mouth and then closed it, biting her bottom lip before she smiled and chuckled a bit. "You have a good day, Mr. Strong. I'll see you Monday," she said, to his father, her eyes still locked on his face. "And I'll see you too . . . Kael."

She was bold. She was defiant. She was take-no-charge. She was in his face. She was challenging him.

The question was to what?

Kael rose up off the wall where he leaned, raising his height another inch or two and closing the gap between them as well. He chuckled and shook his head when she just arched her brow and didn't back away.

In a different time, different place and if he was in a different emotional skin he would have snatched her up and kissed the smugness from her. He knew he could do it. Easily.

Just as easily as he could see himself pressing his lips, tongue and hands to every inch of her body.

"Good-bye, Ms. Rockmon," was all that he said, although many more words rested on his tongue.

She turned. "It's Lisha," she called over her shoulder as she left the room.

He turned his head to watch her exit.

Logan chuckled. "If I was twenty years—no, make it ten—if I was ten years younger and didn't have a bum hip I'd give you a race for your money, son," he said, placing his hands on his knees as he stretched his back and sat up straighter on the bed.

Kael looked over at him. "Race for what?" he asked, playing dumb.

He knew exactly what his father meant.

"That one got your nose so open, you can smell rat shit ten miles away." Logan reached for the black and white 5X7 photo of Ivy Strong on the nightstand. "Your mother had me jittery as hell like that too."

"You might need to lower the dose on those pain meds," Kael said over his shoulder as he walked through the bedroom's open door.

Logan just grunted and laughed.

Kael stopped and pressed his back to the wall when he saw Kelli leaving the kitchen carrying a metal tray with legs. She passed him and he continued on to the kitchen, happy as hell to see his plate of food already served up and waiting on him.

Pushing aside all thoughts of Lisha Rockmon, he sat down at the round oak table, sparing a few seconds to say a quick grace, and then dug in to the meatloaf with brown gravy and mashed potatoes. He stuffed three huge forkfuls into his mouth before he even chewed, swallowed and then took a deep sip from the jelly jar filled with fresh-squeezed lemonade.

Kelli walked back into the kitchen and sat down at the table across from him. "Daddy thinks you want some *trim* from Lisha," she said, folding her hands atop the table as she tilted her head to the side to look at him.

Kael choked on his food and had to cough it up. His sister remained seated in that same pose waiting for him to answer. "Trim, huh?" he asked, using his tongue to clear bits of food from in between the wall of his lower cheek and his gums.

Kelli waited.

"She's a physical therapist . . . not a barber," he drawled, turning his attention back to his food.

"I know what trim is, Kael."

He bit back a laugh. "Yeah, me too," he quipped. "I know it very well."

Kelli held up her hands and made a face of disgust. "Okay, cool it, perv."

Kael just shrugged and used the side of his fork to cut another chunk of the well-seasoned meat-loaf, piercing it with the prong and dragging it through the gravy.

"I don't like her, and after the way Donna slung her . . . trim, I would think you would be a better judge of character," she said, reaching across the table to grasp his wrist. "I just don't want you hurt over another woman."

Kael continued eating even as he felt the heat of her eyes still locked on him.

Kelli finally stood up from the table and turned to leave the kitchen.

He didn't address the issue of Lisha Rockmon because there was no issue. Kael had no intention of getting involved with the woman, far less falling in love. In fact, he decided to stick to his original plan to avoid her at all costs.

Chapter 5

One month later

"Amen."

Lisha undid her prayer hands and stretched her arms high above her, still sitting up in her bed. Old habits died hard—especially good ones—and saying her thank you to the Lord first thing after opening her eyes in the morning was something she'd done since she was five or six. Reverend Rockmon and his First Lady would not have it any other way under their roof and she now felt the same way even under her own roof—albeit rented.

Pulling her knees to her chest, she wrapped her arms around her legs and rested her cheek atop her knees as she looked at the sunshine gleaming through the sheer white curtains at her window. The room was cool from the window air conditioning unit blowing all night and she was grateful for it, knowing the summer heat of South Carolina was unforgiving. Just as unforgiving as the electric company and how high her light bill would shoot up for the privilege of that air.

Thankfully the extra hours she earned for working with Mr. Strong had increased the size of her paycheck. When the time for his physical therapy came to an end she was going to miss the extra money and the time she spent with the man. He was strong and smart and fair-minded. He filled their two hours together with funny stories about his past, the ways of white folks or his children.

She always thought it hilarious when Logan's stories would upset his daughter, Kelli, whom Lisha thought to be a really cool, laid-back person. Lisha had invited her to attend her father's church for worship service, but Kelli stayed with her father during the week and traveled home to her husband on the weekends, leaving her brother over their father's care. But Lisha didn't work on the weekends so she hadn't seen much of Kael Strong in the month since she began working with his father. She may see him arriving home in his truck just as she was exiting in her car, and even that was very infrequent.

Thankfully the smaller doses she received of the man had led to the newness of him and his appeal wearing off. Those nervous jitters at just the thought of seeing him were gone. No extra attention was paid to her hair or makeup. When she went to bed at night he was not in her dreams.

Her mini-fascination with Kael Strong was over.

Flinging back the crisp cotton sheets, she finally climbed from bed and made her way straight out of the bedroom to the bathroom for her morning ritual. Before she even relieved herself she brushed her teeth and got rid of any morning breath. Smacking her lips at the minty taste, she pulled the oversized T-shirt she wore to bed over her head and tossed it into the white wicker hamper beneath the towel rod.

Tucking her hair under a plastic shower cap and turning the shower on to let the heat and the steam build she padded back to her bedroom and across her carpeted floor to her closet. She quickly shifted through the clothes, finally deciding on a butter yellow sundress to wear to church that morning. After retrieving and placing her undergarments and heeled sandals atop the dress, she checked her bedside alarm clock and quickly made her way back to the bathroom for a long hot shower and a facial.

Lisha finally felt fully awake and rejuvenated.

Picking up the phone by her bed she dialed Junie's number. The phone rang a dozen times or more before she finally heard the rumble of the receiver being knocked off its base.

"I'm up. I'm up," she said, her voice still thick and hoarse with sleep.

Lisha said nothing and just hung up. It was their Sunday morning ritual, and regardless of what or whom Junie did on Saturday night, she always made it to church the next morning.

When Lisha emerged from her bedroom thirty minutes later fully dressed with her hair up in a loose topknot, Junie was stretched out on the couch in a floral V-neck dress, laid out on her back, her curly Afro wig twisted to the left and her glossy lips opened wide as she snored in her sleep.

Lisha crept over to the stereo system in the corner of her living room, turned the dial to a gospel station and then turned the knob to max the volume before powering it on.

The sound of organ music and a robust choir blasted through the speakers singing the chorus to Andraé Crouch's "Take Me Back."

Junie sat up straight and looked around with wide eyes like she'd received a jolt of electricity.

Lisha laughed as she turned off the stereo and strolled across the room to shift Junie's wig to its proper position on her head. "Morning, morning," she said loudly and with a lot of enthusiasm.

Junie waved her hands away and stood up. "Go to hell," she muttered.

"Late night?" Lisha asked as they left her apartment.

The heat instantly pressed against them. It was barely after nine and it was already hot as the place Junie had directed her to. They both knew there was no need wasting energy to fan themselves as they walked down the flight of stairs to the parking lot.

Junie cleared her throat as she searched in her blue patent leather handbag. "Very," she replied, unwrapping a stick of gum and biting half of it. She offered Lisha the other half.

She made a face as they reached her car. "I don't know what you had your mouth on last night," she snapped, unlocking the car door.

Junie paused like she was thinking about it and then smiled. "You're right," she said, before wrapping the piece back in its paper and pushing it back into her handbag.

Junie was infamous for going on a popping gum tirade that could battle the sound of fireworks on the Fourth of July. She figured out ages ago that a half stick of gum was just the right amount for her to pop away.

Once they were in the car and headed out of the parking lot of their apartment complex, Junie opened her compact and checked her face. "Ain't we going in the wrong direction?" she asked.

"My father's a guest speaker in Holtsville for the church's anniversary so we're following him there," she said, steering the Nova through town and then onto Highway 17.

Junie made a stink face. "Holtsville?" she said. "I am not putting my shoes in mud in no woods."

Lisha refrained from commenting. It took them less than ten minutes to make the drive and soon she was turning onto the paved parking lot of a small brick church with beautiful stained-glass windows in deep rich colors. The mahogany double doors of the church were open directly into the small vestibule.

Junie was looking around and finally her thin shoulders relaxed. They climbed from the car. The sounds of the church's organ music could be heard outside as they climbed the stairs and accepted the church program and donation envelope from one of the two ushers standing at the door battling the heat.

Lisha was thankful for the coolness of the central air when the next set of double doors leading into the sanctuary of the church closed behind them. She felt the curious eyes on their unfamiliar faces and Lisha plastered on a fake smile and locked eyes with those bold enough not to look away. She was headed for a seat in the front of the church when Junie tightly gripped her wrist and jerked her back a few steps to slide onto one of the empty pews at the rear.

As the daughter of the visiting minster she knew her father expected her on the front pew next to her mother. She gave Junie a hard bug-eyed stare that her cousin ignored as she fanned herself with the church program. "I'm going up to the front," she said, rising to her feet.

She felt Junie's fingertips on her wrist again and she snatched it away, pausing as the church doors opened. Her eyes widened in surprise and pleasure to see Logan carefully walk inside the church with a noticeable limp but without his cane or walker. He looked tall and strong and distinguished in his dark gray suit with his brown complexion and silver hair.

Although she steadily worked with him two days a week for the last month and knew he was able to walk short distances on his own, she'd had no idea he felt confident and strong enough to tackle steps and long distances.

I wonder if he's having pain, she thought, her assessing eyes dropping down to his hip.

Many people in the church applauded or loudly praised God at the sight of him. She knew it was the first time many people had seen him since his accident.

She smiled when he paused in surprise at seeing her before giving her a wink. And then she paused at the jolt she felt at seeing Kael holding the door for his father. The lightweight deep navy suit he wore looked good on him and fit his strong build well.

When his father paused long enough to squeeze her hands she saw his eyes shift to her and the surprise that filled his face . . . just before his eyes took her all in from head to toe in one quick glance that made her breathless.

She forced her eyes away from him and smiled at his father instead. "Good job, Logan," she whispered to him, reaching out to rub the back of his lower arm before stepping back and sitting down next to Junie as her knees weakened.

She forced herself to pay way more attention than needed to the church program.

"Ooooh. Well, will you look at the goodness of God," Junie whispered in pleasure, her voice filled with wonder.

Lisha already knew. *Kael.*

She looked up and sure enough he was there behind his father giving him room to make it on his own to their seats, but still there ready to catch him if he fell. She let her eyes wander over his profile as her heart fluttered like it was filled with butterfly wings.

And she was as far from being over Kael as she could ever be.

He glanced back before taking his seat. Their eyes met. The beating and the fluttering stopped.

She was glad when he took his seat and broke his hold on her. Even though the church was cool, she could swear she felt a drop of sweat race between the deep valley of her breasts. She crossed her legs and reached for one of the paper fans.

"Church ain't never been so interesting," Junie said behind her hand just as the organist began to play as the children's choir marched in singing "This Little Light of Mine."

Lisha shifted on the wooden pew and gave Lisha her back.

"Look at them shoulders," Junie was saying, talking aloud to herself.

Lisha rolled her eyes heavenward, not allowing her eyes to go anywhere in Kael's vicinity. She looked at the children in their pressed white shirts and black pants or skirts as they made their way up onto the choir stand to the left of the pulpit. She leaned a bit to her left to lay eyes on her father in his grand black, gold and white robe because the altar blocked where he sat. She searched both front pews until she spotted her mother's wide-brimmed pink hat as she nodded her head to the music.

"Let it shine . . . let it shine . . . let it shine," the choir sang, the children's voices blending well together.

"I got something I wanna let shine, shine, shine," Junie said, knocking her knee against hers.

Lisha dropped her forehead against her hand. *God, please forgive her.*

"Lisha looks sum'n different out that uniform, huh?"

Kael pretended not to hear his father as they slowly maneuvered down the few brick steps of the church. Still, his eyes zoned right in to where she was walking up to them. For a solid month he had successfully avoided her and now here she was in his direct path and completely unavoidable. And completely beautiful.

With the summer sun beaming down, the yellow of her dress was even brighter, like she had a glow around her. Her hair was up, exposing the length of her neck and emphasizing the highness of her cheeks with her round face. The dress respectfully skimmed her curves but the shape of her body showed nonetheless and her legs were toned and full—just the way he liked them.

When he first saw her in church the surprise was understandable—but the rush of pleasure surprised him. And everything about her that thrilled him that first day came back in a hot second. Everything.

Before he took his seat in church he had given in to temptation and turned to get another glimpse of her. When their eyes met he couldn't look away as his heart pounded wildly in his chest.

"Look at you, Mr. Strong," Lisha said, reaching them, her bright eyes looking up at his father. "Are you in any pain?"

Kael felt the fact that it smarted when she didn't speak or even acknowledge him.

"A little twinge here and there, but no major pain, no," he said. "But you ain't working today so don't worry about me until tomorrow when you're on the payroll."

"I worry about you if I'm working or not," she told him with a smile.

Kael frowned at the jealousy he felt at the easy rapport between them. "That's good to know," he said, wanting to be acknowledged by her.

He succeeded.

Lisha looked up to him, her smile fading just a bit. "How are you . . . Kael?" she asked.

He bit back a smile, knowing she was referring to their last exchange in his father's bedroom. "I'm good, Lisha," he said, his eyes locked on hers.

"And you are looking good."

Kael forced himself to look away from Lisha to the petite woman standing beside her. To be honest, he hadn't even seen her. "Thank you," he said.

She extended her hand as she bit her bottom lip softly. "I'm June, Lisha's cousin. Everyone calls me Junie, but you can call me tonight at—"

Just as Kael reached to take her hand, Lisha walked between them and grabbed her cousin by the arm to pull her away a few feet.

Stevie Wonder and Ray Charles would be able to see that Junie was interested in Kael. He had never been hit on so strongly . . . especially at church.

"I used to have 'em fool just like that when I was your age, son," his father said with a chuckle. "Back in 1945 . . ."

Kael steeled himself for one of his father's stories as he continued to look on as Junie and Lisha had a very heated conversation with a few furtive glances in his direction. He couldn't help but wonder what they were talking about or fight the feeling that it was all about him.

"I was in the market buying some meat to grill when this woman walks up to me. Okay?" Logan asked. "And stood right in front of me and pulled her panties off and gave 'em to me. In. My. Hand."

Kael let his head hang to his chest as he laughed.

"Yeah. Yeah. Yeah-yeah-yeah," Logan said, smacking his son's arm lightly. "Now thank God she was fresh. You know?"

Kael rocked on his heels and looked up to the skies.

"Because that meat market coulda smelled like a fish market . . . just like that," Logan said, snapping his finger sharply. BAP.

Kael frowned deeply.

"You get where I'm coming from, son?" Logan asked, with the utmost serious expression.

"Unfortunately, man, yeah," he said, shaking his head.

Lisha and her cousin turned and made their way back to them.

"One hell of a night, son," Logan said in a low voice like he was reminiscing on it. "*Hell* of a night."

"We're going to be on our way," Lisha said,

looking at Kael quickly before focusing back on his father. "I'll see you tomorrow."

Kael glanced over at the cousin who instantly looked away as she hung back a few feet from them. His eyes squinted until they were almost closed as he thought on that for a second.

"Good-bye, Kael."

He looked back at Lisha, but she had already turned and was walking away from them. Her cousin waved at them briefly before catching up with Lisha as they made their way to a long blue Buick. His eyes took in the swish of her hem against her legs as she moved.

And her legs were smooth caramel with a definite feminine shape and a firmness that would make any man wonder if the rest of her body was just as solid.

"We better get you off that hip," Kael said, even as his eyes were still locked on Lisha as she kissed the cheeks of her parents. *A preacher's kid.*

"Yeah, my La-Z-Boy is calling," Logan said.

"You okay walking or you want me to pull the car up?" Kael asked.

"Man, I'm Logan Strong. I'm good," he said with his usual bravado.

Kael fell silent. He knew the injury had shattered not just his father's hip, but his pride as well. Logan Strong was a strong man and it couldn't have been easy for him to learn to walk again and admit he needed help. Having his son help him in and out the shower had to be a struggle that he fought hard not to show.

And the recent news from his doctor that he may never ride horses again was a total shift in everything he knew about the man he was. Logan Strong had been a ranch hand since his early teens and his love of horses had come to him even earlier than that. Although he didn't discuss it, Kael knew that the news had to shake him to his core.

He reached over and hugged his father around his broad shoulders before patting his back and then moving quickly to ram his hands into the front pocket of his bell-bottom slacks. It was as if he did it quick enough, it was almost like he could fool him into thinking it never happened. His father was not a demonstrative man.

Logan scowled.

"What do you think all of that back there was about?" he asked, meaning to change the subject.

Logan opened the passenger door to the truck, but paused. He shook his head as he stared at Kael. "Son, if you can't put two and two together on that then I'm worried about you."

"What you talking about?" Kael asked, watching as his father stepped up onto the side rail with one foot and then the other before turning to sit on the seat and then swing his legs around.

Logan chuckled. "Lisha pulled rank on her cousin for you, boy. She cooled them hot heels quickly," he said, still smiling before closing the passenger door soundly.

THUD.

Kael felt a smile spread across his face at the thought of Lisha blocking her cousin from coming on to him. But why would she care?

Or did she care?

And the real question was: Why did he care?

Kael came around the bed of the truck, climbing into the driver's seat and starting the truck. Flashes of pretty brown legs beneath a sunshine-colored hem kept teasing his thoughts even as he pondered if his father was right. Both he and his father were silent and obviously lost in their thoughts as they made the short drive back to the house.

He was surprised when he turned off the road onto the drive and spotted his sister's car parked by the left side of the house. She usually didn't drive down until late Sunday night and when she left on Friday they had all agreed that their father was self-sufficient enough that she would only come down every other week.

"I thought she wasn't coming until next week," Logan said, obviously just as surprised.

As he parked, the front door opened and Kelli came out to stand on the front porch. Moments later, another woman stepped out to join her.

"Get my cane, son."

Kael shifted his eyes to his father and noticed

the tightness of his jaw. He knew he was in pain or at least discomfort. He hopped from the truck and grabbed the cane from the truck bed before coming around to hand it to Logan who was sitting with the passenger door open.

His urge was to help his father, but he knew Logan would not want it. So Kael pretended to retrieve something from the truck bed, but in fact had has his eyes locked on his father. Thankfully, he maneuvered out of the truck with just a grunt before he pushed the door closed.

"Hey, Daddy," Kelli said, smiling as he came down the walk and stepped up onto the porch.

"Hey there. We wasn't looking for you 'til next week," Logan said, pausing as he sniffed the air. "What's that I smell?"

Kelli kissed his cheek as she wrapped her arms around one of his. "I got here while y'all were in church and made oxtails. My good friend Bea helped me. Ain't that right, Bea?"

Kael looked over at the other woman and paused to see her eyes were steadily on him.

"That's right. I sure did," she said in a soft voice. "I just love making a good home-cooked meal for a Southern man who appreciates it."

Logan chuckled.

Kael shifted under her direct gaze. "Nice to meet you, Bea. I'm—"

She eased past his father carefully and came to stand in front of him. She was tall and slender.

"Kael Strong. Oh trust me, brotha, I know exactly who you are."

He looked over the woman's shoulder to see Kelli looking on with satisfaction.

"Bea lives in Walterboro. We went to school together. You remember, Bea, don't you, Kael?" she asked, stepping back to open the screen door for their father.

Not quite sure the woman would unblock his path, Kael took a look at her. She was cute enough, but he didn't remember her and said as much.

Bea wrapped both her arms around one of Kael's and pressed the softness of her breast against it as they walked into the house behind his sister and father. "That's cool, baby. We can get to know one another."

Kael dislodged his arm from her tight grasp. "Excuse me," he said, making a face once he was out of her line of vision. He headed straight to his bedroom and closed the door.

He kicked off his shoes and removed his jacket, tossing it onto the foot of his bed before he began to unbutton the navy wide-collared shirt he wore. He was half undone before he stopped and reached over to lock the door.

Tossing his shirt atop the blazer he squeezed between the dresser and the foot of the full-sized bed to turn on the large metal air conditioning unit in the window. He wished he'd left it on so the small room wasn't so muggy and hot.

As a teenager, the room had been fine, but as a grown man used to his own place, Kael felt smothered in the room. Still he'd rather that than be smothered by his sister and her pick for the newest lady in his life.

Lying on his unmade bed, he tucked his hands behind his head and crossed his feet at the ankles, staring at the ceiling as he waited for the heat to subside. His chest and back were already damp with sweat.

Knock-knock.

"Kael, you asleep?"

He puckered his brow at the sound of Bea's voice. *What the hell she want?* he thought.

Knock-knock.

Kael ignored her again. Kelli was in the mood to play matchmaker and Kael was having none of it. The kind of short-lived and uncommitted relationships he had with women these days was nothing his sister would want her prim and proper friends to deal with. Women like his sister were looking for marriage and commitment and Kael was not offering that to anyone. Not now.

He was an honest man, and if there was any woman on his radar to even consider dating, it was Alisha Rockmon, and he was avoiding that impulse like it was the plague.

His trust was shaken.

Kael clenched his fist as he thought of the shock and hurt he'd felt at discovering the woman he loved was screwing another man—maybe even multiple men—in the home he'd provided for them. The hurt was gone. He would never be shocked by anything again. The emotion that remained clawing in his throat was anger.

Even now, when people were new to discover that he was no longer with his ex, some were bold enough to tell him he should be glad to be free of her, or dropped names of men they heard she was dealing with behind his back, or looked at him in pity at having heard how he caught her.

He'd been made a fool of and it was not a good feeling.

Chapter 6

Lisha reached her hands out to her client, a teenaged football athlete recovering from a severe ankle break, as they stood in the heated pool of the clinic that was used for aqua therapy. The buoyancy of the water was ideal for resistance without the stress of using weights and the heat kept the muscles limber. "Okay, lean back into the flotation device and give me twenty knee lifts," she instructed him, seeing his determination in the blue of his eyes.

As she finished the five-minute session with him, she assisted him to climb out of the pool via the steps and rails. The smell of the chlorine in the pool seemed trapped and heady in the glass-encased room and she was ready to head straight to the employee locker room to wash it from her skin. "Good job, Garrett," she told him, drying her hands quickly to make notes on his chart.

He was her last client for the day and the pool

therapy was the last portion of his treatment for the week. She handed his chart to one of the physical therapy aides who handed him a towel and guided him to the client locker room to change clothes.

Removing the white swim cap she wore to protect her hair from getting wet, she grabbed a towel as well and wrapped it around her waist in the red swimsuit and shorts she wore. She looked up before heading through the door leading into the changing rooms and paused at the sight of Kael standing at one of the windows surrounding the pool area.

Why is he here?

She started to raise her hand to wave, but lowered it before she did. He surprised her by lifting his chin to her in greeting. Doing the same, she pushed through the door and paused on the other side to take a deep breath. *That man, that man, that man.*

He was her distraction.

When she was working with his dad at their home she was constantly on edge if he was around and even more on edge if he wasn't there and she didn't know if he would suddenly appear. When she wasn't working she found herself wondering about him . . . and she still barely knew the man.

She quickly rinsed off the chlorine before drying off and changing back into her uniform. She raked her fingers through her loose rod-set curls, applied mascara and lip gloss that she hadn't bothered to put on when she got dressed for work earlier. Checking her appearance one last time in her compact, she pushed her purse back into her locker and went through the other door leading out to the clinic.

Her pulse was racing as she looked around the common area for him. She walked around, forcing herself to remain calm as she did. He was no longer by the area overlooking the pool. She didn't see him near any of the treatment rooms. She even breezed past the office of the owner and head physical therapist of the clinic.

Feeling like a stalker, she gave up the hunt, heading back to the employee locker room to clock out and grab her purse. She felt disappointed as she waved her co-workers good-bye and left the clinic through the entrance leading onto the street. Nothing would ever develop between her and Kael. She was gun-shy and he was uninterested.

A man had a way of letting a woman know he wanted her and besides a few lingering glances and catching him checking out her walk-away on rare occasions, Kael Strong had not made a move. And she wanted him to.

Standing on the sidewalk as the August heat warmed her, she checked for oncoming traffic and crossed the street, looking up at the cloudy sky. It was far too dark out for a little after six on a summer evening.

She barely made it into her car and drove a few feet out of the parking lot before the thunder echoed and the skies opened as the rain poured down. Turning on her windshield wipers, Lisha didn't bother with the radio as she enjoyed the sound of the rain pelting against the windows and the car.

She made the two right turns to get on the one-way street running in the opposite direction. She braked and slowed down when she spotted someone pushing a truck into one of the parking spots on the streets. Squinting, she sat up straight, recognizing Kael and his pickup truck.

Lisha pulled up beside him and reached over to roll down the window on the passenger side. Rain instantly pelted through the opening and dampened the seat and door. She blew the horn.

He looked over his shoulder, the rain already soaking his clothes to his body.

"Need a ride?" she hollered out.

Kael nodded and waved for her to park farther up the street.

She did and then watched in the rearview mirror as he finished pushing the truck into a parking spot on the street. He grabbed something from inside it and then dashed up the street to hop into her car.

Lisha took a breath to calm down. "I didn't see

your thumb, but I thought you could use a lift," she joked, glancing over at him before she checked her side mirror and eased the car out into traffic.

He chuckled. "Appreciate it. My baby let me down," he said, wiping the wetness from his face with both of his large hands.

"Nothing serious?" she asked, trying her best not to let her awareness of him shift her focus from driving safely in the rain. She felt jittery being in such close confines with him. Her heart was racing off the charts.

"No, I think it overheated," he said.

"Overheated, huh?" she asked, her voice soft as she glanced over at him.

"Yeah . . . yeah . . . overheated," he said, glancing over at her.

They both looked away.

Lisha's grip tightened on the wheel as she bit her bottom lip and closed her eyes, feeling even steamier than his truck. She felt so uncomfortable around him. So awkward. So unsure. So unsteady. *This man, this man . . . this man.*

Kael looked back at Lisha, but she was gazing out the window. His entire day had been nothing but a string of surprises, some good and some bad.

Finding out that a section of the roofing on his home needed to be replaced? Bad. That was more money to be spent when he was already cash-strapped from setting up the ranch and not seeing any returns on it yet.

Happening to see Lisha in a bathing suit? Good and bad. The sight of the suit on her curvy frame was good. Trying to forget just how delectable she looked? *Damn.*

His truck stalling on him in downtown Charleston during heavy rain? Bad. Real bad.

And then that good and bad mixed again because he was grateful for Lisha happening upon him and offering him a ride, but now he was in this enclosed space with her and it was hard to fight the attraction in such an intimate setting.

"I'll just have it towed back to the house tomorrow," Kael finally said, trying to distract himself from the sweet scent of her perfume.

The same scent that still clung to the air at the house long after she was gone.

"I was surprised to see you at the clinic. Everything okay with your dad?" she asked, as the rain continued to pour.

"Had to settle a bill."

Coming to a stop at a red light, she smiled at him with a twinkle in her eyes. "I'm the best and the best costs," she teased.

He side-eyed her, liking how her face lit up with her smile. "I'm surprised you can fit your head inside the car," he drawled.

She laughed.

His gut clenched. The sound of her laughter

was light and full, the kind to make someone laugh along with her whether they knew what she found funny or not.

"I'm just kidding . . . kinda," Lisha said, settling down into her seat as she sped up a little when the traffic cleared.

Kael pulled his damp shirt from his chest. "So the pool is for therapy?" he asked.

She nodded. "The pool is heated and there's a ramp that lets the patients walk down into the pool if they're not strong enough or confident enough to use the stairs yet."

"I saw that." Kael thought of seeing her in her bathing suit. It was an athletic cut but still far less fabric than the uniforms he was used to seeing her wear.

"Aqua therapy would be really great for your dad."

Kael snorted. "Logan Strong?" he asked, sounding like he didn't see it.

"Maybe we can talk him into it together," she suggested.

"Probably you more than me," he quipped. "He really likes you."

"Well, I like him too," she said. "He's pretty damn funny."

"That's one way to put it," he said dryly, ready to get home and out of his wet clothing.

Lisha laughed, accelerating the car forward

down Savannah Highway. "I almost died when he told me about the time he got robbed . . ."

"In a juke joint down in Mississippi," they finished together before laughing.

"I heard that tale many times," Kael said, shaking his head.

"But I bet it's just as funny each time he tells it, right?" she asked.

"That's because he adds something new to the story every time he tells it," Kael balked.

"True," Lisha agreed.

They fell silent as she drove. He looked toward her when she reached to turn on the radio. Soon the sounds of Gladys Knight & The Pips singing "If I Was Your Woman" filled the car.

Lisha was softly singing along with the music as she tapped her fingers against the steering wheel.

"'You'd have no other woman . . . . you'd be weak as a lamb.'"

Kael looked to her again, believing one hundred percent that she would be able to weaken a man for any other woman. He opened his mouth to tell her as much, but he smiled, bit his bottom lip and swallowed the words. His eyes dipped down to take in her thick thighs pressed against the thin cotton of her uniform pants. He forced himself to look away.

He could easily see himself reach for her hand and play with her fingers as they listened to the soulful song as she drove. Easily.

Lisha was trouble for him with a capital T.

"'I'd never, never, never stop loving you,'" she sang along, barely audible.

"You ever loved someone that deep?" Kael asked, surprising himself.

When he looked at her he saw that he'd caught her off guard with the question as well.

But then she locked eyes with him and said, "No. Never. But I'd like to."

Kael couldn't look away.

"You?" she asked, a hint of a smile at her lips.

"I thought so," he answered her honestly with a shrug.

"It is better to have loved and lost than never to have loved at all," she told him. "Or however it goes."

"Or something like that," he said, their eyes still locked.

"Yeah."

"Yeah."

The music. The rain. The close quarters. Lisha. The combo was heady.

The blare of a car horn behind them broke the intense moment.

Lisha was the first to look away as she faced the road and accelerated forward from where they had stopped at a light that had long since changed from red to green.

He forced himself to look out the window at the towering trees they passed as they neared Holtsville.

He felt regret that their time together was coming to an end.

Lisha Rockmon could easily get to be addictive.

They rode the rest of the way in silence, but there were many times Lisha would catch his sexy eyes on her or she would feel him looking at her. When she drove into Holtsville and soon turned onto the drive of his father's home, she parked the car and turned in her seat to stare boldly at him.

He pressed his back against the seat and eyed her. "What?" he asked, quickly looking over his shoulder.

She bit her cheek to keep from smiling and kept staring at him.

"Yes?" he asked, his brows furrowing.

"Just giving you a full view of me since you were staring," she said, putting some of her fears of being rejected aside.

She barely heard the rain pouring around them and soulful music softly playing on the radio over the steady thumping of her heavy heartbeat.

Kael's stance relaxed as he eyed her with those eyes that were made to make a woman feel like a woman.

"Do you deny it?" she asked.

"No," he said, shaking his head slightly.

She took a deep little breath through slightly

opened lips and then released it in a huff. *This man, this man, this man . . .*

"You're very easy to look at," he admitted in his deep voice.

Another breath. In and then out.

There was an energy that was almost palpable in the cocoon of the car. It was nothing like Lisha had ever felt before. That scared and excited her all at once.

Lisha looked away, needing a break from the intensity, but only seconds passed before she was looking back at him. Getting lost in him. "You're not bad yourself," she said. "But it's not like you don't know that."

Kael chuckled. "Nah," he said.

"Yeah, right."

They fell silent again.

"Let's get it on . . ."

Lisha's hand shot out as she turned the volume down on the car stereo. It was not a time for Marvin Gaye. Definitely not.

Things were powerful enough because Lisha the virgin who didn't even like to kiss on the first date found her eyes on Kael's lush lips, wanting to know just how they tasted.

Kael liked being in the car with Lisha, with the rain beating down on the car and feeling like they were lost in their own little cocoon. He liked it too much.

"I'm not looking for a girlfriend or anything," he said, needing to break whatever it was that kept him entranced by her and not wanting to leave the comfort of that car and her.

Her eyes shot up from his mouth to lock on his eyes before she looked away. He saw her disappointment and was surprised when he felt his own.

"The . . . the . . . the rain is letting up," she said.

He could tell the smile she gave him was fake, but she forced it on and faced him as she politely invited him out of her vehicle.

"Thanks for the ride, Lisha. I appreciate it," he told her.

She nodded. "You better get out of those wet clothes," she said.

Kael's hand paused on the door handle. "I'm going. You don't have to throw me out of your car," he joked.

Her shoulders became less tense as she laughed. "I'm not," she said.

"You are—in a nice way—but you are."

She looked heavenward before she looked at him again. "Okay, I kinda am," she admitted with a smile that made her eyes twinkle.

He felt good about making the disappointment he caused her disappear with laughter.

Darkness settled around them and Kael honestly wasn't sure how long they had been in the car together. "I'll talk to Kelli and we'll try to convince my dad to go into Charleston for the pool therapy," he told her as he opened the car door.

"Okay, good. Bye, Kael."

He looked over his shoulder at her, loving the way his name sounded on her lips. He didn't trust himself to say anything and just nodded before leaving the car and closing the door. The rain had settled down to a light mist and he made his way up the drive to the house.

He thought it was cute and a sign of her good heart that she waited on him—a grown-ass man—to get inside of the house before she reversed out of the yard with a final light blow of her horn.

"I thought y'all were camping out," Kelli said.

Kael turned from looking out the door, closing it behind him. His sister and father were sitting on the leather living room sofa, watching Walter Cronkite deliver the evening news.

"That was Lisha who dropped you off?" his father asked, looking pleased.

"My truck broke down when I left the clinic and she happened to be leaving work and offered me a ride home," he said, hating the need he felt to explain.

His sister was working overtime to get him married. She was already pushing her friend Bea down his throat. He didn't want her to add Lisha to the list of possible candidates. He was barely winning at avoiding both his attraction to her and his father's constant hints about what a good daughter-in-law she would make.

"Been out there a *long* time, son," Logan said, cutting his eye up at Kael before looking back at the television with a grin.

"Sure was," Kelli agreed.

To hell with this shit.

Kael scooped up his father's keys from where they always sat on the end table. "My roof needs fixing. I'm going to check and make sure it's not leaking with all this rain," he said, before heading straight out the door.

Lisha stepped out of the shower and wrapped a thick towel around her damp body. She didn't bother to dry off as she stood at the sink rod-setting her damp hair in the mirror. She paused as Kael's words came back to her.

You're very easy to look at.

She arched her brow at the sight of her rollers and the dabs of pimple cream on her face. "How about now?" she quipped at her reflection.

And then her eyes got sad.

I'm not looking for a girlfriend or anything.

And just like that, she and Kael were over before anything even began. She did appreciate his honesty, but that didn't quell the disappointment. Her ego had played with the idea that she had caught Kael's eye, but none of that mattered.

If he wasn't looking for a girlfriend, then marriage was definitely off the table, and that was the end goal for Lisha. She wasn't in the market for a lover. She wanted to meet the man she was meant to fall in love with and then marry.

Kael took himself out of the running.

Rolling the last long strand of hair around a roller, she secured it with a large bobby pin and then tied a large colorful silk scarf around it. "Ain't this a sight," she said to her reflection before leaving the bathroom and shutting off the light.

"You done talking to yourself in there?"

Lisha started in surprise. Junie was settled on her couch in front of the TV set on the rolling stand. "I don't use my key to your apartment as much as you use the one to mine," she called out, heading into her bedroom to drop the damp towel and pull on her thin cotton housecoat.

"That's because the last time you did you saw way more of me and my date than you wanted to," Junie said when she walked back into the living room.

Lisha paused and frowned at the memory. "You're right," she agreed before plopping down on the other end of the sofa and digging her hand inside the torn aluminum foil for a handful of Jiffy Pop popcorn.

"No need for both of us to be stuck in the house alone with all this rain," Junie said, flipping through Lisha's copy of the *TV Guide* before walking over to the television to turn the channel to *Happy Days* before plopping back down on the sofa.

Lisha turned and looked out the window at the rain still coming down outside. The sight of the wetness on the window took her right back to being in her car with Kael. His large frame had made the compact car seem even smaller and there had been no escaping the warm scent of his cologne.

She shivered a little at how they had stared at each other for the longest moments. Hot electrifying moments.

"What's happening with you?"

Lisha looked over at her. "Huh?" she asked softly.

She tossed popcorn against Lisha's forehead. "What's on your mind?"

"I had to give Kael a ride from Charleston today when his truck broke down," she said, picking the popcorn up and tossing it into one of the large glass ashtrays on the coffee table.

"Kael, the dude you threatened to beat my ass over . . . ON CHURCH GROUNDS?" Junie stressed.

Lisha held up her hands and shrugged her shoulders. "I did not threaten you," she began. "I just reminded you of that last fight we had when we were eleven."

"Yes, the fight when you punched me in the nose," she inserted with wide eyes. "And we were only fighting over shoes then, so I can only imagine what you were threatening to do to me over *that* man."

"*Anyway* . . . he asked me something about ever being in love—"

"Oooh," Junie sighed with a wiggle of her thick eyebrows.

"But then he told me he doesn't want a girlfriend."

"Ew." Junie frowned.

"Exactly," Lisha said, releasing a heavy breath as she twisted her lips in disappointment.

Brrrnnnggg.

Lisha hopped up and made her way to the kitchen to answer the telephone. "Hello."

"Lisha, hey, this is Shieran."

Her surprise at the human resources manager of the clinic calling her was evident. "Hey, Shieran," she said, her brows puckering as she turned to lean back against the wall.

As she listened, her scowl deepened. "Okay, that's fine. See you tomorrow," she said, very calm and polite even though her heart was pounding away.

Hanging up the phone she strolled back into the living room. Junie was laughing away at the antics of the Fonz but she looked up and did a double take at Lisha's expression. "What's wrong?"

"I guess Kael wanted to make it clear he wasn't interested because I just got pulled off his father's home therapy. Kelli—that's his daughter—is going to bring him to Charleston for treatment now," she said. "My job wanted to make sure I came straight to the clinic in the morning."

"Well, damn," Junie said.

"Well, damn is right," Lisha agreed, feeling warmth spread through her that was a mix of anger and embarrassment.

"Passion is the fire that burns from a heart in love."

—Unknown

Interlude

"*Y que sucedió después?*"

The entire Strong clan turned to look at Garcelle and said collectively, "Huh?"

She threw up her hands. "I *said,* 'Well, what happened next?'"

"Oh," they all said together.

"Let me check the turkey," Lisha said, about to rise from her seat.

"No, I'll get it," Garcelle offered, rising from her seat beside her husband, Kade. "I'll be right back. Wait on me."

As she took steps away from him he held on to her until her the very tips of her fingers stroked his as they pulled apart. She smiled at him and felt all the love she had for the man fill her as she finally turned.

She sang along to the music playing as she walked down the hall to the large kitchen.

The island was filled with lid-covered side dishes, various flavors of pies and a huge chocolate cake topped with chopped walnuts. Garcelle already knew from the height that it had to be seven layers. Just like every Christmas, her mother-in-law, whom she adored almost as much as she did her deceased mother, had to cook all of yesterday to have such a feast ready for her large family.

And family was important especially during the holidays.

Garcelle was happy to be there with Kade, her stepdaughter, Kadina, her toddler son, Karlos, and the in-laws, but she felt a deep pang that her own family was all together in the Dominican Republic for the holidays. Her father, Carlos, teenaged brother, Paco, and her uncles, Anthony and Raul.

Maybe next year, Kade, the children and I will travel with my family for the holidays.

She knew Kade would do it, not because she was vain or demanding, but he was always sure to think of her family as much as she thought of his. She knew he loved her and would understand.

And she loved him endlessly.

They had their own story to tell one day, and she was forever in awe that they had to overcome Kade's grief over the death of his first wife and nearly every woman in Holtsville openly pursu-

ing the handsome and sexy rancher. But it was
Garcelle, the woman he hired to take care of his
daughter, who had captured his heart again.

That had been six years ago and never once did
he make her feel he'd regretted falling for her.
Not once.

And he always made sure to let her know that he
would never forget his first wife, but it was she that
filled his heart now. Always.

She smiled as she opened the oven door and
slid on mitts to quickly check the turkey. She
moaned in pleasure at the smell of herbs and
butter as she basted the turkey before replacing
the lid and closing the oven door with her hip.

"I love those hips."

She smiled like a stroked kitten as Kade strolled
his six-foot, five-inch muscular frame into the
kitchen. The black sweater he wore looked good
against his brown complexion and head full of
silvery curls.

Garcelle popped her hip in the opposite direction before raising her hand above her head and
doing a back and forth belly dance motion. "'You
know my hips don't lie,'" she said as she danced
toward him.

"I've been watching those hips since you did
that dance for me at Kahron and Bianca's wedding," he said, placing his hands on her hips and
jerking her lower half close as he bent to press a
kiss to her neck.

"Can you believe we hated each other up until then?" she asked him in her sultry Spanish accent, closing her eyes with a moan.

"I never hated you," he said, stepping back to twirl her before capturing her around her waist and jerking her body up against him with her feet dangling above the floor.

Their eyes and lips were leveled as she brought her hands up to rub his scalp. "*Te amo,* Kade," she whispered, her eyes flittering over every aspect of his face.

"I love you more," he responded before closing the brief distance between them to cover her lips with his own.

Garcelle deepened the kiss, pulling at his curls as she tasted his tongue with a long sultry purr. She opened her eyes when she felt Kade reach for one of her hands and slide an envelope into it.

She leaned back from him and looked down at it.

"Merry Christmas," he said, looking every bit like Rick Fox.

Garcelle looked confused. "But you already gave me Sugar," she said, speaking of the white horse he'd surprised her with that morning.

"Open it," Kade said, looking pleased as he rocked on his heels.

And she did. "Oh, shit," she exclaimed, stomping her feet before jumping up into his arms again. She began speaking in fluent Spanish that was rapid-fire and Kade just laughed in pleasure.

Garcelle was a wife, a mother, a daughter, a sister, a registered nurse, a great cook, a spicy lover, a skilled dancer and an even more skilled poker player. The tickets to Vegas for a big-stakes poker tournament? Everything. Absolutely everything.

She grasped his face and looked deeply into his eyes as she pressed kisses that were hot like fire onto his face. *"Cuando llegamos a casa te voy a besar desde la cabeza hasta los dedos de tus pies y no voy a olvidar ninguna parte de tu cuerpo,"* she said to him softly in between those kisses that trailed down his body.

She knew her husband had no clue what she was saying to him, but he knew it boded well for a heated lovemaking session later.

"I am about to puke with all this lovey-dovey ish," Kadina said, strolling into the kitchen with Lei close on her heels.

The two had become the best of friends during Kaitlyn and Quint's courtship. Now that Kat and Quint were planning their wedding the teens were about to be family and were even closer.

"Where are the babies?" Garcelle asked as Kade let her body slide down to rest on her spiked heels.

"They're all in the nursery asleep," Lei said, opening the fridge to pull out two bottles of fruit juice.

"Give them all kisses for us . . . when you get back upstairs," Kade said.

Garcelle chuckled at their expressions as she

steered the girls back out of the kitchen and past the living room to the staircase. "*Adios,*" she sang, watching them both climb the stairs mumbling under their breath.

Garcelle paused to look down at the tickets in the envelope. Poker in Vegas? She did a little cha-cha step before folding the envelope and sliding it inside her bra as she joined the family. Kade pulled her back against his chest with one arm and she brought both her hands up to grasp it.

"So . . . I was pissed at this man," Lisha said, pointing her thumb at Kael as she slid right back into the story.

"Even after all that chemistry in the car?" Zaria asked.

"*Especially* after all that chemistry in the car," Lisha said, giving Kael a mean side-eye.

He just chuckled.

Lisha leaned way back in her chair with a shocked expression.

Kael feigned innocence, throwing up his hands as his children riled him. "What? Baby, that was forty years ago. We can laugh about it now," he said, reaching for her hand.

She slapped it away. "Like I was saying, I had some *words* for his behind. . . ."

Chapter 7

Way back in the day

Kael pulled the horse's reins to steer him to the right as he worked along with his part-time ranch hand, Jim, to guide his newly purchased cattle into the corral. Because of his experience and knowledge of ranching, and the fact that he could not afford to hire a large crew, Kael knew most of the work to maintain the ranch would fall on his shoulders. But he was ready.

Instead of his usual work out of town on other ranches, he accepted a full-time position as a ranch hand for local horse trainer Hank King, right in Holtsville. That kept him closer to home and able to work to keep funding his own cattle ranch. For now he would work his own ranch part-time until he made a substantial profit.

He was already skilled at properly fertilizing the land for hay growth and managing the grazing patterns of his herd to make sure both the land and his cattle were healthy. Having worked ranches since he was a teenager, Kael had a good portion of the loan and grant money he acquired set aside for the normal pitfalls of running a ranch and maintaining it. He was realistic that he would not see any true profits from his labor for a year or two and that's why he was going to work his ranch part-time at first and still work other ranches until he was ready to take it on full-time.

He was strong. He was smart. He was determined.

His ranch would succeed.

Kael used his horse to guide the last of the cattle into the corral before motioning for Jim to close the gate and securely lock it. Turning the horse around, he trotted it up to the wood fence and sat back in the saddle to look out at the fifty head of Texas longhorn cattle. All heifers ready to breed by the bull he had in a separate corral.

He was proud of the design of the brand they seared into the cattle. The double circle around a blocked letter S would identify the animals as property of the Strong Ranch.

Kael had just looked up to the skies and then over to the open spot where the cattle barn would go. Even though the cattle would be outdoors for the majority of the time, he knew it was best to have a barn in case of extremely bad weather and medical emergencies.

One day, he thought, looking on as Jim filled the troughs with water for the cattle to drink.

The sound of tires on gravel caused him to look over his shoulder. His eyes widened a bit in surprise as he just barely made out Lisha's red Nova pulling to a stop at his house in the distance. He didn't know she even knew where his ranch was. Turning the horse he rode the distance to the house, staying atop his horse as she turned on the porch to look at him.

The scowl on her pretty face was aimed at him, and as adorable as he thought she looked with her lips pursed and her eyes fiery, he wondered what caused it.

"Hello, Lisha," he said.

"Don't you hello me, Kael Strong," she snapped, coming across the wide porch to stand at the rail.

"What has your knickers in a twist?" he asked as he easily dismounted the horse and tied the reins loosely to the porch.

She looked off into the distance and pressed her lips closed.

Glancing over his shoulder, he saw Jim's tall and gangly figure ride up to begin brushing the horse down and leading him to the horse trough to drink from the clean water.

Looking back at her, he quickly jogged up the steps, his boots making solid thumps on the wood as he reached her. "Come on inside," he said, reaching for her elbow.

She jerked away from his touch.

Frowning, he opened the door and pushed it open wide with a wave of his hand for her to enter before him. She stormed across the hall and into the living room to spin around in the center to square off with him. He closed the door and leaned back against the wall next to it, propping his foot against the wall as he waited.

"I got it loud and clear that you didn't want a girlfriend," she said, her chest heaving as she started to pace.

Kael remained silent, knowing that when a woman was mad it was best to let her reveal her hand before saying a word that might send her to a higher level of anger.

She stopped, pressed her hands to her hips in the jean shorts she wore with a striped V-neck T-shirt that Kael was fighting hard not to stare at. "You just gone stand there and say nothing?"

He closed his eyes and pinched the bridge of his nose. "I was waiting on you to finish," he said calmly, still leaning against the wall.

"Oh, I am finished, Kael Strong," she said in a hard voice as she pointed her finger at him. "I am so finished with you."

"How can you be finished with something that never started?" he said, and then wished he hadn't, but his patience was wearing thin.

Lisha's eyes widened and she gasped deeply before she walked up to him. "You think your shit don't stink, but I know it do after that jive stunt you pulled," she told him, stopping just a foot before him. "Your shit stinks to the core."

Kael wanted to laugh at her words because he thought her adorable . . . but he didn't. "You plan on telling me why the hell you're mad at me?"

"I shoulda left your ass stranded behind in the rain," she said, poking his chest.

Kael captured her hand and held it, stopping her finger assault. Her skin was soft and the scent of her perfume on her wrist wafted up to him. His dick stirred. "What did I do, Lisha?" he asked.

Her eyes were on his hand holding hers, but she shifted them up to look into his face. Something in her eyes let him know that his touch affected her just the way her touch affected him.

"You didn't have to stop your father's home care to keep from seeing me," she said, her anger not as fierce anymore.

Kael frowned. "What?" he asked.

Lisha licked her lips and took a step back from him, trying to tug her hand from his grasp.

Kael didn't want to let her go. So he didn't.

She looked down at their hands and then up at him again. She seemed flustered, like she'd lost her train of thought.

Kael gave in to temptation and let his thumb gently stroke her inner wrist. He felt her pulse quicken and pound beneath his touch. His pulse did the same.

"You made sure we wouldn't see each other anymore," she said, her eyes as soft as her voice. "I got it that you don't want a girlfriend. It didn't take all that to get your point across."

Kael was caught up in her. It was clear that even just a simple stroke of her wrist had her mind unclear and he understood because he felt heady with the idea that the same stroke of his thumb against her nipple would send them both into another headspace entirely. "Wait a minute," he said, lowering her hand but still holding on to it. "I didn't cancel the home physical therapy."

"I was told by my job that your sister would be bringing your father to Charleston for his physical therapy from now on," she said. "They called me last night at home and told me again today at work."

Kael frowned. He hadn't made that call. After Lisha dropped him off and he'd hightailed from his family's questions about her, Kael had stayed at his house painting the walls late into the night.

Kelli. It had to be. There was no way his father did anything to stop Lisha from coming to the house.

Lisha had successfully pulled away from him, but Kael reached out for her again.

"I didn't stop the home care," he said.

She paused and looked confused and then disbelieving.

"My sister must have called and thought she was

helping out, but she didn't check with me and I know my father ain't gonna like this shit," he told her, his thumb pressing against her pulse again.

Lisha shook her head. "I'm not a stalker, Kael. I got the point you don't want nothing to do with me—"

"Oh, I want you," he told her, his voice thick. "I want everything to do with you . . . and that's the problem."

She gasped.

He heard her and it fueled him. He tugged her close to him, wrapped his arms around her body to hold her close. "Damn," he whispered against her open mouth just before he gave in to the desire to kiss her.

Lisha's eyes drifted closed and her fingers tightly gripped his plaid shirt into her fist as he tasted her mouth and then outlined it with the tip of his tongue. Her body jerked before it trembled. She opened her mouth beneath his and Kael lightly flicked his tongue against hers before gently sucking it with small pulsing motions.

Lisha let out a cry that she knew came from deep within her as she felt her body come alive like never before. Her skin tingled. Her belly was hot. Her nipples hardened against his chest. The bud buried between the lips of her core was aching. She was dizzy. She was light-headed. She was lost.

Bringing her hands up to his head, she stroked the softness of his hair as he lifted her body and then turned them to press her back against the wall.

She arched and moaned. "Hmmmmmmmmmm."

It sounded as primal as she felt.

Lisha had *never* been kissed like this. Never.

She had *never* felt like this. Ever.

Kael felt an excitement like nothing before as he continued to float between deep kisses with his clever tongue to gentle brief kisses against her mouth. The deep muscles of his thighs trembled as he felt his dick harden and lengthen against her belly. He was sure all of the blood of his body filled his erection. He didn't care. The rest of his body be damned. He was on a journey that he didn't want to end.

A desire like nothing he'd ever felt before filled him. He wanted nothing more than to be buried deep within her walls and stroking them both to a slow and wicked climax.

Lisha brought her legs up around Kael's waist as he sucked her chin before making a trail of kisses back up to her mouth again. He rolled his hips against hers and the hard length of him stroked against her core.

And she liked it. She liked it *a lot*.

"No," she gasped, breaking the kiss and bringing her hands down to tightly grasp the collar of his shirt before she fought hard to find the will and the energy to push against his shoulders until he freed her.

Dropping down to her sneakered feet, she moved away from him and wiped her mouth as her eyes widened at the moistness of her panties against her pulsing clit.

Kael's chest was heaving and he was panting as he turned to look at her walk away from him. His dick ached and his loins were tight. "Lisha," he said.

She turned and held one of her hands up to him when he started to walk toward her with his hard dick leading the way. "No, no. No-no-no-no. No. NO," she said with emphasis.

Kael stopped with his mouth still open and panting as his heart raced. His eyes dropped to take in the sight of her nipples hard and pressed against the thin material of her T-shirt. If it was at all possible, his dick got harder. "I didn't make that call to cancel the therapy," he said. "And I will get it straight and get it back going. My sister was wrong for assuming what's best for our father and I'm sorry."

Lisha nodded and walked up to him, but she reached for the door. That disappointed him. "I have to go," she said softly, turning the knob.

Kael reached out and gripped the door, keeping it from opening any further. "You make it so hard to ignore you, Lisha. Without even trying," he whispered down to her in that heated intimate space of just a few inches between them.

She looked up at him with her big bright eyes, but he didn't understand the sadness he saw mingled with her desire for him. "I have to go, Kael," she said again.

He nodded and released the door before stepping back from her.

Seconds later she was gone.

He felt the loss of her presence and turned to pound his fist against the wall.

Lisha stopped on the porch of Kael's home. She closed her eyes and pressed her hand against her chest and fought to control the desire she had for him. She fought hard . . . and lost.

Turning, she walked back into the house.

Kael was standing at one of the windows flanking the fireplace. He turned and eyed her as she closed the door. Not looking away from him, she pulled her T-shirt over her head as she walked slowly toward him. Her shorts were next and then her sneakers, until she stood before him in nothing but her pink lace panties and sheer bra.

"Damn," he said, dropping to his knees before her.

She pressed her hands to the back of his head and pressed the side of his face to her naked belly. His large hands grasped her calves before slowly sliding up the back of her legs as he turned his face to press warm and moist kisses across her stomach.

She gasped.

He sucked her belly button as his fingers gently pulled the edge of her panties from her body before roughly jerking the lace down from her full bottom.

Lisha's head fell back and she let out a little cry that was a pressure release. "Kael," she moaned, working her hips back and forth gently as he worked her panties down her legs.

Leaning back enough to look up at her with those sexy bedroom eyes, he smiled wolfishly as he pressed his mouth to the plump mound of her pussy. Not even the thin layer of soft hair covering it stopped him from opening his mouth and playfully biting her.

She tilted her head to the side and stroked his square jaw as she opened her legs and then bent them. "Lick me?" she asked softly.

Kael brought his hands around her thick thighs and used his thumbs to spread her lips and pulled her soft flesh up a bit to expose her clit.

She shivered as he drew his tongue against it and then pursed his lips to blow a cool stream of air against the aching bud. "Yes," she whispered, slightly arching her hips forward.

"More?" he asked, his words heating her flesh.

"Please," she begged with no shame.

He rose to his feet and took off the short-sleeved shirt he wore to lay on the floor beside her.

Lisha brought her hands up to drag her fingers against the hard contours of his chest slightly covered by fine hairs. His hard dark brown nipples. The deep grooves of his eight-pack abdomen. The delicious vee that disappeared behind the rim of his low jeans.

She leaned into him and sucked one of his nipples before flicking her tongue against it.

His hands came up to tangle in her hair as he pressed her head closer. "Damn, Lisha. Damn."

She shifted to the other nipple, her hands easing down his back to his buttocks and around to stroke down the length of his dick in his snug-fitting jeans.

"See how hard you got it?" he asked her.

Lisha looked up at him and shook her head. "I can't in those jeans," she said, before stepping back to lie down on the shirt and spread her legs before him.

Kael's eyes zoned in on her pink flesh as he worked the zipper down over his hardness. As he pushed his jeans and black briefs down his legs, his dark brown dick sprung free and hung away from his body with thickness and weight.

Her eyes widened and she swallowed over a sudden lump in her throat.

He saw her fear. He shook his head as he got down on his knees between her open thighs. "Don't be afraid. Touch it," he told her thickly.

She looked down at the curving length of him and then up at his eyes before reaching out to wrap her hand around him. He hissed as his hips jerked forward at her touch. Lisha bit her bottom lip as she stroked the warm hardness.

He thrust his hips forward again and let his head fall back.

Lisha worked her hand down the full length of him, even lightly dragging her fingertips across his dark nuts as well before stroking back up the length of him to trace her thumb around the hot tip.

"No more," he begged, reaching out to capture her hand. "I can't take that. Not when I have something I promised you."

Kael grabbed her thighs and pulled her body up onto the top of his strong muscled thighs until her knees flanked his head and the sweet softness of her ass pressed against his chest. He pulled her legs apart like a chest press and looked down into her moist flesh as it blossomed before him. Biting his bottom lip, he jerked her body up higher and lowered his head to tongue kiss her flesh.

Lisha's hips arched up. Her feet shot up straight behind him and she had to bite her own lip to keep from hollering.

Kael took his time sucking her clit, loving the feel of her body's reaction. The shivers. The moans. The arches of her hips. The way her fingers clenched at the edges of his shirt. The expressions of sweet torture on her face.

He massaged the thickness of her thighs as he pressed his tongue deeper against her clit and stroked it with the sides of his tongue.

"Ah," she cried out, hissing in pleasure.

Kael gave her one last intimate kiss before lowering her body until his dick sat nestled down the middle of her buttocks. He closed her legs, causing her ass to cup him tightly as he worked his hips, sending it back and forth against her flesh.

Lisha moved her hips in countermotion to his until they were rocking back and forth like their bodies floated on a wave.

"Like that?" he asked.

She nodded. "It's nice."

"Nice?" Kael spread her legs again, inhaling the scent of her pussy before using his hand to guide the thick tip of his dick inside her. He felt himself going a little crazy at the tight feel of her as he looked down at her brown and pink flesh surrounding him.

"Like that?" he asked, his eyes locked on her.

"It's so good," she moaned.

Coming off his knees, he lowered his body, sending his hardness deeper inside her until she was filled with him. He tensed and lowered his head to the floor beside hers, pressing a kiss to her shoulder as he fought for control.

Lisha brought her hands up to tightly grasp his hard buttocks and she pushed down on them, wanting him to move inside her. Wanting to feel his hardness against her flesh. Wanting to stroke her clit with his heat.

Just wanting him.

With one tenuous thrust after Kael felt his explosion subside, he began to ride her as his hand clutched at her hair and he pressed heated kisses to the side of her face and neck.

"So wet," he moaned.

Lisha hotly licked his salty shoulder, not caring that the weight of him pressed her body against the hard floor as he gave her inch after inch of something much harder. Slowly. Deeply. Stroke after stroke.

"Yes," she cried out, her eyes closed as she rode all of the emotions as he rode her.

She wrapped her ankles around his calves as she shifted to hold his face as she tilted her chin up and *sucked his bottom lip. He shivered and she felt his dick get harder inside of her. With a seductive smile she pulled his bottom lip into her mouth as she looked up into his eyes.*

Kael eased the last inch inside of her until she was filled to the brim. Freeing her hair, he slid his hand beneath her buttocks and raised her hip up off the floor as he circled his hips, sending his dick against the walls like he was cleaning a bowl.

Round. And around. And around.

Lisha's head shake said no at the torture, but her body said yes as she spread her legs wide like propellers as she moved her hips in that wicked circular motion with him.

"Wait . . . don't move," he said, pressing his face into her neck as his body went rigid.

She purred as she felt his dick throb against her walls.

When he finally began stroking inside of her again, the movements were slickened and she knew that he had cum a little inside of her.

Pressing her feet to the cold wood floors, she arched her body and pressed against his shoulders. "I wanna ride you," she whispered.

He looked surprised by her demand, but held her tightly around her waist as he turned them over until his back and buttocks were pressed against the shockingly cold wood and Lisha was straddling him with his dick still rooted deep within her.

Pressing her hands into his chest and not caring that her knees scraped against the hard floor, Lisha sat up straight and took over the ride, wanting to take control of pushing this particular stallion across his finish line.

"*You're beautiful," he said, his eyes taking in all of her. The pleasure on her face. Her gently rounded shoulders. The back and forth sway of her full pendulous breasts as she moved her rounded hips.*

"*That's my dick.*"

Kael brought one hand up to massage her breast and tease her nipple as the other clutched deeply at her hip as he enjoyed her work. "You asking me or telling me?"

Lisha locked her feet beneath his thighs and shifted her upper body so that every thrust of her hip milked his dick as she rode him fast and hard until his hands fell from her body and grasped wildly as he cried out and arched his back, nearly knocking her off the dick, as he came with force inside her.

With a cry she fell down onto his chest and continued her ride as her own climax sent her into convulsions and made her clit sensitive. When her release seemed to keep her from moving, his hands returned to grasp her hips and bring her up and down on his dick as he thrust upward, sending her free-falling.

Long endless moments later they both lay panting on the floor, sweat soaking their bodies and their hearts thundering as they waited for the calm after the sexy storm.

"*I guess you told me," he joked in between gulps of air.*

Lisha worked up just enough strength to raise her head from his chest to wink at him.

In a world caught between slumber and sleep, Lisha woke up with a start, sitting up straight in bed and clutching the sheets to her body as she looked around at her bedroom cloaked in darkness with only the light from the living room offering slight illumination.

She was alone and in bed.

Not at Kael's home.

Not making love to him on the floor.

It was all just a dream. Still, with the throbbing of her core and the dampness of her panties she had experienced the climax.

She fell back down on the bed and covered her face with her hands as her cheeks warmed in embarrassment. She could only hope to be so alive and sexy and take-charge when she did make love to her husband one day. The little Lisha knew about sex she got from Junie . . . but riding a man, oral sex, stroking a dick until it almost came in her hand—those were things she had no real experience with.

Lisha shook her head as if to clear it of the erotic images.

When she left Kael's house she had kept running until she was in her car and headed to her apartment in Walterboro. She couldn't believe that she kissed him with such passion and let him know more about her body than she had offered any man she'd been in a relationship with.

And Kael made it clear that they were not in one and he wasn't looking for one.

She'd gone too far and could have easily gone

further if the feel of his hard dick hadn't scared her shitless. Kael was . . . large . . . long . . . lethal. His erection had shaken her out of her sexual daze and she knew she had to get away from him.

And now he was in her dreams.

You make it so hard to ignore you, Lisha. Without even trying.

Her main takeaway from his comment by the door was that regardless of anything, he was trying to ignore her, and Lisha realized that she needed to do the same to him or risk getting hurt.

Climbing from the bed she made her way to the living room and turned on the television before snuggling into a corner of the couch. It was just a little after ten and she wasn't ready to go back to sleep. There was no way she could trust herself in her dreams tonight.

Chapter 8

Kael stood back out of the kitchen and surveyed his handiwork. The wooden floors now gleamed after he worked until well after midnight stripping and then staining them. Wiping his hands on the rag he had stuffed in his back pocket, he nodded in approval. Like most men, he wasn't concerned about décor, but he had to admit that he liked the dark green curtains Kelli had bought for him as a housewarming present.

As he walked down the hall, each footstep echoed throughout the house. The only room he even bothered to furnish yet was his bedroom and even that was just a bed and nightstands. He wasn't planning on moving in until his father was as close to a hundred percent as possible or he finally got the old man to agree to move in with him.

Kael was beginning to wonder if he was anywhere near either one.

He paused as he came into the living room. His

eyes fell on the newly installed phone sitting on the floor in the corner. If he had Lisha's number he would call her.

And say what? Can I kiss you again?

So many hours had passed since their heated moments against the wall and he was still shaken by the fire between them. The feel of her lips on his was branded. The softness of her body was unforgettable. He couldn't believe he almost nut himself just from grinding against her.

"Shake it off, Kael," he told himself, before walking throughout the house and turning off all but the lights in the living room. He pulled his keys from his pocket and left the house, locking the door and jogging down the stairs to his truck.

Jim had long since placed the horses in the trailer and dropped them off to be housed along with his father's horse in the small barn at the far rear of his property. The man was a godsend. He was just as knowledgeable about cattle ranching as Kael, if not more so.

Opening the truck door, Kael took a moment to look back at the large house softy lit by the moon. An image of Lisha walking out the door and waiting for him on the porch played out before him, surprising and pleasing him at the same time. A woman waiting to properly greet her man home after a long day of work.

Before the end of his last relationship, that was

the life he wanted. A wife. Family. Children. A house filled with laughter and love.

But not now. Not yet.

Shaking his head to clear it, Kael climbed into his truck, patting the dash. He'd had it towed from Charleston and after checking it, discovered a leak in his oil line. He did a temporary fix with silicone tape with plans to get it replaced by a mechanic this weekend.

Driving the short distance to his father's home, Kael thought back to the cause for Lisha's anger. No matter her intention, his sister had been out of line. And he planned to let her know about it.

But when he pulled up to the house and climbed out from the truck, he wondered if he even needed to say a word.

"I am a grown-ass man. *Your* father. Don't you forget it, Kelli."

Logan Strong was a man rare to raise his voice and Kael figured his sister going against his wishes would warrant a rare tirade. Even though he was tired from a full day of work at King's Ranch and his own, Kael sat down on the metal bench of the porch instead of step inside the middle of their argument.

"I just think it would be better if you go to Charleston for your treatment," Kelli said. "I was only trying to help."

At the sound of tears in his sister's voice, Kael leaned forward and braced his elbows on his knees as he shook his head. *That should about do it,* he thought. Kelli knew the waterworks worked with both of the Strong men.

"Those crocodile tears won't work this time, Kelli," his father said, his voice still hard and still angry.

Kael sat up straight in surprise, his face incredulous.

"But Daddy—"

"But Daddy, hell. Fix it."

Moments later a door slammed and echoed through the house.

Seconds later the screen door opened and closed. Kael looked over to see which one joined him on the porch. "Hey, sis," he said, moving over on the bench.

She eased down beside him, knocking her knee against his. "I don't think I've ever seen him so mad . . . especially at me. I'm his favorite," she said.

Kael chuckled. "Maybe not anymore," he teased.

She punched his arm before laying her head on his shoulder. "I was only trying to help," she explained.

"How?" Kael asked, seriously confused.

She sat up. "Oh, God. You, too?"

He nodded. "Pretty much," he admitted.

Kelli threw her hands up.

"He doesn't want to make the trip into Charleston twice a week. It's just that simple," he told her.

"Okay. There's physical therapists in Walterboro."

"He likes Lisha." Kael swatted away a mosquito that had landed on his hand. Standing up, he turned off the porch light, hoping not to attract any more of the blood-sucking creatures.

"And so do you."

He paused for a half second before sitting back down. "She really works well with him," he said, leaving it at that even as his gut clenched at the thought of Lisha.

Kelli just sucked air between her teeth.

"Well, you can thank me because it's already fixed. I told Lisha you made a mistake," he said, rising to his feet to walk past her to the door.

"You talked to her? When? Where'd you see her?" Kelli asked, rising to follow him into the house.

Kael frowned. "It's fixed. She'll be back here Friday," he said, before walking into his bedroom and closing the door securely.

He needed a shower, and whatever his sister cooked for dinner smelled good, but Kael just kicked off his boots and lay down on the bed, not even bothering to turn on the air. As he shifted onto his side his eyes fell on the phone sitting atop the phone book on his nightstand next to a picture of him as a teenager in his high school football uniform.

Reaching for the phone and the phone book, he sat up and flipped through the pages before using his finger to turn the rotary dial.

The phone rang three or four times and he felt nervous as he waited.

"Hello."

He smiled. "Hi, Lisha, it's Kael."

She said nothing and the sound of her television played in the background. He sat all the way up, setting his feet on the carpeted floor.

"Lisha, you there?" he asked.

"Kael, I—"

"No, I just wanted to . . . I just . . ."

"Wanted what, Kael?"

He opened his mouth and then closed it, shaking his head. *Talk to you. Hear your voice. Kiss you again.*

But he knew he couldn't say those things no matter how true. Lisha wasn't a one-time chick at all.

"I just wanted to make sure you got home okay," he lied.

"I did. Thank you," she said, her voice husky above the sound of her television playing in the background. "Kael, listen. I'm not expecting anything because of that . . . that . . . that kiss today, you know."

He flopped back onto the bed. "It was some kiss," he said, wanting to know if she felt what he felt too.

"Yeah, it was, but unless you changed your mind about things, that was the first and the last."

"Changed my mind?" he asked, stalling because he didn't want to end the sound of her voice in his ear.

"Yes, Kael," she said gently. "Have you changed your mind?"

"No," he admitted reluctantly.

"That's cool," she said, even though her tone belied otherwise.

Something about her made him want to take the risk. But what if he was wrong? What if everything about her looked and sounded good but it was just a façade? He believed the very best about his ex, denied the things others told him about her because he believed the very best . . . and look at the end result. No, for now he would just give up what the right ones had to offer and focus on his business.

"So I guess I'll see your father Friday, then," she said.

He didn't want the call to end. "Okay."

"Y'all probably should speak with my bosses and make sure we're all back on the same page," she suggested.

He nodded and licked his lips. "Okay. That makes sense."

"Okay, then. Good-bye, Kael."

"Good—"

Click.

He was left with nothing but the dial tone. He hung up the receiver and left his bedroom to walk to his father's. The door was still shut. He knocked once.

"Come in."

Kael opened the door and stood in the doorway. His father was lying in bed doing his leg exercises. "How you feeling?" he asked.

Logan glanced over at him before looking back up at the ceiling as he raised and lowered his leg slowly. "Pissed."

Kael smiled. "Lisha's looking forward to seeing you Friday," he said.

Logan paused in his leg lifts.

"So how you feeling now?" he asked.

Logan nodded and continued his exercise. "Better."

"I figured as much," he quipped before turning to leave.

"All women ain't the same, son."

Kael paused and then turned. "Sir?"

Logan lowered his leg and waved his son over as he carefully turned his body before bending his legs and sitting up on the side of the bed.

Kael came to stand over him.

Logan leaned back a bit and looked up. "Man, sit your tall ass down," he said. "Makes me think you 'bout to knock me out and we both know—bad hip or not—you don't want to fool up with that."

Kael sat down on the trunk pushed against the

wall. A trunk in which he knew his father kept all of his mementos of their mother.

"That Donna wasn't shit," he began.

Kael flinched.

"It didn't matter how much love, how much support, how much money or how much dick you put on her . . . she didn't know how to be faithful."

Kael squinted.

"What she did is all about her and not about you. Hell, she doing the same shit to the man she live with now," Logan said, waving his hand dismissively.

Kael looked surprised.

"But all women ain't her, son," Logan said, locking eyes with Kael.

Kael nodded in understanding.

"I know she hurt you, but you don't let her win by not moving on."

"Is this about Lisha?" Kael asked.

"You damn right it is," Logan spouted. "Hardworking girl, preacher's daughter, pretty as all get out, nice as can be—"

"You're really selling her," Kael drawled.

"You're really missing out on her, son," Logan shot back.

Kael thought about the kiss they shared and completely agreed, although his father meant more than just her sexuality.

"If you can't trust a preacher's daughter, who can you trust?" Logan said.

"Sometimes they're the worst ones."

Logan pointed at him. "All women ain't the same, son," he repeated.

"Dad—"

Both Kael and Logan looked up as Kelli came to stand in the doorway. They fell silent and Kael felt sorry for his sister because it was clear that their father was still annoyed with her.

"Did Kael tell you about Lisha?" she asked, coming in to sit beside him on the bed.

Logan nodded. "Yes. No need to talk about it anymore," he said, reaching over to pat her knee twice.

All was forgiven.

"I thought the actual clinic in Charleston would help you recover quickly," she said. "But I should have talked to you first."

"Lisha did mention adding pool therapy to your treatment," Kael added, trying to help his sister out.

"I'd have to go to Charleston?" he asked.

"We don't have a pool here," Kelli said.

Logan just grunted.

That was a no.

Kael chuckled as he stood up and left the room hoping, as he left his father and sister, that they could mend the small tear in the relationship. Plus he had a lot of his own issues on his mind.

You're really missing out on her, son.

* * *

Knock-knock.

Lisha shifted her eyes from the TV screen long enough to glance at the door. "Use your key, Junie," she called out, far too comfortable to rise from her spot stretched out on the sofa.

"It's Kael."

Lisha gasped in shock as she jumped up in her sock-covered feet. She tiptoed over to the door and pressed one eye against the peephole. Not that she had any doubts, but it was indeed Kael.

"What does he want?" she mouthed even as she rushed into the bathroom to yank every roller off her head and then rinse with mouthwash.

She rushed out of the bathroom and turned, almost slamming into the wall before a quick shift sent her running through the door to yank off her nightgown and quickly pull on a yellow sweat suit.

Knock-knock.

She paused, considering a spray of perfume and a dash of lipstick, but decided against it. Glancing at the clock, she made her way back to the front door and took a breath to steady herself before stepping back to open it.

Kael was heading down the stairs, but looked back.

"Hey," she said, smiling at him even as she felt overwhelmed still by his sudden appearance at her front door.

He retraced his steps, looking handsome in jeans and a dark navy T-shirt that molded to his chest.

The color of the shirt made his complexion and the silvery tint of his hair all the more appealing. She closed her eyes for a second, remembering the taste of his lips with a slight tremble that made her clutch the doorknob tight enough to snap it off.

"I'm sorry to come by so late . . . and without calling," he added, looking down at her from his towering six-foot-five height. "I thought we needed to talk."

"About what, Kael?" she asked, leaning against the door to look up at him.

"Us," he said.

"There is no us," she reminded him gently.

"I wanted to explain why."

Lisha waved him in, closing the door once he stood in her living room. The breadth of his shoulders and his height made the room seem half its size. She lightly touched his arm as she eased past him to turn the television down.

"Nice apartment," he said, looking around at the bright and simple décor.

Lisha bit her cheek to keep from smiling as she watched him, but she said not one word.

Kael finally faced her. "It was nothing personal with my sister," he said.

She nodded. "Once you told me she called . . . and not you, I never thought she had a problem with me. We get along real good."

Knock.

Lisha frowned as she walked over to the door. "Yes, Junie," she said before opening it.

But there was no one there. She stepped out and looked down the hall just as Junie's front door closed. Kael stepped up beside her.

"There's something on your mat," he said.

She looked down between her feet and choked on her own spit at the box of condoms. Lisha kicked the box and it went spiraling across the concrete and under the rail to fly off the second-floor landing. She turned and didn't miss Kael's grin as he turned from her.

"Junie loves playing pranks," she said weakly, feeling mortified.

Kael just held up his hands.

"She is not funny," Lisha added.

He shrugged.

"What did you want to talk about?" she asked, wanting to head to Junie's apartment to pimp-slap her. Twice.

Kael eyed her. "Is that your favorite color?" he asked.

She looked down at her terry-cloth sweat suit. "Huh?"

"You had the same color on at church," he explained.

"Okay, no . . . no, it's not," she said, crossing her arms over her chest when she noticed her nipples were hard and poking through the thin material. "White is actually."

"That color looks good on you."

Lisha started to throw her hands up in exasperation, but caught herself. "Kael Strong, you cannot say things to me and kiss me and look at me like *that* and then be quick to say you don't want a girlfriend. It's not fair because I like you. I mean I really like you and I'm not a part of the sexual revolution like my cousin—regardless of those stupid condoms—so all I know is all in or all out."

"But I can't help but look at you like that and say things . . . and kiss you," he admitted, taking a step toward her.

She held up one hand. "Stop," she said.

And he did.

She was thankful. The room was already charged with their energy even with the distance between them. "I have never felt like this with anybody before," she admitted, hating the tears of frustration that welled up. She blinked them away and lowered her head.

Even a second before his hands pressed against her face she knew he was nearing her from some unspoken awareness and reaction to his body. That chemistry that could not explained.

He raised her head and she looked up into his eyes. His thumbs softly traced along her skin beneath her eyes and she knew some of the tears had fallen anyway. She felt light-headed from his touch. "I hardly know you and I don't understand what this is between us," she admitted in a voice barely above a whisper.

"Me either," he said, curving his lips into a half smile as his eyes took in every aspect of her face. "I wish I met you years ago."

Lisha stepped away from him. "Are you married?" she asked, her voice accusing.

Kael's handsome face filled with confusion. "Huh? No. I'm not married."

She visibly relaxed. "Then what is it?" she asked.

"I just got out of a relationship less than a year ago and I'm just not ready for another one."

"You still love her?" she asked in understanding, reaching out to rub his elbow comfortingly.

Kael scowled and reached out to stop the circles she rubbed on him. "Hell, no," he snapped abruptly.

Lisha looked confused.

"She cheated. I was away from home busting my ass working to provide for both for us and she cheated," he explained.

Lisha saw the anger he felt. She felt it and understood it. No one wanted to be betrayed. No one wanted to be hurt. She reached out and held his wrist. "Hey, she didn't just cheat on you . . . she cheated herself out of what I think is a really good man," she said with earnest.

Kael looked at her in wonder. "And that's why you scare the shit out of me, Lisha," he professed.

She took him in. All of him. "What a dumb girl

she is," she said, fighting the urge to step up and kiss him. Wanting so badly to feel the passion she found in his arms earlier. Wanting so badly to get lost in it all again.

But instead she moved past him to get her equilibrium back. Kael Strong made her feel like she walked a tightrope, caught up in the thrill and the danger all at once. "Thanks for explaining," she said.

"I better go," he said from behind her.

She nodded as she turned.

He opened the front door, but turned to look over his shoulder at her as she walked up. His face was filled with his regrets as he took her in from head to toe. "Bye, Lisha," he said.

"Good-bye," she said, holding the doorknob.

And he was gone.

She closed the door and turned to press her back to it. "Damn," she swore.

Lisha turned back to look out the peephole and was surprised to see him still standing on the top step looking back at the door with all the uncertainty he felt clearly written on his face. Lisha opened the door and rushed up to him, reaching up to press her hands up his chest to grip his shirt in her fists and pulled his face closer to hers before she tilted her head to the side and whispered, "One more kiss?"

She didn't wait for an answer and kissed him instead with a few gentle pecks before she lightly probed his mouth with the tip of her tongue and deepened it with a small moan of sweet release.

Kael wrapped his arms around her waist and easily lifted her body up against him as he opened his mouth a little wider to let Lisha suck the tip of his tongue as she brought her tremulous hands up to grasp the back of his head.

Neither knew how much time passed as Kael leaned back against the wall and held Lisha's body against his as they kissed. With passion. With electricity. With fire.

Lisha tilted her head back as she gasped for breath. She brought her hands down to grasp his broad shoulders as her world continued to spin off its axis. "I really, really hate your ex," she said, before dropping to her feet and turning to walk away without another word or even a look back.

Chapter 9

"Lisha, someone is here to see you about Mr. Strong."

She looked up from the stacks of charts she was updating at a table in the employee lounge. Taking another sip of her bottle of Crush strawberry soda, she nodded at the clerk before rising from her seat and following her out the room.

Lisha thought it was Kael, but it was Kelli standing at the front desk of the clinic. Smiling at the woman, she approached her. "Hi, Kelli," she said.

"Hey yourself," she said, looking pretty in a red sundress with a wide full skirt. "I wanted to apologize for the mix-up and wanted to come down personally to apologize and to make sure everything was okay about you returning on Friday."

"Actually the facility would be a more ideal situation for your father, but I and his physical therapist are very pleased with his progress so far," Lisha said, walking the other woman over to the waiting area to take seats in front of the glass windows.

"That's what I figured and I assumed I could talk him into it even if Kael couldn't," Kelli said. "So you will be starting back tomorrow?"

"Yup."

"Good," she said. "I'm going to get going now. I have to stop by Kael's house and see how all the renovations are going."

"It really is a nice house," Lisha said. "I can't imagine it being torn down. He did a good job."

Kelli crossed her legs and leaned back to eye Lisha. "Oh, you sound like you've been in the house," she said, with a teasing lilt to her voice.

Lisha shrugged. "Just once," she said.

Kelli nodded. "When was that?" she asked with a big toothy grin.

Lisha shifted in her seat. "Why?"

Kelli reached forward and patted Lisha's hand. "I was just curious because Kael is so secretive about the house," she explained.

"I only saw the living room with the big fire-place, but it's really nice. He should be proud," Lisha said.

Kelli stood. "I don't want to hold you up, but we should do lunch or go shopping or something. I don't have many friends in town since I moved when I got married."

Lisha nodded "I would like that."

"Lisha."

She turned at the sound of his voice. One of the X-ray techs from the hospital was standing a distance away holding a large envelope with films. "I better get back to work," she said.

"But we're okay?" Kelli asked.

"Yeah, we're fine," she said like there was never a worry in the world.

"Good."

With one final wave Lisha turned and walked over to the tech. "Hey, George. Are those the films I asked for?"

He nodded.

"Yes, what do I owe you, Mr. Lifesaver?" she asked, glancing up at him as she double-checked the name on the film.

"Dinner would be cool."

Lisha looked up at him and playfully pouted. "How about a sandwich in the cafeteria?" she said. "I might even spot you a soda too."

George laughed even though she knew he was serious with his request. But she had sworn off dating in her workplace any longer.

"Too bad," he said, smiling and revealing two deep dimples in his cheeks.

Cute, but compared to the rugged good looks of Mr. Outdoorsman Kael Strong, the poor man could not compete.

But why is Kael my bar? So what if I kissed him on two different occasions yesterday? So what? I'm still as single as the day is long. He isn't my man and never will be. And if I only meet men at work and I cut that off, I will never fall in love.

"Lisha," he said. "Lisha."

She looked away from some random potted plant she was staring at. "Huh?" she asked, still distracted with her thoughts.

"I said maybe I'll visit your dad's church Sunday and we can grab something to eat afterward," George said.

"You go to church?" she asked.

"I'm a deacon at my church," he told her.

She tilted her head to the side and eyed the man. *Really* eyed him. Not Kael, but not bad. "Let me seriously think about it," she said, reaching out to touch his wrist lightly.

Absolutely no spark at all.

"Okay." He reached in the pocket of his uniform pants and pulled out a pen and pad. "Here's my number."

Accepting it, she focused on looking down at his handwriting as he turned and walked away.

Kael closed the door to the corral and removed his Stetson long enough to wipe the sweat from his hair and his brow with the cloth he kept in his back pocket. It was the end of August and fall was officially a month away but the temperatures were still in the nineties some days even if the nights were chillier.

Taking a deep sip of the ice water in his thermos, Kael checked his watch. He had just another twenty minutes left of his lunch break and he always spent that time working on his ranch. Jim worked every other day and so he really planned on making sure the cattle had plenty of water and minerals, were grazing well and were taking advantage of the cooling shade offered by the trees in their corrals. He checked them all to make sure none showed signs of overheating, like breathing through their mouths and slobbering.

Pouring the last of the water over his head, causing his hair to thin and curl, Kael grabbed the reins of his horse and decided to walk back to his truck and trailer. He missed his father being there with him to help with the animals and the repair of the house. Logan Strong had a way of making the time go fast and right now Kael was feeling pretty damn lonely every time he visited the ranch and the house of his dreams.

Leading the horse to the trough, he removed his girths and sponged him down as the horse drank from the clean water that Kael cooled with small amounts of ice chips. He wanted to make sure the animal did not overheat either.

"Well, hello there, Kael."

Looking over his shoulder, he had to guard his face from showing his disappointment at Kelli's friend Bea standing there holding a picnic basket.

Her hair was pulled back into a ponytail and all the makeup she wore made her pretty face sweat. And it was clear that she wore no bra under her tank top and maybe even no panties under her cut-off jeans.

"Hi, Bea. Can I help you with something?" he asked kindly, before turning back to finish sponging the horse.

"I'm sure there is plenty you can help me with . . . but I'm here to help you," she said.

"Oh, yeah?" he asked, wringing out the sponge and using the hose to rinse his hands.

"Your sister told me you come here every day during your lunch break to work your ranch and I thought, 'Well, Bea, what can I do to help a hard-working man through the day?' and after I got rid of my first idea," she said with a laugh, "I decided food was the *second* thing a man needed."

Kael watched as she turned and walked back toward the house with the sway of her hips going as far and as left as the pendulum of a clock.

Back and forth. Back and forth. Back and forth.

He shifted his eyes up before he became hypnotized.

Bea paused and looked back to bend her finger at him to follow.

Leaving the horse with his reins loosely tied to the base of a tree, Kael then made his way over to the porch where she waited patiently by the door. His steps faltered at the thought of having her in the same living room where he'd been with Lisha, and it didn't sit well with him at all.

"Actually, Bea, I don't have much time left before I have to get back to work," he said truthfully.

She pouted and then set the basket down on the porch before bending over to root around in it. He was given quite a view of the lush cheeks of her buttocks.

Kael was a man. A man with clear vision and a healthy libido. A man who hadn't enjoyed the sexual appetite of a woman since his father's accident over a month ago. He'd be a liar to say it wasn't a helluva sight . . . and a temptation.

His dick definitely kicked up a little as she continued her wiggles and giggles.

Bea pulled out a sandwich wrapped in wax paper and came down the stairs to stand before him and open it. "I made a pot roast last night and I thought it would make a good sandwich for you today, Kael," she said, lifting the sandwich halfway up to his mouth as she kept her eyes trained on him. "Don't you want to eat it?"

He paused.

Bea was offering it up like the church plate on Sundays. All the teasing and innuendos? She was just begging him to give it to her.

And that's why Kael wasn't interested. Still, he opened his mouth and took a healthy bite.

She raised her thumb to lick the tip and then wiped gravy from the corner of his mouth. "Ain't it *so* good, honey?" she asked him.

Kael focused on the taste of something burnt in his mouth. He started to make a face but forced himself to keep chewing and swallowing. With a stiff smile he swallowed down the last of it and just prayed it didn't give him the trots later. "It is so something," he said. "You have something to drink in the basket of yours?"

"Oh, I know how to take care of a man, sugar," she said, turning to head back to her basket.

Kael gathered up all of the saliva in his mouth to spit, hoping the taste of the food went with it. It didn't. He was distinctively thinking Bea needed to spend more time in the kitchen and out of the bedroom if she was going to brag on her cooking skills.

He accepted the bottle she handed him, fighting the urge to gargle with it. "I appreciate this, but I really have to get back to work," he said, looking apologetic even as he made his way back to his truck.

"Kael, take it with you," she called behind him.

He turned just as she ran in her wedge heels, and his mouth opened as she went toppling forward. Kael dashed out and caught her in his arms. "You okay?" he asked.

She nodded as he helped her to her feet. She leaned in to him, pressing her breasts against his chest. "Thank you. I'm so embarrassed," she said.

Stepping back from her as his dick responded to the feel of her breasts, he spotted the sandwich that flew out of her hand. *Good riddance.*

"Let me help you to your car," he said, steering her in the direction of her green Nova that did nothing but remind him of Lisha.

"Thanks, suga," she said, still leaning against him.

He was glad to finally open her car door.

"I didn't have time to deliver for lunch, but maybe dinner at my house? Well, dinner and dessert," she said, licking her glossy lips.

Kael rushed to the porch and grabbed her basket. He opened the passenger door and set it on the seat before shutting the door soundly. "I appreciate the offer, but I'm so busy with work and the ranch and . . ."

She came around the car and stepped in his path to his truck, pulling a pen from her cleavage.

Kael swallowed hard.

"Well, when you get tired of playing with cattle, you come and play with me," she said, grabbing his hand and writing her number in his palm before she lowered her head and kissed it.

With one last wiggle and giggle she climbed into her car and reversed in a semi-arc before pulling off down the tree-covered dirt drive.

Pushing all thoughts of the woman away, he loaded the horse into the trailer and finally headed back to work. As he drove, his thoughts were on Lisha—as they had been since yesterday.

It felt like a lifetime had passed between them and not just a day. So much had happened. So much had been said and done. So much revealed.

He couldn't believe he told her about his ex, and then she said something he would never forget.

Hey, she didn't just cheat on you . . . she cheated herself out of what I think is a really good man.

And then the surprise kiss outside her door.

That surprised him. Surprised and thrilled him.

She completely invaded his dreams with that. Instead of a good-bye, it seemed like a hello to forever.

"Damn," he swore, remembering the feel of her. Again.

I really, really hate your ex.

That made him laugh. And it made him feel good in a sadistic way because even though he wasn't willing to take the risk with his heart, it felt good knowing that she wanted him just as much as he wanted her.

You're really missing out on her, son.

* * *

The next day, Lisha was surprised to see Kael's truck parked in between his father's and sister's vehicles. She glanced at her clock. It was a little after four. She was surprised he wouldn't be at work or least working on his ranch.

As she climbed out from her car, she thought of him having the determination and strength to work that hard to get his ranch up and running. He basically had two full-time jobs. For that she felt he should be commended.

Usually it was a man with a family who struggled to provide that for his wife and children, but Kael was doing it while young, single and without kids. Most men would party their twenties away, but he put all of his energy into working for his future.

She liked that in the man and many other women would too. Someone would scoop him up and Lisha honestly hoped he fell for the right one the next time.

Closing the trunk of her Nova, she hitched her tote bag of equipment higher up on her shoulder. She smiled at Kelli sitting on the porch, but her smile faltered at her lips and left her eyes as the door opened and a woman with a body like it was drawn by a man stepped out onto the porch as well. She had full glossy lips and half-closed eyes that made her look like she was in the throes of sex. Her white shirt seemed to be bursting at the seams and she had no room to pass gas in her skin-tight bell-bottom jeans.

"Hello, hello," Lisha said even as she wondered who the woman was.

"Hey, Lisha," Kelli said.

"Your dad inside?" she asked, all business.

"Waiting on you," she said.

Lisha noticed the other woman studying her and gave her a nod before stepping up onto the porch.

"I hope Kael loves that chicken I fried for his dinner," the woman said. "That stove was hot . . . but he's worth it."

Lisha entered the house, but she couldn't deny that she slowed up her steps.

"My brother deserves a good woman like you," Kelli said.

Lisha stopped and anger made her body hot from her feet and up to the top of her head like mercury rising in a thermometer set in boiling water.

That lying, cheating, manipulating, gray-haired—

"Hi, Lisha."

Mr. Strong stepped into the living room, already dressed in one of the sweat suits she made him wear during their sessions so that his movements weren't constricted by the jeans or the green Dickies uniform pants he seemed to favor. "Hi there.

You ready?" she asked, forcing a smile to her face even as her soul felt crushed.

Logan pierced her with his eyes. "You okay?" he asked, his voice sharp.

"Yes, sir," she answered. And somehow his show of concern kicked the gate off her emotions and tears welled up quickly. "Can I use your bathroom, please?"

"Yes, you know you're more than welcome," he said, stepping back into the kitchen to make room in the hall for her.

She set her bag on the floor by the sofa and dashed past him before the tears could fall. She had just made it to the bathroom door before the first tears raced down her face.

"Who fucked up this chicken like this?" Logan snapped from the kitchen.

Lisha shut the door and closed the lid on the commode before sitting down on it. "I don't want a girlfriend," she mimicked, unrolling sky blue tissue to wipe her eyes.

No, he just didn't want me *as a girlfriend.*

"And I believed his story about being cheated on. Old dusty-haired liar," she mumbled, unrolling more tissue to blow her nose.

Lisha *hated* a liar.

And then to parade his woman in my face. Ole non-cooking heifer.

She actually giggled at Mr. Strong's complaint on her chicken. "Humph. Who can't fry chicken?" she said, rising up to stand in the mirror and make sure her eyes weren't puffy—as they tended to do whenever she got teary.

"All right, Alisha," she admonished herself. "Get it together. He wasn't yours to lose and who cares if he lied. All he gained was a little swapping of some spit . . . and a dry hunch."

Still . . .

Giving herself a shake before she washed her hands and rinsed her face, Lisha reached for more tissue. When the roll quickly went empty, she grimaced even as she patted her face dry. Dumping it all in the trash can, she finally opened the door and walked right out to Kael leaning on the wall.

His face lit up and he smiled at her. "Hey, Lisha. Were you talking to yourself?" he asked.

"What I do in the lavatory is my business," she said coldly before easing past him into the hall.

He grabbed her wrist.

She turned to glare at him.

"Hey, what's wrong?" Kael asked, obviously taken aback. "Are you mad at me?"

Lisha snatched her arm away and quickly walked up the hall.

"Lisha," he called.

She ignored him, walking out onto the porch

where Mr. Strong was standing, talking to his daughter and future daughter-in-law. "All set, Mr. Strong?" she asked. "I thought we might walk to the stop sign down the road and back."

In truth, she wanted to get the hell away from Kael and his girlfriend. This was going to be the longest hour of her life.

He nodded and offered her his elbow.

Lisha took it and they walked down the drive at a good speed together. "Let me know if you have any pain, and be careful of anything you can trip over," she said.

"I'll be fine as long as I don't have to try and rush home to shit out that nasty chicken," he said.

Lisha smiled. "You ready to run now?" she teased.

"No, and that's why if you see me hit the woods, you run home and get me some toilet paper," he said. "Deal?"

Feeling better, she nodded. "*Definite* deal."

Kael's father's home sat on two acres of land and he used the rear section of the land to house his barn and the two horses he used to race. Hating to sit around with idle hands—especially with Bea and Kelli's game-playing—he'd decided to clean the stalls out and replace the hay and water.

He'd actually knocked off work early and left the duties of the ranch to Jim to be home when Lisha came for his father's physical therapy. He changed out of his work clothes and showered to sit and wait on her, wanting to see her again.

And then at the first sight of him she gave him the cold shoulder? That wasn't nothing like the heat of the kiss *she* gave *him* last night.

He did overhear her in the bathroom mumbling something about dry hunching? Kael frowned as he gave each of his father's horses his two carrots to eat from the palm of his hand.

When he was done he walked out of the small barn and secured the gate, leaning the rake and shovel he used against the wall. In the distance he spotted his father and Lisha walking back down the road toward the house.

He eased his hands into the snug back pocket of his denims and honed his eyes in on her as she laughed at something his father said, causing her hair to fly back from her face.

Fresh faced, no makeup and in her uniform, and Kael would choose her over all of the flash of Bea any day.

He made his way across the grassy land, coming from around the house and sitting down on the swing just as they turned onto the drive. He leaned forward and pressed his elbows to his knees, his eyes watching her every move.

"Oh, there you are, suga."

Kael rolled his eyes and ignored Bea. The only thing on his mind was finding out what had Lisha mad at him now. That's all.

Kelli came out onto the porch, wiping her hands on the edge of her apron. "Daddy, you ready to eat?" she called out to him.

His father opened his mouth, but Kael spotted Lisha tug at his arm and say something to him. His brows dipped when his father just said, "No thank you," in the fakest voice.

She even has Daddy wrapped around her finger.

His father had never really cared for Donna. In fact, he had been one of the ones to warn him about trusting in her so much.

As they neared the porch, he eyed Bea and Kelli share a look.

"Y'all were gone a long time," Kelli said. "Lisha, I hope you're not running late to get ready for your date?"

Kael stiffened.

"My date?" she asked, looking confused.

"That cute guy you were talking to at the clinic," Kelli explained. "I overheard him ask you out before I left."

Kael couldn't believe the way his gut felt like he'd been kicked by the hooves of a stallion.

Lisha looked over at him but her face closed up as she glanced away. She shrugged. "I'll be fine," she said.

Kael was floored. Kissing him less than twenty-four hours ago and accepting a date with another man already? He shook his head and looked toward his father. "I guess they are all just the same, huh?" he asked, before brushing past Bea and Kelli to walk into the house.

Seconds later the door to his bedroom slammed and they all jumped at the sound of it.

"Love is passion and fire; it haunts and enchants the one who touches it."

—Unknown

Interlude

"Wow, so Aunt Kelli was a . . . a hater?" Kaleb asked, his face incredulous.

The few lines on Kael's face deepened as his expression changed. Lisha reached over to stroke his hand and wrist. "We didn't know that at the time," she said gently, motioning with her eyes to her family to leave it alone.

And they did.

"How bad was Bea's cooking, though?" Jade asked, trying hard to change the mood.

Kael begrudgingly smiled. "It was bad," he said. "Too bad she didn't cook as good as she looked."

His sons all grimaced or covered their faces with their hands.

The ladies all got fired up and their mingled voices of protests clashed with the jovial sounds of

Destiny's Child singing "Rudolph the Red-Nosed Reindeer."

"Hey, hey, hey," Kael roared in a strong voice, bringing immediate silence.

Everyone in the room looked to him, but he gave the floor to Lisha with a wave of his hand.

She smiled. "No worries, children. She couldn't touch me in cooking, looks or—"

"Hey," Kaeden hollered in protest.

"I was *going* to say in personality, son," Lisha told him.

"Thank God," he muttered, pulling at his long slender fingers—his new nervous gesture since he finally overcame reaching to push up the glasses he hadn't needed since his Lasik surgery almost two years ago.

Jade chuckled and reached over to press a kiss to her husband's smooth-shaven cheek where they sat on the floor in front of the Christmas tree. She enjoyed the scent of the pine and said a silent thanks to God that Kaeden's allergies didn't kick in and send him running for his inhaler.

She still marveled at how different they were but how much they loved one another. She loved adventure and the outdoors, even once co-owning an adventure tour business, while Kaeden was a straitlaced accountant who was pretty much allergic to any and everything in the outdoors. Growing up with brothers who all enjoyed and thrived in the outdoors and who now all worked in ranching had left him feeling like the odd man out even if he did the accounting, bookkeeping and taxes for each of his brother's businesses.

She had been surprised to discover that behind the glasses and the suit was a handsome man with beautiful eyes and a body that was lean and still fit. And his prowess in their bed?

Uhm-uhm-uhm, Kaeden still gives me fever.

She eyed her husband looking ever so fine in his navy blue long-sleeved shirt and dark denims sitting on the floor beside her. A lot of people thought he and Kade looked like twins, and although Jade thought they favored each other, she believed her Strong man was the best of the lot. He was definitely the best for her.

She looked around at the large room filled with family—her family now too—as everyone was seated and centered around Lisha and Kael. They were respected and loved as the elders of the family. From their love had come five children who now all had love of their own.

And children of their own, she thought with sadness as she looked down at the area rug to keep from showing her emotions on her face.

She'd wanted to start a legacy for them as well. Last year she made the decision to pause her work as an adventure tour guide to focus on having a baby with Kaeden, but so far they had not been blessed with a child. Just that morning she had taken yet another pregnancy test, hoping to surprise her husband with good news for Christmas. Instead she put on a brave face and just gave him the newest iPhone.

Kaeden loved gadgets and technology so the phone went over well, but she knew a child would have been the best gift of all . . . for them both.

Tears welled up quickly and Jade climbed to her feet with ease and quick-walked out of the living room and across the hall to leave the house. The cold snap in the air felt invigorating to her, and as she stood at the railing she took deep gulps of it, enjoying the feel of the crisp wind wrapping around her body.

Their home in Summerville seemed empty this last year without the laughter of a child, and although they never spoke of it, she knew Kaeden had to be feeling the same way. They were the only ones to have a home without kids; even Kaitlyn and Quint had Lei.

Jade opened her eyes as something warm was placed around her shoulders. She smiled at the smell of Kaeden's cologne as he wrapped his arms around her from behind. She leaned back against his strength, needing it.

"You okay?" he asked, pressing a kiss to her temple.

She started to nod. She started to lie. "No, I'm not okay," she said, whispering the truth as she looked out at the vast lands of the ranch in the distance. The grounds were white tipped with frost and the skies were cloudy.

Kaeden turned her body around to face him, readjusting her coat around her shoulders. When she looked down at his chest, he used a strong finger to press up against her chin to raise her face. "What's wrong?" he asked, his eyes filled with concern and love. Lots of love.

"I want to make a baby with you," she admitted, her voice breaking as a tear raced down her cheek.

He caught it with his thumb and then pressed his kisses to her lips, warming them instantly in the cold. "And we will, baby. It's just not our time yet," Kaeden said, pulling her body close to his.

"But what if we can't?" she asked, admitting to her newfound fears.

"We *will*," he assured her.

Something in his voice eased her fears a bit.

"After the new year we'll make an appointment to meet with your doctor and we'll go from there and do whatever we have to do to have a baby," Kaeden promised.

Jade's face brightened and she smiled as she lifted up on her toes to kiss her husband. "Maybe we'll get lucky during that vacay to Hawaii you surprised me with this morning."

Kaeden pressed a kiss to her forehead like he did so many times over their years together. "Maybe," he said.

At the loud snap of something overturning

around the corner of the house, Kaeden and Jade walked around the large wraparound porch to find Kadina and Lei stretched out on their backs in their outer gear with a broken table in between them.

"Hey, Uncle Kaeden. Hi, Aunt Jade," Kadina said from the ground.

They rushed forward to help the teens to their feet.

"Are you okay?" Jade asked, her pretty dark brown face filled with concern.

"Yes, ma'am," the girls answered in unison.

Kaeden held up one hand to keep everyone quiet.

A Christmas tune mingled in the air with the raucous voices of the family inside.

Kaeden looked up at the small window overlooking the living room. It was clear the girls used the table to open the window and it gave way from under them.

He easily reached up and closed the window that was designed for ventilation in older homes.

"Uncle Kaeden, we want to hear the story too," Kadina said, giving him her best sad face with pouted lips and all.

Jade bit back a smile.

"That worked when you were four inches shorter and six years younger," he said dryly, waving the girls toward the front of the house.

The girls walked off, mumbling under their breath.

"You sure you want one of those?" Kaeden asked.

"Definitely," Jade said.

They walked back into the house together, secure in their love and their desire to build on it. Hanging up their coats, they moved back into the living room to reclaim their spots on the floor before the tree. They slid right back into the good-natured banter of the family as Kael and Lisha continued telling their story.

"Wait a minute . . . are y'all talking about Bea Olson that lives on Honeysuckle Lane?" Kaleb asked.

Lisha rolled her eyes. "Yes," she said with emphasis.

"I didn't want her then and I *damn* sure don't want her now," Kael drawled, shifting in his recliner and crossing his ankle over his knee.

"I know that," Lisha assured him. "But back then that heifer had me riled up. . . ."

Chapter 10

Way back in the day

Lisha rolled her eyes as she swatted away the hand massaging her shoulder. The arm around the back of the front bench seat of the car was bad enough, but she wasn't trying to have her right breast "accidentally" groped or stroked while trying to watch *Foxy Brown* at the drive-in movie theater. Looking over her shoulder in the darkness she saw Junie and her date damn near stretched out on the rear seat, kissing and doing only God knows what.

As she was turning back around, her date, Tyler, leaned in.

"You too fine to act so ugly," he whispered in her ear.

Lisha shut one eye and made a face at the smell of his breath before she climbed from the car.

"Hey, where you going?" he asked.

"Bathroom," she lied, before closing the door of the Cadillac.

She made her way through the rows of cars and walked toward the light of the concession stand as the cool September night winds whipped around her.

Add no more double dates with Junie to my never-to-do-again-list.

For the last two weeks she had moped around her apartment, still bothered by Kael and his lies to her. She barely knew the man, but it just hurt like crazy that he kissed her like that and said the things he said to her while he was also busy sniffing under the skirts of his sister's friend.

She had been so embarrassed by it the day in his father's yard that she didn't care if he thought she had a date that night. She was only trying to save face. His jumping up with his little slick comment to his father meant nothing to her.

I guess they are all just the same, huh?

She didn't know what he meant and didn't care.

And now when they did encounter each other during his father's therapy, she made as big a point of avoiding him as he did avoiding her. Did it stop her entire body from still reacting to him at the very sight—and sometimes thought—of him? No. Not at all.

A man walked up to the stand shaking a cigarette out of his pack of Marlboros. Lisha stepped in his path. "Can I have one?" she asked, pushing her hair from her face.

"Hey, no problem, baby girl," he said, the wind causing his massive Afro to sway back and forth on his head.

She took the cigarette and placed it between her glossy lips as he cupped his hand around his lighter to light her cigarette and then his own. "Thank you," she said after a deep inhale.

Lisha didn't smoke and barely knew how, but she needed something to do with her hands as she stood around waiting for the double date to be over.

"If my girl wasn't with me I'd ask you to watch the movie with me," he said.

Lisha eyed him through the stream of smoke she released. "Do all men look for more sweets while their hand's already in somebody else's cookie jar?" she snapped.

He held up his hands and took two steps back from her.

Lisha turned and ignored him, smoking *his* cigarette. She was just thankful the movie was near the end. She wanted to go home, take a long hot bath and get ready for church in the morning. She finished her cigarette and leaned against the side of the stand to watch the rest of the movie.

Before she walked back to the car she purchased a pack of Freshen-up gum from the stand. When she got back to the car her date was sitting in the front seat staring forward while Junie and her date were still lost in each other in the backseat.

She unwrapped one of the squares of gum and popped it into her mouth before handing him one. "Here you go," she said.

He eyed her, the gum and then waved it away before focusing his attention back to the screen. Lisha just shrugged and counted down the last few seconds of the movie before he finally removed the speaker hanging on the driver-side window and cranked the car.

"The movie over?" Junie asked, raising her head up with her short hair in total disarray.

Neither Lisha nor her date answered her and neither had anything to say as he drove back toward their apartment just down the road on Highway 63. As soon as he parked, Lisha opened the door. "Thank you—"

He waved his hand at her dismissively.

Lisha swung her door shut hard before tapping on the rear passenger window. "Junie, we're home," she said.

Moments later Lisha stepped aside as the car door swung open and Junie climbed out, smoothing down her shirt over her hips. "Bye, Gary," she said.

Tyler sped off from them with a nasty squeal of his tires.

"Didn't work out, huh?" Junie asked as they made their way up the stairs.

"Bad breath and groping hands do not a good date make," Lisha said.

"I thought you would like him," Junie said, bumping her hip against her cousin's. "Sorry."

"No problem. I needed to get out the house anyway and I did get to see all of the movie . . . unlike other folks," she teased, reaching up to smooth her cousin's flyaway hairs back down.

"I'm glad you feel a little better," she said.

Lisha pulled out her key and unlocked her apartment door, turning on the lights when she entered. "A little bit," she said as she kicked off her shoes and loosened the button on the skin-tight jeans she wore.

Junie followed her inside, heading to the kitchen to grab a bottle of red wine and two goblets. "Can I ask you something?"

Lisha folded her body onto the sofa and accepted the full glass of wine to sip.

"You ever judge me?" Junie asked.

Lisha swallowed her wine before setting the glass on the coffee table. "What do you mean?"

"I'm a little free-spirited with my life and you've sworn off sex until you're married, so like do you ever judge me and think I'm too fast or something?" Junie asked, coming around the sofa to sit on the opposite end.

"Nope," Lisha said. "I love you just the way you are."

"But we're so different," Junie stressed.

"So does this mean you judge me like I'm a prude or something?" Lisha asked, rising to tuck one of her feet beneath her bottom.

"I don't judge, but I do wonder how you do it," Junie admitted before she took a sip. "Like sex is so good and you're twenty-five and you have never . . . like never . . ."

"Never," Lisha assured her.

"You know you're like a unicorn or Santa Claus and the Easter Bunny and shit, right?" Junie asked.

"But you know that the more I deal with men and see the shit they do, the way they lie and mess up, the more I know I'm doing the right thing," she said, her heart aching a bit at the thought of Kael.

Junie bit the tip of her nail as she glanced up at the ceiling and then back at her family. "But who's to say the man you marry won't lie or mess up . . . and then what, Lisha?"

"I don't know," she admitted softly.

"But what if you wait and your husband is horrible in bed. *Then* what?"

"I don't know," she stressed again. "But I do know that I am going to wait for that man that values me enough to propose. And what's *wrong* with that?"

Junie set her goblet down and scooted down the sofa to hug her cousin close. "Oh, nothing at all. I just don't want you disappointed."

"Shit, me either," Lisha spouted.

Junie laughed as she sat back.

They fell into a comfortable silence, drinking their wine and lost in their own thoughts.

"I do want to get married one day too, you know," Junie said.

Lisha's face filled with surprise. "And have babies?" she asked, her voice filled with wonder.

Junie grabbed the bottle of wine and topped off their glasses. "Maybe one," she said. "But that's it."

"But how will you figure out which man is your Mr. Right if you don't settle down with anybody?" Lisha asked in as polite a way as she could.

"Because the right one will make me not want anyone else," she said assuredly.

And Lisha thought of Kael. Since she'd met the man she hadn't been able to muster up even a flirtation for another man. No one compared to him in her eyes. No one.

"I want a bunch of kids," Lisha said, purposefully steering her thoughts away from him. "Like five or six even."

Junie's face filled with distaste. "Oh, no-no-no-no-no."

"Why not?" Lisha asked.

"Girl, you'll be changing diapers, cooking and cleaning up behind them for the rest of your life."

Lisha's eyes lit up. "And loving them, and teaching them and watching them to see what kind of adults they become," she said with excitement. "I was an only kid and it was not fun."

"Hey, I'm an only child too, but we had each other." Junie raised her glass.

Lisha nodded and toasted to her. "Yes, but even you went home and it was still me playing with my dolls all alone," she said, thinking back on it. "No, I want my kids to have each other's back and look out for each other and be close."

"You are going to make some man a really good wife and a bunch of kids a really good mother," Junie said with an earnest expression.

Lisha smiled in thanks. But her doubts were there. Would she ever find love and make all of her dreams of a happily ever after come true?

Two days later, Kael and his ranch hand, Jim, were busy checking the heifers they bred with one of the two bulls a month ago. He was glad for the break in the humidity and heat of summer, particular with the rather intrusive palpitation method of checking the herd. Having his arm deep in a cow's rectum up to his armpit was necessary so he could

decide how many of the open cows he would sell
to avoid the cost of caring for them all winter when
they weren't going to produce a calf next year.

Gently easing his arm and hand free, he shook
his head at Jim as he carefully removed the arm's
length glove and dumped it into the trash. He
wasn't discouraged; his experience in cattle ranching let him know that cows were not that fertile,
and so far he was at an eighty percent conception
rate.

"How's it going?"

Placing another glove on his right arm, Kael
looked up in surprise at his father standing at the
gate of the corral with his cane. "How'd you get
here?"

"I drove," he said with spunk as he leaned forward against the gate.

"By yourself?" Kael asked, coming around the
front of the cattle to walk over to the wooden
fence.

"Yup," Logan said, his eyes squinted as he watched
Jim check the next cow. "How many so far?"

"Just over eighty percent," Kael answered, turning to watch Jim as well before turning back to his
father.

"My doctor approved me to drive, son," Logan
said before Kael could open his mouth. "I had an
appointment just this morning."

Kael nodded. "I forgot that was this morning."

"Son, you and your sister have to stop worrying about me. My hip is doing good. My therapy with Lisha is done in two weeks. You have your ranch to focus on and I'm shipping your sister back to her husband full-time. Trust me, I'm cool."

Kael thought of Lisha at the mention of her name and that now-familiar mix of anger, jealousy and desire filled him. He knew he had no right to not want her with any other man when he was clear on his decision not to get serious with her, but he couldn't lie. The thought of that irked him to the core.

"It's time for the old dog to come off the porch because driving is not all the doctor cleared me for, son," Logan said with a roguish wink and a noise he made with his teeth. "Me and my truck *both* gonna ride tonight."

Kael kicked at a dried cow patty in the dirt. "Aw, man. Come on, man."

"Hey, you may not care that your Johnson stays dry as the Sahara lately, but I'm going to take mine for a dip in a nice sweet pool, buddy," he assured his son.

"You don't know what I do with my Johnson," Kael said, shifting his hat back on his head as he looked up at the afternoon sun.

Logan just grunted.

They both looked on as Jim gave a thumbs-up that the cow he just checked was pregnant.

"Sure gonna miss Lisha," Logan said, giving his son a sidelong glance.

Kael just shrugged.

Logan grunted again.

"How many more?" Kael called out.

"Last one, boss," Jim called back.

Logan shifted his tall frame on his cane. "I'm real proud of you, son," he said, looking around the property. "Real proud."

Kael nodded as he reached over with his fist to lightly tap the top of the hand his father used to grip the railing. "Thank you. You taught me to work hard for what I want. I learned by your example."

Logan blinked rapidly as he looked down at his boot. "Good boy. Real good, son," he said.

Kael looked at his father curiously, swearing he could see a little wetness in his eyes. He stepped up and pressed a quick kiss to his cheek. His father swatted him off and Kael grinned, knowing that would be his reaction.

"You boys done here?" Logan asked.

"Yes, sir," Kael said.

"Come on, show me your house." He turned and walked away with a limp, not waiting to see if his son was going to do as he asked.

Kael helped Jim finish cleaning up and getting the cattle watered before finally walking the distance to the house. His steps faltered at seeing Lisha standing on the porch with his father. He eyed her, liking the way she had her hair straight and framing her face.

He could tell from the look on her face that she didn't want to be there but was acquiescing for his father. Stiffening his back, he walked over to the house and climbed the porch as she avoided even looking at him. Moving past her to unlock the door, he hated how the scent of her seemed to make him feel more alive.

Kael opened the door and stepped inside, needing the space between them widened. He removed his Stetson. "You haven't seen it since I did all the work," he said to his father who stepped inside, nodding in approval.

"You took my advice on the fireplace, huh?" Logan asked, walking over to touch and inspect the new deep cherry stain Kael had put on it.

"Sure did."

"All new windows?" Logan asked, walking across the large expanse of the room to enter the hall leading to the kitchen.

"No, I didn't need to right now. Some were in good shape," he said, following behind his father and leaving Lisha standing in the hall by the front door.

He looked back over his shoulder just as she reached out to lightly touch the wall where they shared that first heated kiss.

"Beautiful kitchen, son," Logan called down the

hall. "Now you just need a woman to cook in it for you."

Lisha looked up. She dropped her hand and looked away at the sight of Kael looking back at her even as his steps carried him toward the large and airy kitchen.

"I don't need the hassle," he said, before looking forward. "*Trust* me."

His father was inspecting the used stove and refrigerator he'd purchased. "They look damn near new," he said.

Kael set his hat on the counter and looked on as his father finished walking the entire length of the spacious kitchen.

"Plenty of room for a big family, son."

"One day," he said, looking back down the hall at Lisha still standing rooted in the same spot.

Logan grunted. "Lisha," he called out.

Kael looked away as she turned and made her way down the hall.

"My son needs a woman's touch in here," Logan said. "What would you do?"

Lisha looked surprised and then her face closed up.

Why is she *mad?*

Kael watched as she walked around the empty kitchen slowly. "Well, if any other man than Kael owned this house and that man was smart enough to ask me my opinion, then I would do bright colors to break up the wood floors and cabinets," she said, before casting a little glance over her shoulder that was sarcastic.

Kael had to fight the urge to storm across the room and literally turn her over his knee. "Well, since it is my house and I didn't ask, I'll wait for the opinion of the woman I do ask."

"Uh-oh," Logan said, shaking his head as he leaned back against the counter.

Lisha whirled. Her bright eyes flashed even more brightly as she glared at him. "Yes, and I'm sure the particular woman you have in mind will make it look just as tawdry as her makeup and just as nasty as her chicken." Lisha finished her words high-strung.

Kael threw his hands up in the air. "What?" he asked, his face showing his confusion and annoyance.

"Your ass, negro," Lisha snapped, walking out the kitchen.

Kael looked over at his father at Logan's chuckle. "What the hell is she talking about? What is she mad for?"

Logan pointed his finger at his chest. "You asking *me*?" he asked. "Now that don't make sense."

"Women are crazy," he said, his brows crinkled.

"Sometimes," Logan agreed. "And sometimes a man drives her crazy."

"Man, hell with it," Kael said, going out the other entrance of the kitchen that led directly into the dining room.

His father followed behind him and they finished going through each of the rooms on the first level, including a den, guest bathroom and a small room Kael planned to use for an office.

Lisha had replanted herself in her spot by the door, making it clear to him she cared nothing about his house. It wasn't until Kael led his father to the staircase in the hall between the living room and den that she quietly moved to climb the stairs behind his father. Her eyes stayed locked on Logan as he carefully used an up and down motion with each step.

"Any pain, Mr. Strong?" she asked, midway up the stairs.

"No," he said. "No pain."

They reached the top and Lisha remained by the door to the hall closet as he and his father walked in and out of each of the five bedrooms. "Which one is yours?" Kael asked his father.

"None."

Kael just laughed it off. "We'll see in twenty years," he said.

"Maybe," Logan agreed, using his cane to open a closet door. "And maybe not."

Kael walked over to one of the many windows

lining the middle room and looked down on the acres upon acres of green pasture.

"The rate you're going, the rooms will be open and available regardless," Logan said, dropping the little gem before he limped his tall figure out the room.

Kael looked out the door behind him, and when his father moved, his eyes fell on Lisha. He smiled at the way he caught her eyes shifting as she looked inside each of the bedrooms. *So she does care.*

He left the bedroom and walked up to her. "Your boyfriend mind you being here?" he asked for her ears alone.

"Why would he mind?" she countered, finally looking at him directly and locking her eyes on his.

"Because of what happened against that wall," he said, pointing toward that spot near the front door even as he kept his eyes leveled on her.

Lisha didn't look, but her cheeks warmed.

"And later that night on the other wall," he added. "Remember?"

She looked up at him sharply. "Cut your crap. I'm not falling for it no more. Okay?"

Logan walked through the double doors of the master bedroom. He stopped as he eyed them. "Do you two need to be alone?" he asked.

Lisha shook her head and walked over to lightly

touch his father's elbow. "Not at all," she said, as she walked with him to the steps.

Kael lowered his head as he pressed his hands to his hips, wondering when the tables had turned for Lisha to be angry at him.

"We are *more* than done," she said firmly.

Chapter 11

"Hold up, Lisha."

She looked up in surprise at Kael walking out onto the porch. She was just about to climb into the passenger seat of Logan's truck and the loud diesel was already roaring with life. "What do you want, Kael?" she asked, more than exasperated with him.

"I want to talk to you," he said.

"Go talk to Bea," she snapped, climbing into the truck and slamming the door.

"Bea?" he asked. "What the hell do I want to talk to her for?"

He came down the stairs and reached for the door handle.

Lisha clutched the top of door through the open window and tugged to keep it closed.

He pulled.

She tugged.

Logan chuckled.

Kael cockily used just one hand and jerked the

door open with one hard jerk that showed his strength over her. He reached in and grasped her upper arms to lift her out the truck and down onto her sneakered feet. Lisha childishly kicked his shin and Kael howled out in pain.

When she turned to climb back into the truck, he reached out and wrapped one strong arm around her waist to hold her writhing body against his.

Lisha tried like hell to loosen his steel-like arm around her, even digging her nails into his brown flesh and pummeling her fists anywhere her arms could reach. Finally giving up, she dropped her hands and released ragged breaths. "Mr. Strong, please tell Kael to put me down," she requested, eyeing him as he sat in the driver's seat and watched them with amusement.

"I will . . . if you promise to stand there and listen to him," he said. "Please."

"I don't need your help, Dad," Kael said.

Logan ignored him and continued to eye Lisha. "Please," he said.

In the weeks since she'd been working with him she knew that one word had not been an easy one for him to say and so Lisha nodded.

"Let her down, boy," Logan said.

"I'm not a little boy," Kael said.

Logan lowered his head to make sure his son could see his eyes. "Let her down, Kael," he said again in that no-nonsense voice that demanded and received respect.

Moments later Lisha was on solid ground. She turned and glared at him. "What do you have to talk to me about?" she asked.

Suddenly the door of the truck slammed closed and the diesel sounded off as Logan revved the engine. "Make sure you get her back to my house, son," he called out the window before accelerating forward.

Lisha whirled again. "Mr. Strong," she called behind him even as his truck got smaller with the growing distance.

Kael chuckled.

"What the hell is funny about being stranded?" she asked him.

"You're not stranded," he said.

Lisha just shook her head and moved past him to sit on the steps of the porch. She was steamed and could steadily feel the heat of her anger rising until she thought the top of her head might blow off. "Look, I'm pretty sure Bea wouldn't agree with you being here with me, so could you take me to my car?" she demanded, looking up at him as he walked over to stand above her.

In his jeans, Lisha could clearly see the outline of his member and she leaned back, remembering the hardness if it.

"I'm not involved with Bea," he said. "I mean

she's throwing herself at me pretty hard, but I don't want it."

"Liar," Lisha said.

"I'm not a liar, Lisha," he said.

"Well, somebody's lying because Bea made it clear she was there to see *you* and be a good woman for *you* and cook chicken for *you,*" she stressed.

Kael came around her to sit beside her on the step. Lisha scooted away from him. "Bea likes me. She's my sister's friend and I don't know what she said to you—"

"She didn't say it to me," Lisha admitted, biting her bottom lip as she looked away.

Kael looked puzzled.

"I overheard her talking to your sister," she admitted.

Kael reached over and lightly grasped Lisha's stubborn chin. "I have never kissed Bea and I don't want to," he said, his eyes searching hers.

Lisha hated how she felt like she was swimming in the brown depths of his eyes. "You don't think she's all sexy and stuff?" she asked, her voice soft and unsure.

"I didn't say that—"

Lisha smacked his hand away.

"But I don't want her," he added. "Not to date, not to kiss, not for sex . . . and for damn sure not for her cooking."

Lisha laughed a little at that and then she remembered something. "Well, you don't want me either," she said lightly.

"Oh, I want you."

Lisha took in a hot little breath as she turned her head to look into his handsome face. Her eyes glazed over and her mouth opened a bit as she saw the way his eyes honed in on her lips.

He leaned in and she swore he was going to kiss her again. She closed her eyes in anticipation of that first fiery spark of his mouth touching down on hers.

When the kiss never came she opened her eyes just enough to see that he had leaned back from her. *Huh?*

"Kissing me and dating other guys?" he asked.

"What?" she asked.

"Your date. Your boyfriend. How is he?"

Lisha waved her hand dismissively. "I didn't go on a date. I just said that because I thought Bea was your girlfriend," she said. "But even if I had a date, would I be wrong? You don't want a relationship."

Kael leaned forward, pressing his elbows onto the top of his knees. "But I can't share you with anyone else."

Lisha licked her lips, feeling both a thrill and a disappointment about his words. "Well, in two weeks I'll be gone and we won't have to see each other ever again."

Kael wiped his face with both of his hands. "I don't want that either," he admitted.

"You don't know what you want, Kael Strong," she said.

"I can't lie. You have had me messed up since that day I saw you in the hospital," he admitted.

"So why fight it?" she asked, looking down at her hands as she twisted her fingers.

He didn't say anything.

"I'm not going to fight for something you obviously feel so conflicted about, Kael," she said. "But I will say I think this is something special and it does feel like a loss to me. It feels like God blessed us with something that could grow into something amazing and you're just throwing it away because of some stupid girl who didn't know how to love—not just you—but anyone probably."

Kael stood up and then pulled her to her feet. He easily lifted her onto the next step so that their eyes were level with one another. "I could fall for you," he admitted in a deep and husky voice as his hands rested on her hips.

She brought her hands up to stroke the sides of his face and traced his bottom lip with one of her thumbs. "Then let's fall together," she whispered to him.

Lisha leaned in and pressed her lips to his, closing her eyes as she stroked the contours of his mouth with her tongue before he opened his mouth and allowed her in. Her entire body trembled and flooded with heat as she stroked his tongue with hers as she brought her hands down onto his shoulders and then his back to tightly grip the material in her fists.

With a moan of pleasure, she gently tugged his tongue into her mouth and worked her chin in tiny up and down motions as she sucked it.

Kael released a moan filled with his own hunger, bringing his hands around to clasp her buttocks, gently kneading the soft flesh as he enjoyed her taking control and kissing him. He honestly felt like he could stand there forever with her in his arms kissing him like that.

Kael made her feel bold and brazen. He brought out her confidence and made her follow her womanly instincts on what to do to please him. As she tilted her head to the side and lightly fluttered the tip of her tongue against his, she brought her hands down his strong wide back and then under the edge of his shirt. The first feel of her hands against his warm skin made him shiver and that pushed her to lightly rake her nails up and then down the expanse of his back.

Kael's hands eased under her shirt as well and she gasped hotly into his open mouth at the feel of his touch. "Kael," she cried out, flinging her head back as he pressed hot kisses to the length of her neck.

She felt his hand coming around to the edge of her bra and she was so lost in their passion that she didn't object when his fingers slid under the lace to touch the brown mounds.

"Boss."

She moaned and her knees weakened beneath her as his fingers gently circled her hard nipples.

"Boss," Jim said louder.

Kael and Lisha broke apart to find Jim standing a-ways back from them, but clearly in full view of them. Feeling flooded with embarrassment, Lisha turned and raced up the stairs, nearly tripping in her haste to reach the inside of the house.

Closing the door she rushed to lower her bra back onto her breasts and then winced when the lace rubbed against her hard and aching nipples. She turned when the door opened and Kael walked in. Lisha made a face of horror. "That was so embarrassing," she said.

"You?" he asked in disbelief. "Can you imagine standing up and talking to my employee—a dude—with a hard-on?"

"Is he gone?" she asked.

Kael nodded and reached for her, pulling her body close and settling his chin atop her head as he rocked her body back and forth smoothly. "God, huh?" he asked, referring to her earlier comment.

Lisha shrugged as she closed her eyes and enjoyed the scent of him and the feel of him as he held her. Everything about it was pure goodness. Everything.

But she stepped out of his embrace a bit and looked up at him. "You know what, Kael, I will lay it all out for you," she said.

He looked surprised. "Really?"

She playfully swatted at him. "Not like *that*," she stressed. "I meant I want to open up and take a risk by exposing how I feel so that maybe you will take the risk by letting yourself be with someone who is impressed by you, who feels protected by you, someone who smiles just by seeing you, someone who shivers at the very *thought* of your kisses. Someone who would never betray you. Someone who believes that she could really, really love you. Like love you hard . . . the way you deserved."

Lisha stood up on her toes and pressed a kiss next to his mouth. "And that someone is me," she said. "But I want you to think about it and you make damn sure I am what you want and need."

Kael picked her up and hugged her close.

Lisha snuggled her face into his neck and pressed a kiss there.

When he eventually set her back down on her feet, she smiled up at him and then presented her hand. "Deal?"

He nodded and shook her offered hand. "Deal," he agreed.

Kael wasn't ready for her to leave him. "Do you want to ride?"

Lisha looked shocked at the suggestion.

"A horse?" he added. "Do you want to ride a horse?"

"Oh," she said, looking slightly relieved.

"You ever rode a horse?" he asked.

Lisha made a face like "please."

He laughed. "Do you want to ride?" he asked again.

"Is it safe?" she asked even as she let him take her by the hand and lead her out the door.

"I won't let anything happen to you," he promised.

She looked unsure, but walked beside him anyway as he made his way across the stretch of land to a large tree where his quarter horse Sampson was tied loosely as he enjoyed his hay and water. The evening sun glistened through the break in the leaves and made his coat golden. As they neared the powerful animal he felt Lisha pull back. He looked down at her and saw the fear in her eyes.

"It's okay," he said. "Come around to the front and let him see you."

She did as he said even as she kept herself safely shielded behind him. He wondered if she was aware that Sampson's eyes were steadily locked on her as well. As he stepped closer to his animal, Kael held his hand up, palm side down. Sampson instantly lowered his head and then brought his nose up against it in greeting.

Lisha jumped and squealed, but Kael just smoothed Sampson's jaw and the bridge of his nose. "How are you, boy?" he said to keep him settled so that he didn't rear up from being startled by her.

"Come on, Lisha," he said. "Stroke his nose just like this."

She stepped closer to Kael.

He reached behind himself and lightly grabbed her wrist to pull her forward. Holding her hand, he opened her palm and guided her to stroke the horse. She jumped at the first feel of him and Kael kept her hand steady until he felt the tension leave her body.

He was surprised and thought Lisha gutsy when she stepped from behind him. "Good boy," she said. "Don't act up."

Sampson nudged her hand with his nose.

"It's his way of saying hello," Kael explained.

"Oh . . . okay. Well . . . hello," she said.

"Ready?"

Lisha looked over her shoulder at him as she continued to stroke Sampson's neck. "Ready for what?" she asked.

"To ride."

Lisha's eyes dipped down to his nether region before looking back up at him with reddened cheeks. "Yeah," she said, turning from him with a mischievous smile.

Kael liked her mix of innocence and sexiness.

Fighting the urge to grab her and kiss her until she undressed and begged him to make love to her, he undid the reins and climbed up into the saddle with ease. Looking down at her, he held out one hand.

Lisha whispered something near Sampson's ear that caused the horse to shift back and forth a bit. She took his hand though.

"Put your left foot on top of mine in the stirrup while I pull you up," he instructed, carefully watching her. "Then lift your right leg over the saddle."

She did as he told her, and with one strong tug Kael pulled her up, leaning back as she straddled the saddle. The plushness of her buttocks settled atop his thighs a bit. He felt his dick stir and hoped she couldn't feel his growing erection as she kept shifting her bottom to find comfort in the saddle.

"Ready?" he asked, settling one arm loosely around her waist as he loosened the reins a bit.

Sampson slowly walked to the left of the tree and down a newly broken path.

Kael found himself leaning a bit to the side to check her expression.

She looked a little trepid, but she was still looking around at the beauty of the summer flowers blooming and the varying deep greens of the heavily wooded area. In time he felt her body relax in the saddle, but that only made her bottom press more deeply against his crotch.

Shifting back so that she landed more securely in the saddle in front of him, Kael nudged Sampson forward.

"What's that?" Lisha asked, pointing.

"The hunting cabin," he answered her. "I think it's been there even longer than the house."

She nodded and Kael nudged Sampson forward toward the more heavily wooded areas.

"Is it safe?" she asked.

"This area is great for deer hunting and that season doesn't open up for another week or so," Kael explained. "Plus it's private land and they are supposed to get my permission before hunting on it."

"Do you hunt?"

"What country boy doesn't?" he joked, leaning a bit again to look at her.

She glanced back at him.

"I have a beautiful ten-point head I'm going to put over the fireplace in the living room," he boasted as he leaned them both back a bit as Sampson skillfully moved down a slight incline.

"Oh, Kael, not in the living room," she said. "Maybe put it in your den, but not your living room. That's the room you dress up and no one uses except on special occasions like family holidays."

"Oh, yeah?" he asked.

Lisha nodded. "Yes," she stressed.

He just chuckled.

"What are you going to do with all this land, Kael?" she asked.

He shrugged. "Expand my ranch one day if I make it," he said.

She settled her hands on top of his and patted it. "You will," she said with ease as she continued to look around.

"You're not making it easier," he said.

She looked over her shoulder at him. "What?" she asked.

"Our deal," he said.

Her eyes dropped to his mouth. "I'm not trying to make it hard for you," she said, her eyes moving back up to view his face.

"I know you're not," he said with honesty.

She leaned her head back with her face still tilted up and puckered her lips for a kiss.

Kael kissed her once and then again and again and then twice more.

He could get addicted to the taste of her lips and wondered if her other lips were just as sweet.

Coming to a glen, he halted Sampson and dismounted. "Hold on to the saddle," he said, guiding the horse to a tree where he loosely tied the reins before coming to lift Lisha down to her feet.

She looked on as he retrieved a clean blanket from his saddlebag and stretched it out near the edge of the glen atop a thick patch of green grass almost as soft as a bed itself.

He sat down on the middle of it and then reached out his hand for her.

"You're not making it easy on yourself either," she said, hesitant to come to him.

"Come here, girl," Kael said.

And she did come to him, taking his hand as she sat down on the blanket beside him. "It's beautiful here," she said, lying down to look up in wonder at the haven created by the towering trees overlooking the cleared spot.

Kael shifted on the blanket to lie on his side. He propped his head in his hand and looked down at her. "You're beautiful," he told her truthfully, leaning down to plant kisses on her entire face. Her forehead. Cheeks. Chin. Mouth. And forehead again.

He shifted on his back and pulled Lisha's head onto his chest, wrapping his arm around her body as they enjoyed the unique feel of the coolness offered by the shade mingled with the glows of the sun's rays that beamed through the trees.

"I always drove by all the trees on the side of the roads and highways and always wondered what it was like deep in the woods," she said, her eyes drifting closed as she enjoyed the steady up and down movement of Kael's chest as he breathed. "I never imagined nothing this pretty."

Kael wasn't surprised when soon the sounds of her breathing changed as she fell asleep. He didn't wake her and selfishly enjoyed having her there secluded in the woods away from the world as she slept in his arms, even as he wrangled with his decision to take a chance on love or risk it all.

When Kael opened his eyes and saw that darkness surround them, he realized that he'd fallen asleep himself and a couple of hours had passed.

"Lisha," he said, gently rousing her.

She released a heavy breath before her eyes opened and she looked up at him before sitting up. "I fell asleep?" she asked in surprise, covering her mouth in case the little nap made her breath less than fresh.

"I did too," he admitted, rising to his feet and holding out his hand to her to pull her up.

"We gotta get back before it gets too dark," he said, moving to Sampson to untie his reins.

Lisha picked up the blanket and folded it, moving over to push it into the saddlebag.

Kael noticed her initiative and liked it.

Climbing into the saddle, he helped her mount in front of him again before steering Sampson around to head back onto the path. Lisha just leaned back against his chest the entire time with his arms on either side of her as he held the reins and the horn of the saddle. It took them about twenty minutes or better before they saw the tip of the house in the distance.

"Thank you for showing me your land, Kael,"

she said, as he brought Sampson to a stop near the horse trailer.

"You're welcome," he said, as he dismounted and then reached up to help her down.

Lisha looked on as he quickly sponged the horse down and then used the hose to rinse out the trough and fill it with enough water for Sampson to drink his fill. "Your door locked?" she asked.

Kael considered before shaking his head. "I don't think so."

"You got your key?" she asked, already turning to cross the front yard and jog up the steps.

"Yeah."

Lisha opened the door and turned the lock.

He looked on when she suddenly disappeared in the house and returned a few moments later with his Stetson on her head. That made him smile as he finished loading Sampson in the trailer and then hopped in the driver's seat of the truck to pull around in the yard and stop in front of the steps for her to hop in.

"Looks good on you," he said. "You might have a little cowgirl in you."

"Yee-haw," Lisha joked.

Kael laughed as he pulled off down the long dirt road. They said nothing as they drove to his father's for her car, but he held her hand on the center of the bench seat. Just the feel of her supple skin beneath his calloused fingers made him happy.

But what if it all crashed and burned?

When he parked the car in his father's yard, he was reluctant to let her hand go, but he did, and Lisha climbed from the truck. "Tell your dad I'll see him Wednesday," she said, before quickly walking around her car and climbing in to crank and reverse quicker than a Nascar driver.

Kael turned and watched her leave, fighting the urge to stop her and tell her not to go. He watched her car until it disappeared down the road from his sight.

Someone who would never betray you. Someone who believes that she could really, really love. Like love you hard . . . the way you deserved.

Kael wondered if maybe, just maybe, he was missing out on something special. He had never even felt so connected to his ex as he did to Lisha. This groove between them was new to him and it worried him because that meant he would put his heart at even more risk.

"Bea called."

Kael turned and found his sister standing on the porch. "All you are doing is setting your friend up to get her feelings hurt," he said as he strolled up to the house.

Kelli nodded. "I think you're doing the same thing with Lisha," she said.

He froze. "Excuse me?"

"After that bullshit with Donna I just don't want to see you hurt and I think she would hurt. Just from talking to her and being around her while she was here working with Dad, I just don't think you really see her for who she is," Kelli said, reaching out to grab his hand. "Let's be honest. Your judgment sucked for the last woman you spent five years of your life with."

Kael flinched.

"I think you are overlooking a good woman in Bea because your head is clouded with Lisha," she stressed. "I don't want to have to come back and say I told you so when you walk in and find her with the next man too."

"I'm a grown-ass man, Kelli. Back off," he warned, staring at her hard. "If you want a man to bully and push around and have jump to your every whim, then maybe you need to go home to your husband."

With that he turned and walked back to his truck. "Tell Dad I'm staying at my house tonight," he called out the window to her before reversing down the drive.

Chapter 12

"I can't believe I let you talk me into this," Lisha said as she followed Junie into the country club.

"You always make me out to be the bad guy," Junie said as she smoothed the turquoise jumpsuit she wore over her hips and looked around at the people milling about in the expansive foyer of the once-exclusive country club. "But it's never that hard to talk you into it."

Lisha ignored her as she looked at the attire of her fellow attendees, hoping the black halter dress she wore was appropriate. She didn't know how to dress for a charity bachelor auction—especially at a country club that probably wouldn't have allowed her through the doors ten years ago. "I am not bidding," she insisted in a whisper to her flamboyant cousin who was too busy waving and greeting many of the people she worked with at the hospital.

The annual auction was to benefit the hospital's charity care fund to help those without medical insurance receive care without concern over hefty medical bills. There were women of all races, all shades of races, and all socioeconomic backgrounds—that was evident from the clothing.

It was a cause Lisha could believe in, but to sit back and bid for a date for an eligible bachelor . . . ? Definitely not. *I'll enjoy their food though. I might as well get my five dollars worth.*

"Be right back," Junie said, walking away and disappearing into the crowd of women.

Lisha tucked her clutch under her arm and headed for the buffet table along the glass windows overlooking the greens of the golf course. She eyed the selection of finger foods as she picked up a saucer and fork. She decided on fruits, raw vegetables with dip and mini-sandwiches. "It'll do," she mumbled, turning up her nose.

"Ladies, here are our wonderful volunteers for tonight's bachelor auction," someone said from behind her.

Lisha dipped a celery stick into the dip, not even bothering to turn around and see the men that were causing the gathered women's chatter to become lively. "I'm good," she said.

"It's rude to let everyone know you hate the food."

Lisha paused with a piece of broccoli before her opened mouth at the sound of Kael's deep voice. Instantly on edge, with the hairs on the nape of her neck standing on end, she dropped the crudités and licked the corners of her mouth before finally turning to face him.

Lisha literally took a step back at the sight of him looking devastatingly good in a suit that was so deep a blue that it could have been black, with a matching open-collared satin shirt. She always thought he looked his very best in blue. *Shit.*

She set the plate down as the rattling of the fork against the china revealed her frayed nerves. "Hi, Kael," she said.

"You look good, Lisha," he said, his warm chocolate eyes taking her in from head to toe.

"I've looked good all week," she said with a smile as she tipped her head to the side as she looked up at him.

Lisha hadn't laid eyes on the man since the Friday they spent kissing on the porch, horseback riding and then napping in the woods. Not since the day they made the deal.

"But your voice sounded good during the phone calls we had all week," he reminded her with a grin.

"True," she admitted, loving their laid-back flirty air. "As brief as they were."

He had called her over the last six days, but only

for a few moments to say hello or to make sure she got home from work okay or in the fuzzy moments just before he went to bed at night. The call was never for long, but a call did come once a day.

Kael licked his lips and wiped his smiling lips with his hand as he nodded. "True. I just . . . uh . . . wanted to think over our deal. You remember our deal, right?" he asked, reaching up with his finger to move her hair back from her face and behind her ear.

Lisha's skin warmed from the slightest touch of his hand brushing against her cheek. "Oh, I remember it well and I am eagerly awaiting the resolution," she hinted, lifting her brows as she licked her lips and gave him a look.

Kael laughed. "I think you'll like it," he assured her.

Lisha's heart fluttered. "I think I'll like it even sooner," she teased, reaching over to hold his wrist and stroke her thumb over his pulse. She liked that it was pounding away. The attraction and chemistry was going in both directions.

"Gentlemen, every woman here wants a chance to meet you, so please mingle a little."

Lisha looked around and a lot of the eyes of the women were on her and Kael. She frowned and looked back at him. "Wait a minute. Why are you here?" she asked, looking around again and noticing the men all had numbers pinned to their shirt.

Looking back at Kael, her eyes fell on the number eleven pinned onto his wide lapel. She kicked her hip to the side and pressed a hand to it as she looked at him. "Oh, so you're an eligible bachelor up for sale?" she asked, very tongue in cheek.

"And you're one of the women here ready to bid?" he countered.

"Junie dragged me to this," she said, setting him straight.

"And my sister volunteered to be on the committee hosting this auction so she begged me just this morning to do it because they didn't have enough volunteers," he explained, reaching to touch her elbow.

Lisha grunted softly as she looked past his broad shoulders to see several women openly eyeing them. Women she thought may have complained that she was getting all of Kael's time. "Ooh, and they are hungry for your . . . date," she said, purposefully looking down at his crotch during the pause.

"Hey, don't be that way," Kael said, his eyes becoming serious. "I'm just helping out my sister, not looking for love."

"Oh, trust me, I believe you ain't looking for

love," she said with a wave of her hand toward herself.

"Oh, I'm looking right at you," he said.

A petite white woman came up to them surrounded by a cloud of strong perfume. "Hello, bachelor. We really need you to mingle with the other ladies a little before the auction officially starts," she said.

Lisha raised her hand up and twirled her finger. "Yes, Kael. Do mingle with the ladies. That's what you came for, right?" she asked.

He reached out for her hand, but Lisha shifted away from his clasp and moved across the room. She spotted Junie talking to some of her co-workers and decided not to intrude so she took a glass of wine offered by a uniformed waiter circling the room and stood looking at the white woman leading Kael around the room, introducing him.

Humph, looking more like a slave auction to me right about now.

Her eyes widened when Bea stepped forward to smile up at him and press a hand to his chest as she laughed.

"Lisha, I didn't know you were coming to the event."

She shifted her eyes from Kael and Bea to find his sister, Kelli, standing beside her. They shared a hug. "My cousin works for the hospital and she invited me," she explained.

"We have some fine brothers in the mix too," Kelli said, nudging her as she pointed to a thin light-skinned man with an Afro.

"Oh, I won't be bidding," Lisha assured her, taking another sip of her wine as she watched Kael move on from Bea even as the woman's eyes stayed locked on him.

"Well, you never know, you might see someone you like . . . but Bea has my brother all wrapped up," she said. "It's already arranged, girl."

Lisha squinted as she looked at the other woman. "Like I said, I won't be bidding," she said again, the softness from her voice gone. "Excuse me."

She moved away and followed the gold-trimmed signs directing to the bathroom. Inside she stood at the sink and raked her fingers through her hair before reapplying her lip gloss and adjusting the varying length of gold chains she wore draped across her cleavage.

It's already arranged, girl.

Lisha sucked air between her teeth before she left the restroom. She paused in the doorway to see Kael leaning against the wall. He stood up at the sight of her.

"I see Bea's here," she said with a smile that was far from flirty or real.

"That's my sister's bullshit," he said, digging his wallet out of his back pocket and removing the cash in it.

"Yes, I see that now," she agreed. "But it doesn't change the fact that you're going along with the bullshit."

Kael shoved the cash in her palm. "Bid on me," he stressed.

Lisha pushed the money at him. "Why should I?" she asked with a little attitude.

"Oh, there you are," the white woman said, coming up on them quickly. "The auction is about to start."

Kael closed her fingers around the money. "Man, just bid on me," he said again.

Lisha shook her head. "Oh, no-no-no-no-no. What would you have done if I wasn't here? I mean, this is why you're here. To be auctioned off to women, right?" she asked, breezing past him. "Enjoy!"

"Lisha, stop playing," he called from behind. "Lisha!"

She pushed the cash into her purse, not even counting it as she walked back into the reception. Junie spotted her across the room and came over. "Girl, it's about to start," she said, guiding Lisha inside the now-open double doors of the dining room.

All of the tables and chairs were staged in a circle with a microphone in the center of it. They sat at a table in the second row. Unfortunately it gave Lisha a clear sight of Bea and Kelli sitting in the first row to her immediate right. Their heads were huddled close together as they flipped through the program.

Lisha stopped the waiter. "Can I have a glass of white wine, please?" she asked.

"That'll be two dollars. It's a cash bar now," he explained.

Opening her purse, she moved aside the wad of cash she planned to give back to Kael, and pulled the money for the wine from her wallet. "Two glasses, please," she said, getting one for Junie.

The petite white woman moved through the tables to stand before the microphone. "Hello, ladies. As most of you know, I'm Eloise Riley, the chair of the ladies' board who is having this wonderful bachelor auction to benefit the hospital's charity care program," she said.

The waiter appeared at her shoulder and Lisha turned to set first Junie's glass of wine and then her own in front of them as the women clapped and some even let out raucous whoops that made the event feel more like a strip show.

As the first bachelor was introduced, Lisha eyed the tall and handsome man with his reddish brown hair, tanned complexion and green eyes. "Not bad," she murmured into the glass with a little shrug of her bare shoulder.

"I think I want some milk in this coffee," Junie whispered to her.

"This is Hank Ingrams. This six-foot-one cutie with green eyes is a firefighter who knows how to put out your flame, ladies. And when he's not busy working his hose, he likes to ski, backpack and play tennis. His idea of a good date is a walk on the beach after the dinner he will cook for you."

Lisha sat back and Hank began to walk around the circle as the women raised their cards to bid on him. They were mighty fired up for the red-haired fireman and his *hose.*

Even Junie placed a bid for him, but bowed out quickly. A pretty blonde with a curvy figure won the bid for fifty dollars. Hank made his way over to her, looking pleased himself.

And the night went on like that with bachelor after bachelor being plucked up by one of the women. Even a pudgy dude with a receding hair-line got scooped up.

"Okay, ladies, here's our last bachelor for the night," Eloise said, turning to wave Kael closer.

The murmurs of the women grew a little louder as it had with the intro of each new bachelor.

Junie nudged her. "Ain't that—"

Lisha rolled her eyes. "Yes," she stressed.

"I didn't know he was—"

"Me either."

"This is Kael Strong. He's six-foot-five, ladies, with brown eyes and silver hair—and remember, ladies, where there is smoke there is plenty of fire. This twenty-six-year-old cattle rancher is one cowboy who knows how to *ride,*" Eloise said, actually raising her hand to pretend she was working a lasso as she circled her hips.

Lisha thought Eloise had partaken of the wine a little much, but she enjoyed it as Kael smiled uncomfortably. His eyes were shifting about the room and she could tell he was looking for her. Looking over at Bea, she saw the woman sitting back comfortably with her eyes locked on him.

"Kael's idea of a romantic date is dinner on a yacht under the stars."

The ladies all swooned, but Lisha knew from his fleeting confused expression that Kael did not offer up that info. *Some more of his sister's bull.*

"Let's open up the bids," Eloise said, pressing a hand to Kael's back to urge him to walk the circle.

"Fifty dollars," Bea said, holding her card up.

"You are serious, huh?" Eloise said with a high-pitched laugh.

"Well, damn," Junie said.

Kael did move around the circle then looked at the faces in the crowd until his eyes lit on her. "Bid," he mouthed, his face urgent.

Lisha looked away from him and took another sip of her wine.

"Do we have fifty-five dollars for this sexy cowboy in blue?" Eloise asked.

"Fifty-five here."

Lisha's eyes darted across the room from her left.

Kael continued around the circle, but his eyes were on her.

"Sixty," Bea said.

Lisha eyed the woman, looking smug in her strapless gold dress as she slid hands with his equally smug-looking sister.

Kael shook his head.

"Sixty-five," another woman in the crowd called out.

Kelli opened her pocketbook and counted the cash before whispering to Bea.

"Eighty," Bea countered.

Kael walked around the circle again and squinted his eyes at Lisha like he wished he could spank her like a child. She raised her glass to him in a toast as he continued back to his spot by Eloise.

"If you wasn't my cousin and I wasn't worried about your fist on my nose . . ." Junie said into her glass of wine as she watched Kael closely over the rim. "Jesus, Jesus, Jesus."

Lisha ignored her and opened her wallet to count Kael's cash and her own. The fact that his sister and Bea were being so slick and sure about the shit spurned her on. Well, that and the fact that Lisha didn't want the woman to win. Period.

She snatched up Junie's card and waved it. "Ninety," she said, leaning back in her chair to eye both Bea and Kelli who pierced her with their eyes.

Kael looked relieved.

"A hundred," Bea countered, rising to her feet to press a hand to her hip as she eyed Lisha.

"Give me your cash," Lisha told Junie.

"What? Huh?"

"Give me your cash," she repeated, never taking her eyes off Bea.

"I want my money back," Junie said, reluctantly sliding a fifty-dollar bill across the table to her cousin.

Lisha stood up as well. "Two hundred," she said, after totaling Junie's money to the cash she had on hand.

The women looked on with *oohs* and *aahs*.

Eloise cried out like she saw Jesus. "Two hundred dollars! Can we get two hundred and ten?" she asked, turning to look at Bea.

Everyone including Lisha looked at Bea. She dropped back down in her seat.

"Sold for two hundred dollars to the lucky lady in the black," Eloise said.

All of the ladies except Bea and Kelli applauded as Kael made his way over to Lisha. "You owe me and Junie fifty dollars," she told him just before he wrapped an arm around her waist and pulled her body close to his.

"And I owe you this," he whispered against her lips before he kissed her.

Lisha brought her hands up to his shoulders as Kael covered her mouth with his own, deepening the kiss with a deep moan of hunger. She trembled and entwined her arms behind his head as the women clapped.

"Well, looks like their date is going straight to the end," Eloise said into the mic.

Kael eyed Lisha as she unlocked the door to her apartment. She turned and held the doorknob as she looked up at him. "Thank you for the ride home," she said.

"Thank you again for saving me during that auction," he said, pushing his hands into his pockets as he rocked back and forth on his feet.

"I shouldn't have," she said, reaching to tug at his shirt.

"You didn't want anyone else to win me," Kael said with confidence.

"I don't have a say. Do I?" she asked in a soft voice.

Kael smiled and licked his lips as he looked away from her and then back at her again. "You have a say," he told her, loving the brightness of her eyes.

"What does that mean, Kael?" she asked.

He reached up to stroke her cheek with his

finger. "I need someone who will never betray me. Someone who believes that she can really love me hard . . . . the way I deserve and the same way I can love her."

Her eyes softened and she smiled in pure happiness, and that look on her face, that look that shone in her eyes, made him happy. And that's what he wanted. To make Lisha happy.

Kael stepped close to her and reached behind her to shut the door before he picked her body up against the door and then stepped forward to press his lips and his body against hers. And the softness of her lips made him hard in a rush as he enjoyed the feel of her hands wrapped around his waist to splay against his back.

Her fingers gripped the material and she moaned as he felt her body melt against him. "Kael," she sighed against his mouth. "Kael, Kael, Kael."

He loved the sound of his name from her lips. "Yes, baby," he answered her.

Kael wrapped one arm around her securely as he reached and opened the door to the apartment, stepping inside and yanking the keys from the lock to fling away before closing the door with a kick of his foot.

Lisha dropped her purse from under her arms as he carried her to the couch and pressed her body under him.

Kael wanted her. He wanted to kiss her, taste her, stroke her, come in her . . . and then do it all over again. He could hardly think straight as he reached behind her to undo the tie of her halter. He shifted down to press kisses along her neck and then from one shoulder to the other before moving to that intimate space between her breasts.

"Ah," Lisha cried out, arching her back.

He inhaled the scent of her perfume as he pressed his face against the soft swell on the side of one of her breasts. "Lisha," he said, the hardness of his dick making him ache. "Damn, Lisha."

Kael shifted to his side on the sofa, loving the look on her face as he eased his hand down to the hem of her dress to massage her soft thighs. He bent his head to use his teeth to nudge the top of her dress down, exposing her full breasts and the chocolate tips of her breasts to his eyes. "Shit," he swore, dipping his head to lick at one taut nipple.

Lisha cried out again.

He sucked it deeply.

She gasped for air.

He fluttered his tongue against it.

She raised one arm above her head to clutch wildly at the arm of the sofa.

He sucked the brown nipple with his lips and teased the nipple with his tongue.

"Shit," she swore fiercely, bringing a hand up to press his head to her breast.

He watched her closely as he smoothed his hand against the lacy trim of her panties as he licked away like a cat to milk at her breasts. He pulled the panties to the side and stroked his index finger against the split. His mouth formed a circle at the wetness and the heat. "Damn," he said in awe before easing a finger inside her.

"Wait, Kael," she said, sounding drugged as she pressed her thighs close, trapping his hand.

He still circled his finger around the entry of her core as he kissed her breasts wildly.

Lisha winced in pleasure even as she fought to keep her legs pressed. "Baby, wait, we can't. Not yet. I—"

"You not ready?" he asked, his voice thick and his eyes half-closed as he looked up at her.

She shook her head. "I have to tell you—"

Kael allowed himself one last feel of her wet tightness before freeing his hand from her thighs and smelling her juices on his finger.

Lisha looked amazed when he sucked his finger into his mouth and moaned deeply at the taste of her.

"You've never had anybody taste you before?" he asked, licking his lips.

She shook her head.

"Anyone ever ate you?" he asked, sitting up higher to look down at her.

Her cheeks flushed and she turned her head to tuck into his armpit as she shook her head.

Lisha's sudden shyness surprised him, but he smiled as he reached for her chin and turned her face so that she looked up at him. He kissed her mouth. "So have you ever tasted a man like that before?" he asked as gently as he could.

Her eyes bugged out. "Noo," she said with emphasis.

He liked that. He liked that a lot. "Then I'll have to teach you," he said low in his throat. "Do you want me to teach you one day?"

Lisha closed her eyes as she nodded. "*One* day," she said, opening one eye to look up at him.

He chuckled. "No worries. Today I have something else to teach you about," he said, carefully rising off the couch.

Lisha's exposed breasts jiggled as he turned her body on the couch, standing between her legs before he knelt. "Kael," she said.

"Sssh." He massaged her inner thighs before rubbing his hands up her hips to gently ease her panties down.

"Kael," she said, her hand shooting out to press to his chest.

"I'm just gonna eat it," he said simply.

"And nothing else?" she said after a very long pause.

"Nothing else you don't want," he said, using his hands to lift her hips and ease the panties down her buttocks, thighs, knees and then ankles to fling over his shoulder.

His eyes devoured the sight of the soft and tight V of curls covering her before he pushed her legs up and spread them, exposing her fleshy and moist core to him. Using his finger, he outlined her lips and her inner folds, loving the way the muscles of her core flexed in response to him.

Bending down, he used his fingers to press the flesh up and expose her swollen clit. With pursed lips he sucked at it gently before circling it with the tip of his tongue.

Lisha's hips jerked at the first feel of his mouth on her intimacy.

He sucked harder in a slow pulsing move, moving his hand to massage her thick lips. Her legs wiggled on each side of his head and her cries of pleasure let him know he was taking care of the right spot. And well.

"Kael," she cried out.

He felt her clit warm and swell in his mouth. *She's about to cum.*

His dicked throbbed until his thighs felt weak and he sucked and licked her core and clit until her body quivered and he had to lock his arms around her hips to trap her in place as her cum filled his mouth and she fought to back away from the pleasure.

Kael was relentless. He continuously sucked and wildly licked at her clit, driven by the taste of her, the feel of her and the sound of her hoarsely crying out.

"I'm comming," she gasped, her eyes rolled back in her head. "I'm commmminnnnnng."

He didn't stop until the constant quivering of her body slowed down to sporadic jerks before she went slack. Rising up, he looked down at her with his mouth glistening from her juices. Needing to be with her, he unzipped and lowered his pants down around his hips, freeing his thick and long dick.

His pre-cum had the tip wet and slick as he used it to lube his dick before pressing the thick tip to her pussy.

Lisha's eyes opened at the first feel of him probing her wetness. "No, Kael. I'm a virgin," she gasped, her eyes wild for another reason.

"What?" he asked. His heart stopped in his chest as he posed with dick in hand ready to bury deep inside her walls.

Lisha sat up, lowered her feet to the floor as she pressed her face against his neck. "I'm a virgin," she moaned against his flesh.

Shit, shit, shit.

Kael closed his eyes and let his head fall back as he still held onto to his throbbing hard dick.

"I'm sorry."

At least that's what he thought she mumbled against his neck.

"Just not a good time to tell me, baby, that's all," he said, raising his free hand to push his fingers through her hair to rub her scalp.

Kael was proud of his control. Later, when all the blood hadn't left his brain and rushed to his dick, they could discuss it in detail.

"Just touch it," he said thickly, taking her hands and pressing it around his hardness.

"You ever stroked a dick 'til it came?" he asked, pressing kisses to the side of her face.

Lisha shook her head no as she sat back a bit and looked down at the full and curving length of him in her hand. She squeezed it tight. "Like this?" she asked, glancing up at him.

Kael brought his hands up to cover hers. "Loosen it up a little," he said. "Not so tight. And work right under the tip, like this."

"Like this?" she asked, flexing her wrist back and forth the way he'd shown her.

"Yes," he said through clenched teeth, rolling his hips to send his dick through the circle she made with her fingers.

"Wet it," he said in a husky tone as his heart thundered like it outraced Sampson and won.

Lisha bent over and circled her tongue around the hot tip.

Kael gasped and moaned as his buttocks clenched with the forward jut of his hips at the feel of her tongue. He froze as his nut surged forward. He didn't want to fill her mouth with it. Not yet. Not tonight. "I meant wet your hand," he said, tilting his head to the side to watch as she gently sucked the tip with her moist lips. "But I ain't complaining."

Lisha said something, but his dick muffled the words.

He bit his bottom lip and enjoyed the pleasure, fighting not to urge her to take more of his inches into her mouth. Feeling his nut surging again, he freed himself from her lips as he cried out hoarsely with each jolt of his release against her hand until he was weak and spent.

"Love in its essence is spiritual fire."
—Lucius Annaeus Seneca

Interlude

Kael and Lisha stared at each other mischievously, stroking each other's hand as they shared a private soft chuckle at their heated memory of the night after that auction. Marvin Sease sang a soulful "Merry Christmas."

"I think I fell in love that night," Kael said to her with a roguish wink.

"Oh, Kael," Lisha sighed, stroking his wrist with her thumb as she leaned over to press a heated kiss to his lips.

He smacked his lips. "Just as good as it was forty years ago," he assured her.

"Ain't it?" she agreed.

They were lost in each other and the past that had built the strong foundation for their marriage and their family.

"Hello? Excuse us. Room full of family here."

Lisha and Kael looked away from each other and saw every one of the family members staring at them and patiently waiting for more of the story.

"Wait a minute. So what happened after the auction?" Meena asked, looking quizzically at her identical twin, Neema, before glancing back at her step-grandparents.

"Y'all just got kinda quiet and got googly-eyed after you told us how you won the auction," Neema added. "Then what happened?"

"Nothing," Kael and Lisha said in unison, keeping that part of the story for them.

"Your mama and daddy nasty," Zaria teased in Kaleb's ear where they sat on the love seat beneath the wall of framed family photos. "You'd think they still do it."

Her husband flexed his chiseled chest in the red fleece jacket he wore over a crisp white long-sleeve tee as he looked at her. "I know I will be tearing that ass up when I'm sixty," he said, glancing down at her bottom in the dark denim jeggings she wore with thigh-high boots.

Zaria made a face. "But I'll be in my seventies," she said.

"And looking like you're in your fifties," he said, moving his hand around her to tap the side of her ass.

"Right!" she agreed, her gold hoop earrings dangling.

Zaria was in her early forties and her husband

in his late twenties but even with more than a fifteen-year age difference, they had worked past their major differences to be together. Kaleb had been the one to help her settle down and leave the partying alone, instead of the other way around. Her college-aged twin daughters had struggled with the relationship, but in the end it was their interference that had brought Kaleb and Zaria back together. Now they were a big family with the addition of their son, Kasi Dean, who was two years old.

After her marriage of twenty years shattering, Zaria had thought she may never find love again, but then came Kaleb and he taught her more about loving and being loved than she could ever dream.

They were good but . . .

Shaking away the doubts that had been plaguing her for the last week, Zaria looked over at her daughters, both beautiful and smart and so supportive of their once-wild mother. But what would they have to say when she gave them all the news?

"What's wrong, Ma?" Meena asked, coming over to squeeze onto the love seat beside her as she played with her mother's hair.

"You enjoyed your Christmas?" she asked, picking up the locket she and Kaleb gave both twins.

"So far, good. We gotta see what Dad got for us at his house," she said.

"Y'all 'bout to go?" Kaleb said, turning to look at his stepdaughter.

"Yeah," Neema said, walking up to them. "We promised our dad we'd eat with him and the step-mama."

Zaria's eyes scolded them. "Don't call her that," she said.

"Do you call me the stepdad behind my back?" Kaleb asked.

"No, but we love you," Meena said.

"It's not right," he told them.

"Okay," they said in unison.

It forever amazed her that there was less than a ten-year age difference between her daughters and her husband but the respect they showed him belied that. When Kael spoke they listened. Period.

He stood up. "Let me check them tires again before y'all get on the road," he said, moving across the living room to grab his coat and leave the house.

And it was things he did that built up the respect for him.

"Twins, y'all leaving?" Kael asked, addressing them as one unit as he always did affectionately.

Meena nodded.

Neema spoke. "We just stopped by before we head to our father's house," she said.

Kael waved them over and they each kissed his cheek before turning to give Lisha hugs.

"Drive careful," she said.

Neema nodded.

Meena spoke. "Yes, ma'am. And thanks for our iPads."

"You're welcome," Kael said.

And that's why Zaria loved her in-laws. They loved her children because they loved Kaleb and they included them in with all the other grandkids— even if they were in their twenties. Her girls got the same birthday cards, gifts, random phone calls, hugs and kisses as all the rest.

Following the twins out the door, she didn't bother with a coat as she stood on the porch. "Y'all drive careful, please," she said, accepting a hug, squeeze and rock from each one.

Kaleb jogged up onto the porch and offered each one his fist for their customary pound. "You should be good, but stop and fill up on gas first," he admonished them. "You got your gas card?"

Meena nodded.

Neema tapped her small red Coach crossover bag.

"Hey, before you go I have another Christmas present for everybody," Zaria said.

Three sets of eyes fell on her.

"Uhmmm . . . remember I was going to go back to school to take some business classes so we can expand the dairy store," she said.

"Aw, Ma, that's good," Neema said.

Zaria shook her head and looked at each of them.

"No school?" Meena asked.

Kaleb just looked on with an ever-growing more serious expression.

"Maybe in another nine months *or so,*" she said gingerly, her eyes darting from face to face to face.

They all looked confused.

"Twins," she said, pointing to her belly.

Three sets of eyes widened in understanding.

"Oh, shit," Kaleb exclaimed, stepping up to lift Zaria into his arms.

He twirled her and then stopped. "It's not hurting the babies, is it?"

She massaged his muscular upper arms and shook her head, loving his happiness. For the news. "No, not at all. This is good?" she asked, her eyes unsure.

"Yeah, baby, we love each other. This is good," he said. "The more the merrier. As long as you're healthy and happy then hell, I'm good."

Zaria looked over her shoulder at her girls.

They shared a long look. "We're good," Meena said. "But this is it, right? I mean you're forty-four—"

"Hey," Zaria hollered.

"Well, at least we don't have to worry about another delivery on your wedding day," Neema said, pressing a hand to her mom's belly. "But this *is* it, right?"

Zaria just laughed. "You two get on the road.

Come by the house when you get back. We should be home by seven or eight," she said.

With one final wave the twins moved down the stairs and into the car.

"It's cold, let's get back inside."

Kael set her on her feet in the hall and closed the door.

"Twins, huh?" Kaleb asked, still holding her in his arms.

"Twins," she agreed. "Heaven help us."

"Heaven blessed us," he stressed.

"Uhm, let's not tell the family yet," she said, reaching for his hand. "Jade told me she and Kaeden are trying and nothing yet so I don't want —"

Kaleb nodded in immediate understanding. One Strong for all and all for one. That was the way they were born and bred. He would never hurt one intentionally, and just like his wife, Jade was a Strong.

Zaria frowned when she spotted a movement in the den. Walking down the hall to the right, she caught Kadina and Lei just as they were about to scurry across the room to hide behind the leather sectional.

"Girls, aren't you supposed to be—"

Kadina held up her hands. "Upstairs. Yes, Aunt Zaria. We know," she conceded.

"Good, now make it happen," she said, crossing

her arms over her chest with a fake stern expression that she dropped as soon as they left the room.

Pressing her hands to her belly, she closed her eyes. "Lord, I thank you for our gifts, but please bless Jade and Kaeden as well," she mouthed for His ears alone.

Zaria let her hands drop and headed back into the living room to reclaim her seat.

"Merry, merry, merry Christmas . . . to you."

"So what next?" Kaitlyn asked, removing a peppermint cane from the tree.

"We fell in love," Kael said.

Lisha nodded. "That we did. . . ."

Chapter 13

Way back in the day

Lisha checked her makeup in the mirror, but she was unable to apply her red lip gloss because she was too busy smiling like crazy. She was happy. Without question. Without fears. Without equivocation. She was boldly happy.

Being in love was everything she'd ever dreamt and much more.

"I love Kael," she said softly to her reflection, lightly touching her hands to her lips as she smiled. "I love him."

The last three months had passed so quickly and she knew three months was nothing compared to three years or definitely thirty years but after so many years fearing she would never find the man willing to wait, she couldn't help but feel . . . happy. Just simply happy.

Knock-knock.

After tousling her hair she left the bathroom and made her way to the front door, opening it with a smile. A smile that faded at the sight of Junie.

"It's good to see you too," Junie said, looking offended. "I did knock."

"That's because I took your key," Lisha reminded her.

"Kael here?" she asked, twisting her lips as she looked around.

Lisha hid her smile as she closed the door. Her relationship with Kael had cut into the time she spent with her cousin. Although Lisha had always fallen back to allow Junie all of her little adventures, her cousin was having a problem doing the same for Lisha. She was happy for her but didn't like the intrusion of Kael on her "Lisha-Junie" time.

"No, but he's on his way," Lisha said. "I cooked him some oxtail stew."

"Didn't you say he has a big old house, so why cook here?" she asked, strolling into the kitchen and washing her hands in the sink before she grabbed a bowl and fixed herself some food.

Lisha straightened the cushions on the sofa and adjusted the tilted lamp shade. "Yes, but I don't want to scare him off, thinking I'm trying to get him to propose so soon," she said, coming into the kitchen and checking that the beer Kael liked was cold. "He's not pressuring me *too* hard for sex and

the last thing I want to do is have him think I'm
invading his home. I got my own place and we can
visit each other."

Knock-knock.

Junie added splashes of hot sauce to her bowl.
"I'll get it on my way out," she said, pausing to grab
a bottle of strawberry Crush soda from the fridge.

"Bye, Junie," she called behind her, turning the
pilot light under the stove higher to make sure the
food was warm.

"Bye, Lisha. *Bye,* Kael," she said with emphasis.

Moments later the door closed and Kael's energy
filled the room before he eventually stepped into
the kitchen. Wiping her hands on a towel, Lisha
turned and smiled at him, looking real fine in a
ribbed navy turtleneck and bell-bottom jeans.

"She still mad at me?" he asked with a smile as
he leaned in the doorway.

Lisha finished stirring the pot and set the large
spoon on the saucer on the stovetop. "She'll be
fine," she said, coming to him. "I have sat home
alone many a night when she has a friend. And I
mean *many* a night."

Kael reached out for her when she was close
enough and pulled her the rest of the way to press
several kisses to her mouth.

She leaned back in his arms and looked up at
him. "Hungry?" she asked.

"What you got for me?" he asked, wiggling his

brow as he playfully swatted her buttocks in her snug-fitting jeans.

Lisha eyed him. "Are you sure you're okay with the no-sex thing?" she asked, her insecurity showing.

They had enjoyed plenty of kissing and even some heaving petting, but nothing even close to the passionate things they did to each other the night of the auction.

"Do I want to make love to you? Hell, yes," he stressed. "But is it a deal breaker for me? Hell, no."

"You are too good to be true, Kael Strong," Lisha said, feeling all the love she had yet to reveal explode in her chest and warm her soul.

Kael took her fingertips in his hand, holding them even as he moved to the stove to turn the fire down under the pot. He then led her into the living room to pull her down onto the sofa beside him. "How was your day?" he asked around a yawn that he covered with his hand.

"My day was good," she said. "And yours?"

"Not good. Not good at all," he said.

Lisha kicked off the satin slippers she wore and climbed on the back of the sofa to straddle his back. "What happened?" she asked, deeply kneading away some of the tension she felt in his neck and shoulders.

"Oh my God, that feels good," he moaned,

leaning forward to pull his shirt up around his neck. At the first feel of her hands against his skin, goose bumps raced across his back.

He closed his eyes and enjoyed the special treatment. "The roof of the new barn has a leak. One of the cows had a miscarriage and we had to quarantine her and have the vet come to make sure it wasn't caused by a contagious disease. Jim is sick and couldn't work this week so I've been handling the ranch alone. I'm still waiting on my disaster check from Farm Service for the heat this summer destroying some of my lands. Shit, what else? You want it? I got it."

Lisha leaned forward and pressed a kiss to his nape. "You'll figure it all out; you just have to put it in God's hands and think it through," she reassured him, massaging his lower back.

"I know. It's just hell when a ton of shit comes down on you at one time."

"Just relax. I got you," she said.

Kael pulled his shirt off completely and tossed it onto the armchair in front of the living room window. He pushed his worries aside and focused on the feel of her hands on his back and just feeling confident that she had his back. In the months since they welcomed each other into their lives he had no regrets.

"My sister and her husband are coming home for Christmas," he said.

He hollered out when Lisha's nails dug in and

almost broke his skin. "Hey," he protested, looking over his shoulder at her.

"I'm sorry," she said, leaning down to press her lips to each of his shoulders where she'd pained him.

Kael eyed her and saw something in her eyes. Standing up, he turned and stood before her, reaching to dig his fingers through the loose waves of her hair to stroke her scalp the way he'd learned she liked. "What's wrong?" he asked.

She pressed her lips together and shook her head, not meeting his eyes.

He remained quiet, having made a point to learn more about her in the last three months. She wasn't one to be pushed to talk.

"You're having dinner at your house and I just think your sister wants you with Bea, so is she gonna be sitting there with us Christmas Day?" Lisha snapped. "Is she gonna make a pan of her *nasty*-ass chicken wings to bring?"

Kael wiped his mouth to keep from laughing. "I will make it clear that if Kelli wants to see her friend for Christmas then she needs to go to Bea's house to eat her nasty-ass wings," he said, bracing his hands on her knees.

Lisha nodded in agreement as he spoke. "Yes," she said enthusiastically.

Kael playfully opened and closed her legs by her knees. "I want you there with me for the holidays."

"But what about your sister?" Lisha insisted.

"I've always been nice to her. I thought we were friends, so I don't know what she has against me."

There was truth to what Lisha said, but Kael wanted her to have a good relationship with his sister. "I don't think she even knew we liked each other, Lisha," he said.

She just shrugged.

His heart tugged. "If my sister says something to you that is wrong, just let me know and I'll take care of it," he promised her, pressing her cheeks with his hand to cause her lips to pucker like a fish until she finally swatted his hand away and laughed.

Hours later Lisha and Kael lay on the floor together with their heads propped on pillows as they watched the ABC Movie of the Week *Get Christie Love!* They both were caught up in the made-for-TV movie about a black female undercover cop battling a ring of drug dealers.

"You want something from the kitchen?" Kael asked, easily rising to his feet.

"No, baby. I'm good," she said, biting the side of her nail as Christie fired her gun.

Lisha looked up when Kael returned with a can of beer. He sat down on the floor, leaning back against the sofa as he took a deep swig from the can of Pabst beer. She liked that he was comfortable enough in her home to move about without asking. She moved about the same way at his house.

Reaching over to tug at one of his toes, she looked back at the television. "You feel better?" she asked.

"Yeah, I'm cool," he said, before taking another sip.

At the sound of his voice she looked over at him before she rose up to go and straddle the top of his thighs. "You don't ever have to put on a strong front for me," she told him. "I swear to God you can be as strong or as weak as you need to be with me. 'Cause see, right here in this little world of yours and mine, we made it safe."

Kael studied her with his eyes for a long time. "I am scared shitless that the ranch is gonna fail," he admitted, setting the beer down on the edge of the coffee table and reaching for one of her hands to hold. "I'm scared I don't know what I'm doing. That I don't know how to be a boss and run a business and make decisions and take the weight all on my shoulders."

Lisha nodded in understanding.

"I put all my money—and it wasn't much—into that ranch. Loans. Grants," Kael said, releasing a long, heavy breath.

"I think you can do whatever you set your mind to. I believe in you because I see that you are a hardworking man with plenty of sense. I believe in you because you're young and your focus is building a future for yourself and the family you'll have one day. I believe in you because you are the strongest man I know. You live up to your name, Kael Strong."

"I can't fail," he said, his face serious as he reached up and stroked her cheek with his hand.

"And you won't," she said with confidence, reaching down to massage his thighs.

"Because you said so, huh?" he teased.

Lisha smiled brightly. "Of course," she told him. "And your daddy thinks so too. He's so proud of you."

Kael looked surprised. "He told you that?"

Lisha reached for his can of beer and sipped it. "You were just about all we talked about during his therapy. 'Kael was so good in sports in school. Kael was so mischievous when he was little. Kael can shoot a rifle blindfolded better than most men can with two sets of eyes,'" she said, imitating Logan's gruff voice and stern expression.

Kael looked even more surprised.

"I knew plenty about you before we even spoke," she said.

"I don't want to let him down," he admitted, his voice low as he looked down at his hand entwined with hers.

Lisha's heart tugged at the insecurity he was willing to show her. It was her turn to reach out and lift his head by his chin. "Trust me . . . you can't."

Kael reached for her and pulled her body up his

thighs to settle her head in the crook of his neck as his hands massaged her back. "Thank you," he said warmly.

She pressed a kiss to the hot pulsing spot there and inhaled the scent of him. The love she felt for this man and in such little time filled her until she thought she would burst. She raised her head and opened her mouth to whisper her feelings to him, but she just kissed his earlobe instead. The fear of discovering without certainty that he didn't feel the same was too heavy to bear.

Kael raised the hem of Lisha's shirt and pressed his fingers against the small of her back. He didn't say any words but his thoughts were full . . . and so was his heart. He loved her. He was in love with her.

And he was afraid.

The success of his ranch wasn't the only thing he doubted or questioned.

Loving her the way he did so soon was not a part of his plan. With love comes the ability for the one you love to hurt you. Break you. Destroy you.

Even in the few and far between moments they argued, his anger would momentarily fade and be replaced by a need to kiss the irritation away from her to see a smile on her face. Lisha was by no means perfect. She had a fiery temper. She was slow to admit she was wrong and she was openly defiant. Yet, with every passing day he believed she was perfect for him.

He thought of her constantly through the day. He missed her around his home when she wasn't there. He worshipped the apple scent of her hair from her shampoo and the familiar scent of her body from her perfume. She made him laugh. She made him think. She made him better. She made him whole.

Letting his head rest on the seat of the sofa, he closed his eyes and reveled at how much just being in her presence made him content. It was a mad mix of exhilaration and fear all at once. Like sky-diving or deep-sea fishing. Like a moving pendulum, his emotions swung back and forth until he didn't know if he was coming or going sometimes.

Lisha could float between roles with ease. He was still amazed that she spent her days off working beside him on the ranch, wading through cow chips as big as three of her feet, even though she had never spent a day of her life on a ranch with farm animals before meeting him. So how could he not love a woman so smart, so independent, so loyal, so protective, so strong, so supportive, so affectionate and so passionate?

He adored her. He cherished her. He loved her.

He dreamt of making love to her for the first time and the fact that she held on so dearly—even in the face of all of the temptation created by their passionate chemistry—was not a turn-off but a turn-on. She stood for something and he admired that inner strength because he knew she would love to have him buried deep inside her just as badly as he wanted to be there.

He loved her.

I love her.

"Lisha."

She sat up and looked at him with sleep already in her eyes. "Huh?" she asked softly.

Tell her. Just say it. Say I love you.

"You ready to eat?" she asked, already moving to climb from his lap as she yawned.

He shook his head, stopping her.

She settled back atop his thighs and looked at him still, her eyelids drooping as she fought sleep.

I love you, Lisha.

He bit back the words. "You're sleepy," he said instead.

She shook her head. "No, I'm not," she lied, trying to swallow back another yawn.

"Hold on," he said, using the steely muscles of his body to rise as she wrapped her legs and arms around him.

Kael carried her like that into her bedroom, laying her atop the covers in the darkness. She reached for him. "Don't leave. It's early," she said, looking up at him.

He bent to kiss her mouth. "I won't leave," he promised, feeling like he could mean forever.

* * *

Lisha awakened with a start, lifting her head off the pillow. The bedroom and the rooms of the apartment were dark save for the illumination from the television still playing in the living room. Stretching, she reached out and turned on the lamp on her nightstand. She looked at the clock as she sat up in bed.

It was just a little after ten.

Kael must have left.

Climbing from the bed, she left her room. In the living room she headed straight for the television to turn it off.

"I'm watching that."

Lisha shrieked in fright before turning to see Kael stretched out on her sofa. With her heart still pounding, she moved over to sit on the edge of the sofa near his feet. "I thought you left," she said, wiping sleep from her eyes.

"I told you I wouldn't leave," he said, his eyes on her.

His words kicked her regular heartbeat into another crazy pattern.

Boom-boom-boom.

"Do you want to stay over?" she asked, unable to keep the hope from her voice.

"Do you want me to?" he asked.

"Do you want to?" she countered, her pulse racing.

Kael chuckled. "You are one stubborn woman."

She nodded. "We're matched that way."

"I'll stay."

"Good. I wanted you to," she admitted with a smile.

He raised his foot to lightly tickle her side.

"Did you eat?" she asked, rising to head into the kitchen. "Because I am starving."

Kael grunted as he stood up. "I better eat because I've seen you throw down and there may be nothing left."

She turned on the light in the kitchen and glanced over her shoulder at him. "You're no slow leak with a fork and plate your damn self," she said, turning the eye under the stove on medium and doing the same with the small pot of white rice she made.

"Especially not the way you cook," he said, as he reached in the cabinets for plates and glasses.

They moved around together in her small kitchen like they had done it for years. Lisha warmed up the food and fixed their plates. Kael opened the bottle of wine to pour in their glasses.

Once they were seated at the table and eating, they didn't bother with too many words. Both were focused on their food.

"How is it?" she asked.

"You know it's good," he said, before shoveling a forkful into his mouth.

"Yes, I do," she boasted.

When they finished the meal they tidied up the kitchen together with Kael washing and Lisha drying the dishes.

"We make a good team," she said, leaning against the counter in her jeans and striped T-shirt.

He walked up to her and pressed kisses to her mouth before moving past her to set the dried glasses back on the counter.

Lisha thought he would deepen the kiss and was disappointed when he didn't. She glanced over at his side profile. "You can sleep in my bed if you want," she offered.

He stopped and then glanced down at the V between her legs before looking back up at her in question.

"Just to sleep and cuddle," she emphasized.

"Then no," Kael emphasized as well.

"Hey," she said in protest, reaching for his face and pulling his head down from its six-foot-five height to trace his mouth with her tongue.

"Lisha," he moaned into her open mouth, picking her up to sit on the counter and step between her open legs.

She swung her legs excitedly as he took control of the kiss, but then he broke it again and stood back from her. "What's wrong?" she asked, her lips still pulsing from the pressure of his mouth.

He pointed down at his erection running along the seam of his jeans and lying on the top of his upper thigh. "Look, baby, you're killing me," he admitted.

"I want to make love to you. I want to have sex with you. I want to . . . bad," Kael said. "So you can't expect me to be able to lie in bed with you all night and not want to."

"But—"

"The couch will be fine," he told her, walking out of the kitchen.

Lisha's shoulders slumped as all of her old fears and insecurities about being a virgin resurfaced. *Uh-oh, here we go.*

"Baby, you'll get me a pillow and a blanket," he called from the living room.

She came to stand behind the sofa and looked down at him. "Are you sure you're okay with not having sex? I understand that it can't be easy for you," she said. "It's not even easy for me."

Kael got up on his knees and reached over the back of the sofa to grab her hips and pull her forward. "No, it's not easy. It's hard as hell. I mean right now my dick is about to poke a hole in this sofa, it's so hard, but I respect that you want to wait."

She pressed her hand to the sides of his face.

"But I really would like to wake up next to you, Kael."

"Do you want to stay a virgin?" he asked point blank.

"Yes."

"Do you know how hard it is to kiss you and taste you and have you taste me and touch me and never get to slide inside you?"

Lisha opened her mouth.

Kael held her finger to her lips to stop her words. "I can do things to you to make you forget about your virginity. I can make you so hot that you'll beg me to make love you. I can make you feel so good that you won't have any regrets until I'm gone."

Lisha gasped at the thought of it all.

"I cannot sleep in the bed cuddled up with you because I will seduce you. I will turn you on. I will make love to you," he promised with heated eyes. "And you will love it. Trust me."

Lisha's pulse raced and she bit her bottom lip. "Wow," she said softly.

Kael turned his face into her palm and kissed it as he shook his head in denial. "Right now I do what I have to do to get the pressure off me, but please believe that jacking my dick is not like being inside you, Lisha," he explained. "And when we do things together and take it right to the edge I go a little crazy because I'm about to jump off that motha."

Lisha felt her clit pulse. She licked his lips and then blew a cool stream of air against it. "I could do the other thing," she offered lightly before biting her bottom lip.

"You'd wear your damn jaw out trying to do it every time you made me horny," he told her, smiling as he pinched her chin.

Lisha smiled and then pouted her lips. "So what are we going to do? Because I don't want to lose my virginity, but I don't want to lose you," she admitted.

"You won't lose me."

She planted kisses all over his face before allowing them a long and heated kiss that deepened as they both moaned in pleasure.

"I am so wet," she sighed heatedly into his mouth.

Kael grimaced and lowered his head to her shoulder. "Good night, Lisha," he said.

"What?" she asked innocently. "It is."

Releasing a long heavy breath, he lay down on the couch on his back. His erection stood up like a soldier through the flap of the boxers that could not constrain it.

Lisha panted a bit at the sight of it. Long and hard and dark with a thick tip. She felt her pussy jump to life as she gasped.

"The covers and the pillow, Lisha," he reminded her, trying and failing to cover it with his hands.

It would be so easy to give in. Just enjoy the ride. The pleasure.

She licked her lips, surprised at the urge she felt to feel it against her tongue and lips.

"Lisha."

Shifting her eyes up to him she felt dazed by the dick. "Uhm, yeah. I'll be right back," she said, forcing herself to walk away from the dick.

She grabbed an extra pillow and blanket from her linen closet and brought them to him. He shoved the pillow under his head as she opened the blanket over him and the back of the sofa.

Bending to kiss him, he turned his head. "Good God, Lisha, it just went down. Don't wake it back up," he said gruffly.

She walked to her bedroom but turned at the door. "'Night, Kael," she called over to him.

"'Night."

She stepped into the room and began to undress.

"Shut the door . . . *please.*"

With the hint of a smile, she did as he asked.

Chapter 14

Lisha sang at the top of her lungs along with the "The Twelve Days of Christmas" song playing on the radio sitting on Kael's counter.

Kael grimaced as he walked into the kitchen via the mudroom. "Good thing you know how to cook because singing ain't your thing," he said.

She turned down the volume on the radio as she watched him leave his boots at the door. He looked handsome in his usual garb of Wrangler jeans and plaid shirt, but she couldn't wait to see him in the suit she convinced him to wear for dinner. "Did you get enough wood for the fireplace?" she asked, using the back of her hand to brush her bangs out of her face as she opened the oven door to check the turkey.

He nodded. "I had a bunch down at the hunting cabin. It's all on the back of the truck."

After basting the turkey and removing the oven mitts she'd purchased for him, Lisha turned the radio back up. Her face lit up as a jazzy rendition of "Have Yourself a Merry Little Christmas" played.

Kael frowned as he came over to inspect the contents of the four pots bubbling away on the stove.

"Hey, that's Ella Fitzgerald," she explained, turning the volume up more as she reached for his hands and pulled him into the center of the kitchen to sway to the music.

Kael gave in to the festive holiday spirit and swayed with her as the sounds of horns filled the kitchen. Lisha spun away from him and snapped her fingers in sync to the music as she worked her shoulders before spinning back to him as Ella's voice filled the air again.

Lisha sang along, not caring that her voice was off-key. She absolutely loved Christmas most of all. And spending the day with her family and his here in Kael's house was perfect.

Kael picked her up and Lisha wrapped her legs around his waist tightly and crossed her fingers behind his neck to lean back as he spun her until the song ended. With a sigh filled with happiness she tried her best to stay stable on her feet when Kael let her down. She stumbled even in her flats and Kael caught her by her hips to help keep her steady. "Merry Christmas, Kael," she said out of breath with her face alive and bright with delight.

He kissed her. "Merry Christmas."

He kissed her again. And again. And again. The

fire that constantly simmered between them was stoked with each touch of their lips.

Lisha licked her mouth before he kissed her yet again.

"This feels so right," Kael told her.

"I don't want it to end," she admitted.

And another kiss. Plus one more.

Lisha pressed her fingers to her lips when he released her. They were warm and pulsing to her touch.

"You better go get dressed," he said. "I'll watch the food."

She wondered if there would ever come a time her heart didn't act so crazy around the man. "I'll be right back," she said, walking out.

"You might need this."

Lisha turned. Her mouth fell open at the gold chain hanging from his finger. Dangling at the end of the chain was a diamond heart. It was so cliché, but the winter sun glistened through the windows and hit off one side of the heart, causing the diamonds to twinkle.

Kael came across the kitchen and clasped the chain around her neck, the heart settling right at the tip of her cleavage.

She pressed her hand against the heart. "Kael, this so nice, but you need all the money you can for the ranch. I can't take this," she said, reaching to undo the clasp.

He brought his hands up to stop hers. "It's pretty rude to turn down a gift," he said.

"Kael," Lisha said. "I—"

"Rude as hell."

She looked up at him, feeling overwhelmed. "Thank you," she said, acquiescing. "I love it."

And I love you.

Kael slapped her buttocks as she left the kitchen still rubbing her thumb against the diamond heart. As she walked down the long bare hall she stopped and picked up her overnight bag from by the door where she'd left it earlier that morning when she'd arrived. She was still fingering her heart when she walked into Kael's master bedroom.

She barely took in the huge king-size bed that dominated the room as she walked into the bathroom and stood looking at her reflection in the mirror over the sink. Her eyes locked on the heart. She loved it.

Everything was too good. Too right.

Lisha hated that all of the goodness of their relationship made her feel like she was just waiting for the other shoe to drop.

"You ready, Lisha? Everybody's supposed to be here in a few minutes," Kael said, reaching into his closet for the jacket that matched the plaid pants he wore.

"Almost," she called back.

He opened the box atop his dresser for his watch. "What the hell?" he said softly, looking down at the small box wrapped with red paper and a gold bow. He picked it up, turning the dangling tag over.

"'Merry Xmas from Lisha,'" he read.

Kael tore the paper and opened the cardboard box to pull out the gold link ID chain nestled atop the cotton. It was inscribed.

Strong Ranch est. 1974
A legacy for the many generations to come

"Aw, damn," he said, touched by yet another show of confidence by her in him and his dreams.

Kael draped it over his left wrist and clasped it securely with his right as he walked into the bathroom. He looked on as Lisha stretched her lips across her teeth as she applied lip gloss. She smiled over at him as he stood in the doorway while she tousled her hair.

"Ready?" he asked.

"You think I'm ready?" she asked, turning to face him in the lined wide-leg red satin pants she wore with a matching shirt and a thin gold belt with several chains around her neck.

"Are we having Christmas dinner with our families or going to a disco?" he asked, waving his hand at the plaid suit he wore with an open-collared chocolate shirt.

"You don't like it?" she asked, her bright eyes widening with worry.

Kael stepped into the bathroom with her and pressed a kiss beside her mouth, not to get her gloss on him. "I love it and I love my bracelet," he said, raising his wrist to show it to her.

She reached out for his wrist and touched the bracelet. "Did you see the inscription?" she asked, her eyes gleeful.

He nodded. "I did. Thank you. I really love it."

And you.

"Good," she said. "Junie helped me pick it out."

"Is she still coming?" he asked, walking out of the bathroom and reaching to pull Lisha behind him.

"Yes, so it should be interesting," she said from behind him.

They took the stairs down together.

"The house looks good," he said, taking in the major furniture pieces Lisha helped him pick out, but not missing the bareness of the wall. "Not finished, but nice."

"The tree I picked looks good," she told him, before rushing down the hall to the kitchen.

"Yes, the tree I cut and dragged does look good," he called to her.

Knock-knock.

"Yes, the tree that I decorated while you watched TV looks real good," was her reply.

Kael laughed as he opened the door, the scent

of pine from the fresh wreath on the door filling his nostrils.

"Merry Christmas, boy," Logan said, looking tall and strong as he stepped inside the long hall.

"No, no, you are stepping into the home of a grown-ass man," Kael said with a wide toothy grin as he extended his hand to his father.

"I hear you, I hear you," Logan said, playfully begrudging as he removed his wool coat and newsboy cap to hand to Kael. "Where's Lisha?"

Kael smiled at Kelli and her husband, Willie, as they stepped inside the hall as well. "Hey, sis," he said, kissing her cheek.

"Where's Lisha?" Logan asked again, his voice booming in the still near empty house.

"Please hurry and tell him where he can find his precious Lisha," Kelli said with a friendly smile as she hugged her brother.

"She's in the kitchen," he said, accepting his sister's coat as well as extending his hand to his brother-in-law.

Kelli's husband, William Thorne, was a man of average height, weight and looks. The perfect friendly-faced attorney and politician. "Merry Christmas, Willie," he said, accepting his brother-in-law's coat and feeling his arm dip with the added weight of the heavy wool.

"Will," he corrected Kael. "And Merry Christmas."

"Yeah, sure."

"Your sister made that peach cobbler you like so much," Will said.

Kael grimaced a little. "Well, I told her not to bring anything and Lisha made a cobbler but . . . the . . . uh . . . the more the merrier," he said. "Do me a favor and take it in the kitchen for me, Willie—*Will*—while I hang these coats up."

"No problem."

Kael opened the empty hall closet door but then remembered he hadn't purchased hangers. Closing the door he jogged up the stairs and laid the coats across the bed in one of the other guest bedrooms.

Ding-dong-deeeeeeng.

The doorbell. Just one of a hundred other things he still had to get fixed in the house. Kael jogged down the stairs.

"Son, that sounds like a donkey getting castrated," Logan said.

"Yeah, Pops," he said to pacify him.

Lisha appeared at his side as he was about to open the door. "Your father won't give a sermon if my father slips up and and cuss will he?" he asked, deadpan serious.

She just laughed and swatted away his hand to pull the door open wide. Lisha and Kael stepped back and tilted their heads up to take in the towering thin man accompanying Junie. She barely reached his belly. He had to duck to fit inside the doorway.

"Lisha and Kael, this is Benny. Benny, this is my cousin, Lisha, and her man, Kael," she said, bumping her hip against an obviously surprised Lisha.

"Man, you can dunk on Kareem Abdul-Jabbar," Kael said, shaking the man's hand.

"I wish," Benny said.

Lisha and Kael shared a look as he closed the door after Junie and her date walked into the den.

"I better go and make introductions," she said.

Kael caught her by the waist and pulled her close to press a kiss to her neck. "You look real good around here playing the lady of the house," he said, reaching up to lightly press the heart against her chest.

"Oh, I do?" she asked. "Well, thank you."

"I would kiss you, but you have all that goop on your mouth," he said.

Lisha raised the edge of her apron and wiped all of the gloss from her lips. "What's your excuse now, Mr. Strong?" she asked, bringing her hands up to his broad shoulders.

"Not a damn thing," he said, leaning in to her.

Ding-dong-deeeeeeng.

Lisha broke free and turned to open the door wide, leaving Kael standing there with his bent arm empty and his lips still puckered.

"Merry Christmas," she said with plenty of love and warmth.

Kael stood behind her as first her mother and then her father stepped inside the house.

"Mommy and Daddy, this is Kael," she said, standing in between them with her arms entwined with theirs. "Kael, this is Reverend Rockmon and my mom, whom everyone calls Lady because she's *the* first lady."

Kael smiled at them as he extended his hand to both. "Merry Christmas. Nice to meet you both," he said.

"Merry Christmas," Rev said, still holding onto Kael's hand with a strong grip. "Heard a lot about you."

Okay. Kael looked down at their hands as the man's grip tightened even more.

"Daddy, let him go," Lisha advised, stepping up to pull their hands apart.

Rev gave him a smile. "You and I need to have a long talk, son. Don't you think?" he asked, with a soft expression but hard eyes.

Kael met his stare. "Whenever you want, sir."

With that, Rev nodded and turned away from him. "Do I smell your cornbread stuffing?" he asked his daughter.

"Yes, sir," Lisha said. "Come on and meet Kael's family, y'all."

As they preceded Kael and Lisha into the den, she hugged his arm close. "He's just being a daddy," she assured him. "Trust me, my mama's the one to watch."

They stepped into the entryway of the den.

It was quiet. Eerily quiet. Everyone was settled around the room and all eyes were on them.

"Ready?" Kael asked her.

Lisha licked her now-bare lips and nodded as they stepped further into the room.

"That was delicious, Lisha," Logan said, wiping his mouth with a paper napkin.

"Yes, it was," Rev agreed. "You did real good."

Lisha beamed from her seat at the end of the large dining room table. "I'm glad everything turned out so good," she said.

"It was delicious," Will said. "I really liked those yams. Can I get some more?"

"Sure," Lisha said, accepting his plate.

Kelli pulled his arm back and shook her head. "He really can't. The doctor is watching his sugar and they were a little sweet."

Lisha set the spoon back in the bowl of yams. "That's more than fine, Kelli," she said, and then turned her head to look down the length of the table to pierce Kael with a hard stare.

"Well, they were perfect to me and I'll take some more," he said.

She lifted the bowl and passed it to her left to Will who passed it to Kelli who promptly set it down on the table, squeezing it between the serving bowls of collard greens and dressing.

Logan eyed her hard before he picked the yams

up with one hand and passed them to Kael who stared at his sister just as hard.

Kelli had been throwing jabs at her cooking throughout the entire meal while her husband spoke so much of his career, his opinions and his life that Lisha was tired of both of them. But it wasn't her home to invite anyone to get the hell out.

And she hated that Kael appeared to be oblivious to his sister's bullshit.

"We're gonna just leave the dessert in the kitchen and everyone just kind of get what they want when they feel like it," she said, rising to walk across the dining room to the swinging door leading into the kitchen. "I'll go make sure everything's warm."

"I would bring everything to the table, Lisha," Kelli said, setting her napkin atop her barely touched plate of food. "Don't do your guests that way."

"They're not my guests. They're Kael's guests," she said as Kelli came to stand beside her. "And he decided he wanted dessert served that way. Didn't you, Kael?"

Both women looked to him.

"I sure did, baby," Kael said in between bites of yams.

"Baby?" Rev said sternly, his round face lined with disappointment.

"Uh . . . I mean Lisha," he said, sounding unsure.

Logan chuckled at it all.

Kael fought not to kick him under the table.

"I'm not ready for dessert. I want another go at this dinner," Logan said.

"So do I. My daughter can cook, can't she?" Rev said.

"Sure can," Logan agreed.

"Me, too," Benny chimed in.

"Lisha, you go on ahead and I'll fix these plates for you," Junie said. Four empty plates were shoved in her direction at once.

Kelli reclaimed her seat and Lisha continued on to the kitchen where she kicked the air to keep from screaming out in frustration. "I knew that had to be working a nerve," Lady said as she strolled into the kitchen.

Lisha held up her hands.

"You got to remember that for a long time she was all the woman in the house her brother and her father needed and then here comes you," Lady said, reaching into her pockets as she looked around the kitchen and then moved straight for the door leading into the mudroom. "And trust me, daughter, you're a lot to take for a woman not steady in who she is. You know?"

Lisha leaned against the counter and looked on as her mother pulled a silver cigarette case from the pocket of her deep green suit jacket. "Daddy knows you smoke, Mama," she said, turning to slide both cobblers and the four sweet potato pies she made back in the oven on low to warm them.

"I know," Lady said as she released a stream of smoke. "And he knows that I know. It's a little game we play. No need to fret."

Lisha nodded her head as she pressed her hands to the counter and looked out the window at the frost barely making the ground white. "So she is afraid they won't need her anymore?" she asked, changing their conversation.

"Yup," Lady said, before taking another drag.

Lisha looked down at the pans of food she cooked from scratch. Ham, turkey, greens, macaroni and cheese, cornbread stuffing, yams and potato salad. Plus four sweet potato pies, a chocolate cake and peach cobbler. "So that's why she made her famous peach cobbler even though Kael told her not to bring anything?" she asked.

"Let her lay out her cobbler," Lady said, walking across the mudroom to drop her cig to the porch before squashing out the ember with her shoe. "It's not worth it or at least it shouldn't be worth it to you even if it's worth it to her."

As much as Lisha wanted to take the cobbler and make Kelli sit in it she knew her mother's wisdom should not be ignored. So she used the mitts and pulled her cobbler out of the oven to slide into the fridge with a roll of her eyes.

Lady walked back into the kitchen and she laughed at the expression on her daughter's face.

"Now you and I have some other desserts of yours we need to discuss," she said, picking up a clean fork to scoop some of the stuffing straight from the roaster pan on the stove.

"What's that, Mama?" she asked.

Lady licked her lips and hummed in pleasure. "Almost as good as mine, Ali," she said, reverting back to Lisha's childhood nickname.

"I'll take that," she said, accepting the fork her mother handed her, sliding it into the sudsy dishwater in the sink.

"And what all has Kael *taken* while you're running around here looking real comfortable as the lady of the house?" Lady asked.

Lisha's cheeks warmed at how close they came to crossing the line. "Not a thing," she assured her. "I live in my apartment and he lives here. He wanted Christmas at his new house and we wanted to spend it together so I offered to cook. We are not shacking by any means."

Lady eyed her for a long time before she nodded. "You guys seem to be moving mighty fast for just three months."

"I love him, Mama," she said, looking away at the look of surprise on her mother's face.

"Well, that's a first," Lady said, coming over to hug her daughter close.

"And I hope the last," Lisha said with a wistful smile.

* * *

Darkness reigned by the time Junie and Benny, the last of their guests, said their good-byes. Kael stepped up behind Lisha and held her from behind with his chin lightly resting atop her head.

"Your father has a way with words," he said.

"What did he say when you two were at the car?" she asked.

Kael chuckled. "He kept it real short," he said. "'Hurt her and your black behind is mine.'"

Lisha covered her face with her hand. "I'm sorry. He wasn't always saved," she explained.

"I understand," he said, removing her hands and holding on to her wrists. "I'm going to be the same way with my daughters."

"Oh, really?" she asked.

"I'm a man just like your father and we know what other men want," Kael explained. "As a father you have to at least try to scare men off from wanting the goodies."

"Did it work? Did my father scare you off?" she asked with the hint of a mischievous smile at her lips.

"Hell, no."

Lisha laughed. "Just remember it won't work for the man you're trying to keep away from your daughters either," she reminded him.

"I got a rifle to help facilitate my conversation though," Kael assured her.

They fell silent as they looked out at the acres of land stretched out before them under the moonlight.

"Our first Christmas," he said, glancing up at that full moon that seemed close enough to reach out and touch.

"First of many, I hope," she admitted, as she massaged his hands where they rested against her body.

Kael hoped for the same. "If things work out I can see us old and gray with a houseful of kids and grandkids enjoying the holidays together."

Lisha turned in his embrace and looked up at him. "How many kids?"

"Ten," he said.

Her eyes widened. "Ten!" she exclaimed. "Maybe five."

Kael chuckled. "All boys."

"Too messy," Lisha said, bringing her hands up to rub his back. "All girls."

"Too much whining," Kael countered.

"You'll probably spoil them all though."

"Daughters? Definitely," he assured her.

Lisha tucked her hands into his pockets and leaned back to look at him. "Do you think we're moving too fast? Are you okay?"

"I am more than okay."

"Good, because that matters to me," she said.

"And I believe that."

She came back towards him and pressed her head against his chest as Kael hugged her tight. "It feels like your arms were made just to hold me," she said.

"Maybe they were," Kael said. "Maybe God meant to move my ex out of my life to make way for you."

Lisha closed her eyes as warmth and happiness spread across her body like melted butter. "You're talking some mighty deep words right now, Kael Strong," she said.

"I like to go deep."

She looked up at him.

"I can go even deeper," he promised her.

"Are you talking about sex because—"

"I'm talking about how I feel for you, Lisha," Kael said, his voice deep and serious as he brought his hands up to warmly clasp the sides of her face.

She got lost in his moonlit eyes.

"I'm talking about how much I love you," Kael stressed. "Because I do."

Lisha's body froze but her heart thundered. *Did I hear him right?*

"I love you," Kael said again, before dipping his head to taste her mouth, warming them both even as the night winds of winter snapped coldly around them as they stood together on the porch.

She felt overcome with her love and she had to blink rapidly to keep tears from falling as she reached for one of Kael's hands and pressed the palm against her heart. "And you have been inside my heart for the longest time, Kael," Lisha admitted, feeling freed by the truth of her words. "I love you, too."

He smiled as he bent his legs to pick her up. "Best Christmas ever," he said low in his throat, his words feathering against her lips just before he kissed her.

Lisha nodded, wrapping her legs around his waist and her arms around his neck as Kael turned and pressed her back against the large post of the porch and kissed her with a passion that left no doubt to his words.

Chapter 15

The last month had been the happiest of Lisha's life. Having her dreams of finding a man who accepted her love and returned it was a blessing for which she was thankful. She and Kael had settled into a nice groove over the weeks. Once they both stepped up and revealed their love for one another, they each did a million little things over the days to show that love. Phone calls. Love notes. Flowers. Dates. Laughter. Long looks. Hand holding. Just being together whenever they could. Missing each other whenever they could not. Needing each other. Loving each other.

Life was good.

She smiled as she thought of Kael's attempt to cook dinner for her last night. Nothing but her love for him helped her finish that bowl of chicken and dumplings. *Bless his heart,* Lisha thought, as she made notes to her client's chart before clicking her pen and handing the chart to the clerk.

She turned and walked into a solid wall that was warm and smelled familiar. Her heart instantly pounded harder. Looking up, a smile spread across her face at the sight of Kael. "Hey you," she said, her surprise and pleasure illuminating her face as she took in all of him looking handsome in all black.

Kael reached up to lightly tweak her chin as he looked down at her. "I thought I would surprise you and take you out to lunch," he said.

She loved how his eyes studied her face. "You drove an hour to take me to lunch?" she asked, reaching to press a hand to his chest.

Kael's eyes looked beyond her for a few moments before redirecting his gaze back to her. "I had to come to Charleston to get some supplies and I timed it for lunch with you," he said, his eyes shifting again as they filled with confusion.

"Okay," Lisha said, glancing over her shoulder. She did a double take at the sight of almost every female staff member openly staring at them—or rather him. They did the same thing when he came to the clinic that day and saw her in the pool.

"Hello, ladies," Kael said.

"Hello," they said in unison. They were almost in perfect harmony.

"You're quite the cat's meow, Mr. Strong," she teased, as she wrapped her arm through his and steered him out the clinic and into the tunnel connecting it to the hospital.

"Jealous?" he mused, stopping in his tracks and causing her to stop as well.

Lisha arched a brow. "Why? They only get to look and I get to touch," she said, reaching up to caress his cheek before lightly patting it as she smirked.

"Shit, touch me," he invited, holding up his hands as a wicked smile spread across his handsome face.

Lisha reached a hand out to him but paused just millimeters from his chest. "I'd rather touch a plate of food in this cafeteria," she teased, turning to walk away from him before giving him a coquettish smile over her shoulder. "Coming?"

"I wish," he drawled as he followed behind her, his eyes dipping down to take in the back and forth movement of her hips even in her shapeless uniform pants.

Lisha turned and walked back to him as people passed by them in the hall of the hospital. "I think you did that last night," she whispered up to him.

"Not inside you," Kael said, his voice deep and low and husky.

Lisha felt her entire body flush with warmth and she licked her lips to ease the sudden parch. She started to say something flirty but just turned and led him to the cafeteria instead even as her heart continued to pound away.

She thought of those heated moments they shared last night on her couch. The movie he came over to watch on the television served no purpose but to offer just enough illumination in the darkness of her living room so that he could see the tips of her hard nipples as he sucked them. And licked them. And then sucked them some more.

And it had felt so good that through the haze of desire she had barely been able to focus on stroking his hardness until it stiffened and then jerked in her hand as he came. And came. And came some more.

It was a hot, passionate, climatic, sticky mess.

Lisha pursed her lips and released a long steady stream of air she hoped released some of the desire that quickly built up in her like steam pressure. The same pressure and tension that caused the swelling of her clit in a rush of desire. They hadn't completely crossed the line or even pushed it as far as they did that first night, but she—*they*—lived in a world filled with building sexual tension.

Kael Strong couldn't burn in the kitchen but Lisha took comfort that he had to be skilled in the bedroom. And that knowledge, those glimpses into his prowess nagged at her throughout each and every day of her life since she met him. The thought of him, his body, his lips, the length of his dick kept her steamy and aware—so very aware—of the sexual limitations she put on them. The man made taking a shower torture because thinking of him as she used a sudsy bar of soap to rub across her breasts and her intimacy was a special kind of blend of heaven and hell.

Lisha let out a little moan in the back of her throat as she found them a table while Kael got in line to select their food. She smiled and waved at people she knew and tried not to fidget guiltily as she crossed her legs to halt the throbbing of her clit.

But those fleeting moments of bliss were chipping away at the once solid mental wall surrounding her virginity. It was getting harder and harder to bring the passion to an end and she was close—too close—to giving Kael her gift.

And she meant *really* giving it to him in a hot, steamy, dirty way.

"Hungry?"

Lisha jumped a bit in surprise, looking up as Kael set the tray he carried on the table before sliding onto the seat across from her. "Huh?" she asked, picking up one of the steaming bowls of beef stew.

"I asked if you were hungry?" Kael asked as he handed her one of the plastic utensil sets.

For you? Yes. Very hungry.

Lisha shrugged even as she shifted in her seat and pressed her thighs even tighter together.

Kael frowned at the stew and then began to chuckle as he raised a spoonful. "And you acted like my chicken and dumplings were the worst dish you ever saw," he said dryly.

Lisha looked down at the stew and then up at him with a smile. "I said the chicken and dumplings were good," she said.

Kael chuckled. "You lied," he insisted.

"I plead the fifth," she said, biting back a smile.

"Hi, Alisha."

She froze and looked up at Byron standing above where they sat. She fought not roll her eyes. Her suspicions that he spread the word on her virginity had been true. Lisha wasn't ashamed but it was not his business to tell. "Goodbye, Byron," she finally said with emphasis.

"I'm Byron Long," he said.

She jerked her head up as he extended his hand to Kael. "Byron, no one cares who you are and you are interrupting our lunch," she snapped.

Kael looked from Byron to Lisha as he roughly wiped his napkin across his mouth before dropping it onto the table as he rose to his full height, towering over Byron by several inches. "Kael Strong," he said, taking Byron's hand in his and grasping it tightly as he shook it. "And I believe the lady—in her own way—asked you to leave us alone to enjoy our lunch."

Lisha's mouth opened a bit at the hard stare with which Kael pierced the man even as he delivered a cold smile.

"That is what you meant, baby?" Kael asked, looking down at her even as he held on to Byron's hand.

"Baby?" Byron asked, glancing down at the tips of his fingers reddening from the pressure of Kael's hand.

"That's exactly what I meant," she said, taking a bite of the stew. "Goodbye, Byron."

"Have a good one, Byron," Kael said, finally releasing the man's hand and bending his body to reclaim his seat.

"Man, take it from me you're just wasting your time," Byron muttered.

Kael froze.

Lisha's eyes widened as his jaw clenched. She reached out to rest her hand on his. "Ignore him. He's a spoiled little boy in a grown man's body," she said.

Byron had turned away but he turned back at her words. "You, Little Miss Virgin, are calling me a little boy?" he said snidely.

Kael stood up and stepped close to Byron. Placing his large hand on the man's shoulder, he whispered a few words in his ear and then leaned back just enough to lock eyes with him.

Byron's face filled with an odd expression before he turned and walked out of the cafeteria so quickly that he could have blazed a trail of fire from the soles of his shoes.

"What did you say to him?" Lisha asked, looking on as Kael took his seat and resumed eating his lunch.

"Just a little talk among men, baby," Kael said

calmly as he broke his dinner roll in half and dipped it into the stew. "But know this—a real man knows when a woman is worth the wait."

Lisha's eyes dipped from his as she felt her cheeks warm with a blush and her heart warm with love.

Lisha pulled her Nova onto the drive of Kael's father's home. She climbed from her vehicle and removed the Tupperware containing the beef stew she'd made for Kael's dinner. She'd thought Logan could appreciate a home-cooked meal as well and so she brought him the savory dish before she headed to Kael's.

She quick-walked up the pathway and knocked twice before she reached for the doorknob because she already knew it was open. Every morning like clockwork, Logan rose at five o'clock and walked out onto the porch to check the day's weather. When he came back inside he didn't bother to lock the door. As he made himself a strong pot of coffee, two fried eggs and toast, he listened to the morning news.

Every morning. Like clockwork.

She frowned when the door wouldn't budge. "It's locked," she said in surprise.

Knocking, she glanced at her watch. It was after seven. *Maybe he's not home.*

Lisha had just turned to head back to her car

when the door opened. She turned back and smiled. "Hey, Mr. Strong," she said.

He let out a string of coughs before waving her in.

Lisha was surprised to see that he was in his pajamas. "Turning in early or just getting up?" she teased.

"A little of both," he said. He pointed at the Tupperware. "What's that?"

"Some homemade beef stew," she said, taking it into the kitchen to slide into the refrigerator. "I thought you might like some."

He coughed again and it sounded like it rattled something wet deep in his chest. "You thought right," he finally said.

Lisha's eyes became pensive as she closed the door to the fridge and faced him. "That sounds like a nasty cough."

He nodded and pulled a cloth napkin from the pocket of his pajama pants to wipe his mouth as he dropped down into his recliner. "Nothing a hot toddy won't break up," Logan said, closing his eyes as he let his head rest back on the recliner.

Lisha removed the floor-length overcoat she wore before heading back into the kitchen. She rummaged through the cabinet beneath the sink and pulled out a small pot to fill with water from the sink. "Where are your tea bags?"

"I keep 'em in the fridge," he said.

She paused at how tired he sounded. "This

toddy ought to put you out like a light," she said, retrieving the tea bags and a cup. "Sounds like you could use some sleep."

"I'll be over it in a day or so."

Lisha busied herself making him a cup of tea and then pouring a liberal amount of brandy from the breakfast bar into it. Setting it on the tray, she also made him a glass of water and a glass of orange juice after warming up the stew and adding water to thin the thick broth.

"You not my nurse anymore, Lisha," Logan said.

She set the tray on the coffee table in front of him. "I was never your nurse," she corrected him with a smile. "But I've always cared about you and ain't nothing changed about that."

Logan leveled his eyes on her. "You love my boy, don't you?"

Lisha thought back to that night a month ago that Kael professed his love for her. When she raised her eyes to his father she didn't care if everything she felt was in the depths of them. "Yes, sir," she answered.

"I knew since that day in my hospital room," he assured her around another cough. "I just been lying back watching it all go down."

"Oh, yeah?" she asked, sitting down on the sofa with a side eye as he sipped the tea and winced from the shot of liquor.

"Oh, yeah," Logan said with a wink.

Lisha stayed with the older man until she made

sure he drank all the tea and half of his orange juice and most of the broth from the stew. Once he dragged himself back to bed she locked the front door on her way out.

Once she reached Kael's home, she looked out in the distance at the corrals and surrounding fields to see if he was outside. She could see his truck was parked down by the barn. Parking her car she hopped out and headed in that direction.

Lisha found Kael and Jim in the barn replacing the water in the trough for the cattle and horses. He looked up and smiled at the sight of her.

"Hi, fellas," she said to them, fighting not to frown at the scent of animal and fresh waste as she made her way to Sampson's stall at the rear of the barn.

"You stopped by my daddy's?" Kael asked, from his stooped position beside a cow.

Lisha stroked Sampson's nose as she looked over her shoulder. "Yes, he has a bad cold," she told him.

She raised her hand up to eye level with Sampson and he used his nose to nudge her palm in greeting. Feeding him a sugar cube the way Kael taught her, she gave him one last pat before she left him and walked over to the stall where Kael worked.

She arched a brow as she watched him reach his arm under the cow to her privates. "Should I be jealous?" she quipped, resting her arms atop the door to the stall.

Jim laughed.

Kael snorted in derision. "If I could satisfy her then you would be in major trouble," he told her.

"Now *that's* the truth," Jim agreed, setting his Stetson back on his head.

Lisha frowned at the image of Kael having a corkscrew penis like a bull. "On that note I'm going to warm up this stew. Have some, Jim?" she offered, already headed out the door.

"No, ma'am."

Lisha used the hose outside the barn to wash her hands before making the sizeable trek back toward the house. She stopped at her car for the Tupperware containing the stew and made her way inside the house. By the time Kael joined her in the kitchen she had heated the stew in a pot, baked fresh cornbread and made a pitcher of sweet tea.

He pressed a welcoming kiss to her temple before washing his hands. "I sure appreciate this," he said.

Lisha rubbed his back as she set the steaming plate in front of him and moved back to the sink.

"You not eating with me?" he asked, looking over at her.

"No, I'm not hungry," she explained.

Lisha left the kitchen and made her way to the linen closet in the hall outside the bedroom upstairs. She had just pulled out a stack of washcloths when she heard a noise from inside Kael's bedroom. Thinking something fell she crossed the hall and opened the door.

At the sight laid out before her, Lisha backed out of the room, shut the door, did a five count and opened the door again.

Instead of lying across Kael's bed in a red lace crotchless teddy, Bea was now walking toward the door.

"How can you be fast in the ass and slow in the brain all at once?" Lisha snapped, stepping into the room to stand toe to toe with the woman.

Bea eyed her up and down with a demeaning eye. "Like you giving up what he want," she said mockingly.

Lisha hated the all too familiar feelings of insecurity that nipped at her, but she stiffened her back and eyed the other just the same. "Like he want what you giving away like free cheese," she said slyly.

"What the hell is going on?" Kael asked as he ran up the stairs.

Lisha glanced over her shoulder at him. "Put down a trap, baby, and catch this rat that snuck into the house," she said, arching her brow.

"Bea, how did you get in my house?" he asked.

Lisha's mouth opened when the woman stood in her face and struck a sexy pose. Turning, she slowly raised her hands. "You know what, baby.

Don't worry about calling anybody. I'll handle this," she finished firmly, pushing both her hands into Kael's chest and shoving him hard until he stumbled back on his feet.

Lisha stepped farther into the room and swung the door shut before he could recover. As she turned the lock his knocks echoed. Lisha ignored him. "Enough is enough," she said coldly, pressing her finger into Bea's chest. "Kael is my man and regardless of what you think I am or am not giving him is none of your business, but you can bet he loves it just the way it is."

"So why did he tell me to come here?" Bea countered.

"Liar," Lisha said with a wave of her hand. "The truth ain't in you. Nobody told you to pull this stunt but his sister and both of ya'll can kiss my ass."

Bea opened her mouth.

"Shut up lying some more," Lisha snapped. "Get your clothes and get your raggedy ass out before I drag you out."

"Don't start nothing you can't finish," Bea said, the few long strands of her nappy unkempt bush pressing through the lace.

Lisha made a fist and stomped her foot like she was about to throw.

Bea backed up and covered her face with her arms.

Crossing her arms over her chest, she looked at

the other woman in satisfaction. "This is your last chance to get your clothes before I send you out into the world just as you are," she said, using her foot to kick an errant shoe toward her.

Bea retrieved her pile of clothes from the floor on the other side of the bed.

Lisha had a million and one questions for her, starting with just how long the other woman had been in wait, but she didn't even bother, knowing she would get nothing but lies. She shook her head as she waited for the woman to cover her near nakedness with her skintight jeans and plunging V-neck sweater that still left little to the imagination.

Bea continued to eye her up and down as she moved past Lisha to the door. "You lucky I don't make it a habit to fight over men, sugar," she said.

"Especially one that's not yours," Lisha countered, following the woman out of the room past Kael and down the stairs.

"Ain't no ring on your finger," Bea said, opening the front door. "So he *ain't* yours either."

The January winds were biting and crisp as she followed the woman out onto the porch. "You know what, Bea? Beneath all that over-the-top behavior and low-cut clothes could be a woman made to be a wife. No man would know because of the way you present yourself. And giving away your goodness like it's worth no more than pennies ain't the way either . . . *sugar*."

Bea said nothing else before she walked down the stairs and around the house. Lisha came down a few steps on her way to follow her, but before she could touch her feet to the ground, Bea drove her green car from around the house and soon it disappeared down the road.

Lisha turned and Kael was leaning in the doorway. "You have to do something about your sister," she said, walking up the rest of the steps to brush past him and into the house.

"My sister?" he exclaimed from behind her.

Lisha did a spin pretty close to that of the Tasmanian Devil as she faced Kael as he closed the front door. "Your sister is on a one-woman crusade to see you with Bea from the beginning. It took me a minute to wake up and see the truth, but now you have to get your head out of your ass and see it too . . . and then handle it before I do."

"So you think my sister told Bea to stroll her crazy ass up to my house and lay in my bed half-naked?" he asked, his face incredulous.

"Yes," Lisha stressed. "I damn sure do."

He walked up to her. "My sister would not pull a stunt like that. She knows we're together."

Lisha held up her hand. "Did you tell your sister I was a virgin?" she asked him.

"What?" he asked, confused.

"Or did you tell Bea? Because either way what does or does not happen between my thighs is no one's business—not even yours."

"I disagree on it not being my business, but I would never go under your clothes . . . to *anyone*." Kael reached for her and held on to her even as Lisha struggled against his strength. "Hey, I will ask Kelli about it, but please believe I don't think she had anything to do with it and I hope you know I didn't want Bea in my bed."

Lisha said nothing as he kissed her temple because she wondered if Kelli would forever be a problem in their relationship and if Kael would ever see the truth.

Kael wanted to check on the horses and the herd for the night. Lisha changed clothes and tagged along even though it was clear her demeanor had changed after the incident with Bea.

"Everything all good?" she asked when Kael stepped out of the barn with a grim expression.

"Sampson got out through the rear door," he said, already striding toward his truck.

Lisha hurried behind him, barely getting in the truck and closing the passenger door securely before Kael pulled off toward his land slowly. "Use that flood-light," he told her. "Point it toward the ground because the light in his eyes can startle him."

Lisha lowered the window and hung her upper body out, swinging the portable flood-light back and forth across the land. "I hope he didn't roam too far," she said.

"If the terrain was all flat I wouldn't really worry," he said.

Kael drove slowly and Lisha continued to sweep the light back and forth on the ground, hoping to find Sampson on the land grazing or resting. He drove as far as he could with the truck but parked at the path between the tall trees. "We gotta foot it from here," he said, reaching for the flood-light before he climbed from the truck and then came around to help her out.

"I hope he's okay," she said, as the freezing winter chill seemed to settle in her bones and cause her to shiver even as she huddled close to Kael's arm.

"Yeah, me too," he said.

They came up on the path leading to the hunting cabin and Kael steered them in that direction. "Let me check around the cabin," he said.

The path opened up into the dirt-packed yard and the break in the cluster of trees caused the moon to light the area.

"Look, it's cold," Kael said, leading her to the door. "I'm going to light the fire and you stay here while I look around some more. I won't be long."

"Kael," she protested as they entered the cabin.

He moved away from her, leaving her by the door as he used the flood-light to reach the stone fireplace. Smiling, he knelt by the fireplace and pulled the box of matches he brought along out of his pocket to light the logs. He stoked the fire and soon the cabin's interior was lit and warmed by it.

"Oh my God." Lisha sighed as she took in the small and cozy interior made all the more charming by the crackling fire and the flower petals heavily strewn on the floor and atop the white sheets covering the love seat in the middle of the room.

She took a deep breath as Kael moved around the room lighting candles. On the fireplace mantel. The table in the corner. Along the edge of the floor. Each ember warmed the room's ambience even more.

"When did you do all this?" she asked, turning slowly to take it all in.

"This morning when I came down for the logs," he explained, before lighting even more candles.

"I wanted to create a moment that you would never forget," he said, looking over his shoulder at her. "Because I have something I want to ask you."

She looked to him. "What's that?" she asked, her irritation and anger still on the edge of her voice.

Kael walked back over to her and looked down into her eyes. "I love you," he began.

"I love you too," she said, sounding more aggravated than emotional.

"Well, act like it," he snapped in irritation.

The stiffness around her shoulders slackened a

bit, but he could still sense she was not over what happened with Bea or the silly notion that his sister was involved in that stunt.

"I said I would talk to Kelli, and I'll tell her if I catch Bea back on my property I will call the police," he said, moving away from her to stand at one of the two windows in the one-room cabin. "Can we enjoy the damn night *now?*"

Moments later, he was aware of Lisha as she moved across the room and came up to stand behind him. When she touched his arms, he looked over his shoulder at her but said nothing. And when she came around to press kisses to his neck, he softened his hard stance but his hand gripped the small box in the pocket of his jacket even as he lowered his head to kiss her.

It was his disappointment that had fueled his annoyance.

Kael had set the stage to propose to this woman he loved, but he felt the moment had come and gone with Bea's shenanigans and Lisha's unwavering anger. He wanted the night to be perfect and there was just no way to remove the stain of what Bea had done.

Not tonight, but soon, he thought as he released the ring box and brought his hand up to press against her face as he deepened the kiss.

"Love is a burning desire, that makes your heart light on fire."

—Unknown

Interlude

Lisha stroked the diamond heart she'd worn around her neck nearly every day since Kael gave it to her that Christmas. Like her wedding ring it was a constant . . . just like the bracelet she'd bought him. She looked down at his left wrist and there it was peeking out a bit from the cuff of his sweater.

"You were going to propose after just four months, Daddy?" Kaitlyn asked, from her spot where she was lying on the floor in front of the fireplace.

"Sure was," Kael said, reaching for Lisha's left hand and rubbing his thumb against the engagement ring she moved to her index finger when he upgraded her ring on their twenty-fifth wedding anniversary.

"When you know, you know. Right, Pops?"

Quinton asked, sitting on the floor with Kaitlyn's booted feet on his lap.

Kaitlyn's head was propped on her hand as she looked from her parents to rest her eyes on him. "So you knew, huh?" she asked with a soft smile and warm eyes.

Quint nodded. "That's right," he said without equivocation. "When you love a woman, time doesn't matter. Nothing matters . . . but her."

The men in the house all backed him up with affirmations.

Kaitlyn sat up, crossing her legs Indian-style as she leaned in toward her fiancé. "And when a woman knows, she knows too," she said. "That's what love is all about. Giving and taking. Forgiving and forgetting. Loving and loving some more."

The women co-signed that.

Quinton nodded as he leaned over to meet her halfway to taste her lips. "Love you, Kat," he said low in his throat.

"I know that's right," she said. "Love you too."

Even with the sounds of "Silent Night" playing, everyone in the room heard them. "Awwwwww," they said collectively.

Quint paid them no mind. He was just months away from wedding Kaitlyn and becoming an official member of the Strong family. Having her as his wife would make his life complete and a big part of her was her love for her family.

He was grateful to them all because if they

hadn't tried to reverse their years of spoiling Kat by cutting her off financially, then she wouldn't have ever moved to the apartment complex where he lived and worked as the manager. He wouldn't have ever met with her, argued with her and ultimately fallen deeply in love with her.

Everyone liked to say that meeting him was the best thing that had ever happened to Kat. That his love for her changed her from the reckless and spoiled woman she used to be. That he made her better.

Quint thought just the opposite.

Knowing and loving Kaitlyn made him better.

She was his biggest supporter, his friend, his lover and the person he knew he would spend the rest of his life loving. In time his heart and his love for her made him see past the façade she put up to the woman she kept protected behind it.

Quint did acknowledge that she was different from the woman who assumed the world owed her everything plus some more. The only time she had been unselfish was with his daughter and it was the way she put Lei first that thawed his heart to her. And now this woman he first thought could love no one but herself, was the type of loving, fiercely protective, supporting mother his daughter had needed.

As the family laughed over Kaitlyn being cut off after a spending spree in Paris, Quint felt his heart swell with love for everything she used to be, everything she now was and still yet everything she was growing to be.

He looked at her, ready for the days to sweep by so he could stand at the altar and make her his wife. She had given him brand-new tools for his business of custom woodworking, but the gift he truly cherished was the love she gave him and Lei every day.

Kaitlyn stood up. Quint's eyes followed her as she made her way across the room to the guest bathroom at the end of the hall. She was slender but curvy and took pride in maintaining her shape.

Quint couldn't wait to see her face, hips and belly swell with pregnancy. He was ready now and Kaitlyn asked them to wait one year after their wedding date to toss the birth control. Both he and Lei were anxiously awaiting adding to the small family.

Wanting a moment alone with his fiancée, Quint left the room. He walked down the hall and into the den to cross it to reach the guest bathroom. Kaitlyn was walking out just as he reached for the door.

He eased her back inside and closed the door. "Did I tell you how good you look in that red dress?" he asked, pulling her into his arms and pressing kisses against the deep vee as she leaned back in his strong embrace.

Kaitlyn nodded even as she shivered from the feel of his lips. "It perfectly matches my new Fendi shoes and bag Santa brought me," she said as she let her fingers enjoy his muscled physique.

Quint raised his head. "Santa is cold and needs something warm to dip into," he moaned against her ear.

"Well, Ms. Claus got what you need, Santa," Kaitlyn said saucily as she wiggled her shoulder and hips.

"Ho-ho-ho," Quint said.

They both jumped as the shower curtain suddenly opened with a snap. Kadina and Lei stepped out of the tub. "This is where we exit," Lei drawled.

"Exactly," Kadina added.

Kaitlyn gasped in horror. "So you two were in the shower while I was peeing?"

The teens pushed between Kaitlyn and Quint. "We were hiding before you sent us back upstairs."

"That is where you're supposed to be," Quint said sternly.

Lei stopped in the open doorway with an impish smile. "Don't worry. We won't tell if you won't," she said before making a comical face and closing the door on her father and soon-to-be stepmother.

"Lei almost saw a side of us she never saw before," Kaitlyn said, checking the mirror to arrange her clothes before following Quint out into the hallway.

They laughed together as he took her hand and massaged it between both of his.

"So, Daddy, you have one daughter," Kaleb said, giving Quinton a side glance as he and Kaitlyn walked back into the room. "Did you have the talk with Quint with your rifle on hand?"

"I can answer that," Quint inserted, comfortably a part of the family and their camaraderie. "He did . . . but hell, you all did too."

"That's right," the brothers all agreed easily, their voices deep and resonating.

"And we all will do the same for Kadina, Lei, Meena and Neema," Kahron said.

"Just like your mama taught you, boys," Lisha said with a smile.

"That sounds like a plan I want to be a part of," Quint said, dreading the day little boys hungering sweet kisses from his daughter turned into men wanting much more.

"Of course, brother," Kade said. "One for all . . ."

"And all for one," everyone finished in unison.

Lisha nodded in approval, her eyes soft as she looked at her gathered family. "This is what your father and I wanted from the very beginning—"

"Once we got our shit together," Kael added.

Lisha nodded in agreement. "And that took some doing. . . ."

Chapter 16

Way back in the day

"Well, hey, stranger."

Lisha smiled at she handed Junie a can of her favorite sugar-covered butter cookies. "Hello to you, *family*," she stressed, doing an exaggerated shiver as the winter winds caused her hair to fly across her face. "It's so cold."

Junie begrudgingly accepted the cookies and stepped back to allow Lisha entrance into her studio apartment. Where Lisha was more laid-back in personality and lived in a world of vibrant colors, Junie had a wild personality but her home was decorated in white.

"You and Kael gave each other a break," Junie said dryly as she walked into her kitchen.

"I'm heading over there later," Lisha said, sitting down to the breakfast bar separating the kitchen and living area. "I had to catch up on some laundry, clean up a little bit and check on my favorite cousin."

Junie used a butter knife to break the plastic seal around the lid of the can. "I'm still right here and alive where you left me for the last four months," she said, setting the can on the bar before pulling a jug of milk from the fridge.

"Junie, I see you every night and every Sunday in church," Lisha said, reaching into the can for a cookie.

Junie shrugged one thin shoulder as she set a glass of milk in front of her. "Okay, yes. But—"

Lisha paused in the act of dunking her cookie into the milk. She glanced up at her cousin.

"What's wrong?" Junie asked, her expression serious.

"Nothing," Lisha said.

"Liar," Junie said. "Do me and my nunchucks need to talk to Kael's balls?"

Raising the now-softened cookie from the milk, Lisha bit into it with a deep moan of pleasure as she closed her eyes. "No, but you can chat with his sister's ass for me," she said, wiping milk from the corners of her mouth.

Junie raised her fists. "All I need is this left and that right to handle that bougie heifer," she said. "She almost met them Christmas."

Lisha reached for another cookie. "I can take her smart-ass comments. Thank God I rarely see her," she said. "It's Kael acting like she's perfect. Like he doesn't see the shit she does."

"Two cuss words dang near back to back. You must be pissed," Junie said, turning to grab the can of Nesquik from the cabinet.

Lisha smiled and accepted the spoon her cousin handed her to scoop two big heapings of the chocolate powder into her milk.

"Doesn't she live three hours away?" Junie asked.

Lisha nodded. "But she's been coming back every weekend lately," she said into the glass before taking a deep sip.

"My suggestion of whooping her behind probably won't help, but that's all I got," Junie said. "So what are you going to do?"

"I'm tired of talking to Kael about it," Lisha said, reaching for another cookie.

"Then skip the middle man and talk to Cruella."

"Kelli," Lisha corrected her.

"Whatever."

Lisha smiled. "Wanna go with me to the Laundromat?" she asked. "I know you got dirty clothes."

"I gots a-plenty . . . but I have to pass. Benny and I are going out eat."

Lisha dropped her cookie in her milk. "Benny's still around?" she asked, obviously surprised.

Junie nodded as she swallowed the rest of the milk. "You and the silver fox look so happy so I am trying this couple thing . . . plus he is hung like a—"

"I'm happy for you," Lisha interrupted her. "So it's your turn to leave me hanging for your dude, huh?"

"I figured with his height everything had to be long on him . . . and I was right," Junie said, shifting the convo right back. "I just love climbing that tree."

When her cousin stared off into the distance with a naughty bite of her bottom lip and a little shiver, Lisha stuck her fingers in the milk and then flicked some at her.

Some of the milk clung to Junie's lips.

She licked it. "Now that reminds me of the night I—"

"And on that note, I will check you later," Lisha said, heading out the door as Junie laughed.

Lisha walked to her apartment, her extreme bell-bottoms flapping in the January winds. She spent the next hour cleaning her apartment. She was walking backward out of the bathroom as she mopped the floor when the shrill cry of the telephone broke the quiet.

Setting the mop in the bucket just outside the bathroom door, she took off her rubber gloves as she made her way to the kitchen to grab the phone. "Hello," she said.

"Hey, baby. What you doin'?"

Kael. She pressed the phone closer to her face as she leaned her shoulder against the brightly covered wall. "Playing Alice from *The Brady Bunch*," she said.

"Yeah, Kelli is at my house doing the same," he said.

Lisha stiffened. "Your sister is in town . . . again," she said lightly, even as her hand clenched and unclenched the rubber gloves until water was wrung and splattered against the hem of her pants and the floor.

"Yeah, she's staying with me this time though."

Lisha rolled her eyes. "Isn't that nice, coming all the way from Greer to clean up her brother's house," Lisha said. "Isn't she . . . something?"

The line went quiet.

Lisha didn't bother to fill it with words.

"Are you coming by the house?" he asked. "Kelli's cooking."

"Oh, not her world-famous peach cobbler again," she said, unable to hide the tinge of sarcasm.

"Lisha," Kael said.

"And did she arrange for Bea to come by again and put on another strip show?" she asked.

Silence again.

And again Lisha let it remain that way.

"I told you I asked Kelli about it, and she hated that Bea did that just as much as we did," he said.

"I thought you were a smart man, Kael Strong," she said, massaging her forehead with her fingers.

"Are you calling me dumb?"

"When it comes to your sister . . . yes," she said, not backing down.

"I'll let you get back to your housework," he said, his voice hard.

"And I'll let you and your sister get back to playing house," she snapped, her anger rising.

"I know damn well you're not accusing me—"

Lisha slammed the phone down and then slammed it again. To be honest, she had yet to release the anger she felt over Bea's intrusion in their lives last week, and because of it things were strained between her and Kael.

Needing to be free of the apartment, she grabbed her short leather trench and the hamper of laundry before heading down to her car. She saw Logan's cane on the backseat. He'd ordered a new one through the clinic and Lisha had brought it home for him the day before.

Climbing into her car, she headed to Holtsville first. She figured if Kelli was in town she wanted to avoid her, and since she was at Kael's trying to show him just how much he didn't need Lisha, it was the opportune time to drop in on Logan and get back to Walterboro.

Lisha's annoyance burned her stomach and didn't ease off even when she pulled her Nova in front of Logan's house fifteen minutes later. Leaving the car running, she grabbed the cane and rushed through the cold winds to the front door. She knocked.

She was about to open the door when Logan opened it instead. He waved her in and turned as he coughed into his handkerchief. "You still got that cold?" she asked, eyeing him.

Logan nodded as he folded the handkerchief.

Lisha's heart double pumped in alarm as she thought she spotted blood mingled in with the mucus in the handkerchief. She set the cane on the sofa and came over to stand by him, pressing a hand to his forehead and tilting his head back to look into his eyes. They were cloudy.

Logan chuckled weakly. "I'm fine," he said, trying to raise his hand to brush hers away.

He tried and failed. He was weak.

Lisha rushed into his bedroom and grabbed a pair of shoes from the floor of his closet and a winter coat. She spotted sweater hats on the top shelf and grabbed one of those as well and the blanket folded across the foot of his bed.

Heading back into the living room, she set the shoes on the floor. "Let's go, Mr. Strong," she said.

"Go where?" he said.

"The hospital," she said, her voice firm because she knew his stubbornness and resolve were firm as well.

"For what? A cold?" he asked, moving his feet when she kneeled down to put his shoes on them.

"Pneumonia . . . I think. But I don't know for sure," she said, holding his wrist as she stared up at him. "I do know it's more than a cold."

Logan opened his mouth.

Lisha shook her head. "Sometimes you got to know when to hold 'em and when to fold 'em, Mr. Strong," she said. "It's time to fold. *Please* let's go."

"You're wasting your time," he said, bending to reach for his shoes and slide them on his feet by himself.

"Any time I spend with my favorite ex-client is not a waste," she said.

"Future daughter-in-law," he corrected her before another round of coughs.

Lisha didn't respond as he stood and she handed him his coat to slide over his ever-present Dickies uniform. She noticed him wince when he raised his arms. "I'll call your kids," she said, turning to the end table to pick up the black rotary phone.

Logan made his way to the door.

Kael's line rung endlessly, but no one picked up. "Kelli's not answering at Kael's and he's probably outside."

"Kelli's at Kael's?" Logan asked as they left the house.

Lisha bit her lip to keep from saying something smart. "Yes, sir, she must have gone straight there because I know if she saw you like this she would've taken you to the hospital too."

A few steps from the car Logan stumbled forward and fell onto the hood. "So weak," he admitted, his breathing labored.

Lisha rushed to his side and tried her best to help him stand upright, but Logan Strong was tall and sizeable and his weakened state made his body like deadweight.

"Can't . . . breathe," he said, closing his eyes as he let his forehead rest against the rumbling hood.

Lisha covered him with the blanket she still held and rushed into the house to call for an ambulance and then tried Kael's number again, slamming the phone down when it was never answered.

Rushing back to his side as the winter winds continued to brutally whip around them, she prayed over and over again for the ambulance to hurry. Before it was too late.

Kael raked the stalls of the barn like a madman. He was fueled by his anger at Lisha's words. What did she want him to do, stop speaking to his own sister?

"Never," Kael mumbled.

Blood was always thicker than water.

"Here you go, Bubba."

He looked up as Kelli strolled into the barn carrying a thermos. "Thank you," he said, turning the top to take a sip of the steaming coffee straight from the thermos. "You told Daddy you was home?"

"I talked to him earlier, but I didn't tell him I was at your place," she said, stepping up on the bottom rung of the door to the stall. "I thought we'd surprise him tonight."

"How's his cold doing?" Kael asked, handing her back the thermos to finish cleaning the stalls.

"Not good. But he keeps saying he's fine," she said. "I made him some chicken noodle soup."

Kael nodded in approval.

They fell silent.

"You still working for King?" she asked, drawing her coat closer around her tall thin frame as a cool draft of wind found exposure in the wood to fill the unheated barn.

"Just part-time now," he said.

"Willie is running for the city council," she said.

Kael grunted. He paused in his raking to look at her. "I thought he said to call him Will?"

Kelli shrugged. "He lets me call him whatever I like," she said with confidence.

"I bet he does," he said.

"How's Lisha?" she asked.

Kael nodded. "She's good."

"I'm sorry again about that stunt Bea pulled," Kelli said as she climbed up in her jeans to sit on the top rung of the stall's door. "I told her about her and I told her to put her feelings for you aside because you were with Lisha now."

Kael said nothing, his thoughts still filled with concern that Lisha seemed to have something against his sister. He started to voice his concerns to Kelli but knew that might make things worse. And he wanted his only sister and the woman he planned to marry to get along.

He thought of the engagement ring nestled among his socks in the drawer of his bedroom. This last week things had been so strained between them that he put the notion of proposing aside. He didn't want the moment he proposed to be overshadowed by hard feelings by either of them.

And now he was wondering if the issue of his sister was more than he was willing to swallow for any woman.

"Lisha coming over?"

He shrugged. "Not sure," he answered.

"Everything all right?"

Kael opened his mouth and then closed it.

"Hey, you can talk to me," she said.

"Lisha doesn't think you like her," he said, looking over at his sister.

Kelli's eyes widened in surprise. "I didn't think she was the girl for you—and I still don't, to be honest. But I like her just fine," she said. "Did I do something to make her feel that way? If I did, I'm sorry."

Kael shook his head. "That mess with Bea didn't help."

"Bea?" she said. "I didn't have anything to do with that."

"I know."

Kael finished up his task and made his way to the barn door with his sister at his side.

"I hope Lisha isn't stirring up some mess to come between blood," Kelli said. "And I hope you know better than to let her."

"Maybe you two should hang out together a little more," he offered.

Kelli nodded. "Okay, if you think that will help, I'll invite her to eat or to go shopping or something."

He brought his arm up to hug his sister to his side. "I think that's perfect. Thank you, Smelly Kelli."

She pinched his cheek. "Go ahead and change and let's head to Daddy's."

They walked the lengthy distance back to the house. As soon as they walked in, the blaring of the telephone met them. "I got it. You go on up," Kelli offered, moving across the living room as Kael jogged up the stairs.

Kael took a short but steaming hot shower before changing into jeans and black turtleneck. Walking over to his dresser drawer he pulled out a pair of black socks and his hand brushed against the black velvet of the box holding Lisha's engagement ring. He picked it up and pressed his thumb against it to pop it open. The round half-carat solitaire gleamed on the thin gold band.

He would have loved to afford a bigger ring to

truly reflect the bigness of his love, but he knew Lisha would love it just the way he knew she loved him. Stroking the diamond with his calloused thumb, he wanted to see it on her finger never to be removed until the one day he could afford bigger and better.

He wanted Lisha Rockmon to be his wife. The mother of his children. The one he spent the rest of his life with.

Then just ask her.

Once Lisha and he were back on solid ground, he planned to do just that. They were the only ones keeping him from claiming his destiny. Not his sister or anyone else. Closing the box he shoved it back amongst his socks.

Knock-knock.

"Come in," he called out, pulling on his socks.

The door opened and Kelli stepped inside, still in her coat. "Daddy's in the hospital," she said, her face lined with worry.

Kael dropped the leather ankle boot he'd just picked up. "What happened?" he asked.

"Lisha called and said she had an ambulance rush him to the hospital and we should hurry up and get there," she said.

Kael jerked on the boots and quickly zipped them before grabbing his leather coat from the closet. "Let's go," he said.

"I already got my car running," she said, rushing down the stairs with Kael close behind her.

They left the house and climbed into Kelli's VW Beetle. "Is it his hip?" Kael asked. "How did Lisha find him? Was he in Walterboro?"

Kelli's knuckles were nearly white from clutching the steering wheel tightly as she drove. "All I know for sure is it has to do with that cold being worse than we thought," she said.

Kael nodded and fell silent.

The sun was just beginning to set and the skies were darkening from a deep blue and lavender to ebony as they made their way up Highway 17. Kael was anxious to get there, but didn't bother to urge his sister to drive her little car any faster. She was going as fast as she could with the line of cars ahead of them.

When they finally pulled into the small parking lot of the county hospital, Kael remembered the day he came there all those months ago. "Daddy must be sick if he let them bring him here," he said as they rushed into the emergency department.

The same nurse was at the desk, and when she spotted them she stood up. "He's here this time," she said.

"You remember me?" he asked.

"Who could forget you?" she said, pointing

behind him to the door. "The second room through that door. His daughter is with him."

Kelli pierced the woman with her eyes. "I'm his *only* daughter," she snapped.

Kael stopped and turned to grab his sister's elbow. "The woman with him is my wife," he lied, before steering his sister through the door. He knew Lisha lied about being his father's daughter because only close family would be allowed.

Lisha was standing outside the closed curtain of the room and she looked relieved at the sight of them. Running into Kael's arms, she hugged him close. "Thank God," she sighed.

"What happened?"

Lisha stepped back from Kael, wringing her hands. "I went by his house to take the cane and he didn't look good and I thought it could be pneumonia—"

"Pneumonia!" Kelli exclaimed.

"I walked him to the car to bring him to the hospital and he got really weak so I called an ambulance," she said, still wringing his hands.

Kelli moved to open the curtain but Lisha reached out a hand to stop her. "They asked me to step out while they examined him," she explained.

Kelli brushed away Lisha's touch before wrapping her own arms around herself. "I'm going to find a phone to call Will," she said, before turning to open the door and disappear through it.

The curtain was pulled back. A short pudgy woman with reddish hair waved them in.

"I'll go find Kelli," Lisha offered.

Kael nodded as he stepped inside the small examination room. His father was on the bed with the head positioned up. He had on an oxygen mask and his eyes were closed as he struggled to breathe.

"I'm Dr. Horowitz," she said.

"I'm Kael. Kael Strong. His son," he said, feeling completely rocked by the sight of his father.

"We're going to run some blood tests to confirm, but I believe your father has congestive heart failure and my exam leads me to think he may have some pretty serious heart damage as well," she said.

Kael locked his knees when he felt them weaken. He glanced at his father and felt a pang of hurt to find his father's eyes open and resting on him. He stepped closer to the bed. "So it's not pneumonia?" he asked, resting his hand on his father's arm.

"No, the symptoms for both are very similar. All of the coughing is caused by a buildup of fluid in the lungs, but regardless, it is a good thing your sister called the ambulance and got him in here as quickly as she could," she said. "I'm having him moved to ICU, and as soon as I get the labs back I will come to his room and talk to you. Okay?"

The curtain opened and a nurse entered. He looked on as she began to draw blood from his father.

Lisha looked around the small waiting room as she stepped through the doorway. She spotted Kelli just as she was turning away from the pay phone on the wall. Lisha made her way over to her.

"Kael's in the room—"

Kelli brushed past her and raced through the door.

Lisha paused and tried her best not to feel slighted. She tried and failed, but she still set it aside as she made her way to the door.

"Your husband is delicious looking."

Lisha stopped and looked at the nurse. "My husband?" she asked, not really focused because of her concern over Logan.

"The young man with the silver hair," she said. "Good pick."

Lisha just smiled a bit and kept on to through the door and to the exam room, not knowing or caring what the other woman was talking about.

She was just passing the row of curtain-covered rooms when Kael and Kelli stepped past the curtain of Logan's exam area.

Kael looked past his sister at Lisha, causing the other woman to look over her shoulder to see what had caught her brother's attention. At the sight of Lisha she eyed her up and down and rolled her eyes before turning back to Kael.

Lisha reached them and stretched up her arm to lightly tap Kelli's shoulder. "Do you have a problem with me?" she asked her.

Kelli turned. "Excuse me?" she asked with attitude.

"Lisha," Kael said, his voice and eyes concerned.

She ignored him. "I said, 'Do you have a problem with me?'" she repeated.

"Are you kidding me right now?" Kelli snapped. "You have the audacity to question me like that right outside where *my* father is laying up in a hospital fighting for his life? Are you crazy?"

"I am well aware of where we are and why since I had sense enough to recognize that *your* father needed medical attention," Lisha told her coldly. "And I ask again. Do you have a problem with me?"

Kael stepped in between them and looked down at Lisha. "Is now the time for this? What are you doing, baby?" he asked, his voice low.

Lisha leaned past him to continue to eye Kelli, some of her anger being fueled by the stunt Bea had pulled last week. "And my question remains," she said, waving her hand.

Kael sidestepped in front of her. "Lisha," he said, his voice filled with warning.

She leaned to the left of him. "Maybe if you

were more focused on *your* father and less focused on minding your brother's business you would have known he was sick."

Kelli gasped in shock.

Two of the hospital nurses stepped up. "We have other patients here," one of the nurses said.

Kael grabbed Lisha's upper arms. "Stop it," he said shortly.

"What did I do to deserve her attacking me like that, Kael?" Kelli said, her voice pained.

He turned to his sister and hugged her close to his side.

Lisha threw her hands up at how gullible he was.

"If you had carried your sneaky behind straight to *your* father's house, you could have seen he was sick," Lisha continued even as Kael stopped comforting his sister to guide her to the door.

Lisha snatched away from him as she glared. She pushed past him to walk to Logan's room. His eyes were still closed, but she slid her hand into his and pressed a kiss to his brow.

"What? Is she attacking Daddy now?" she heard Kelli say from beyond the curtain.

Her anger dissipated. "I'm sorry. I shouldn't have made a scene. I was wrong. I hope you feel better soon, but I'm going now. I love you, Mr. Strong," she said, pressing another kiss to his forehead.

She turned and his hand tightened on hers.

Lisha's eyes filled with tears. Of regret. Of shame. Of anger. Of sadness.

She eased her hand from his and turned just as Kael and Kelli stepped into the room. Shaking her head at the pain of Kael escorting her out, she didn't even look at him as she passed him. "Your sister believes she is your everything. Maybe you believe that too. Either way, there's no room for me in your life, not with her around," she said softly before leaving them behind.

Chapter 17

One month later

Kael didn't how long he sat in his father's room the day of his passing. And now nearly a week later he was back in his father's room. He just wanted to feel close to his father again. He wanted to pretend that on that day his father was alive and well and he was just waiting for him to come home. He wanted to pretend the yard was not filled with those who came to pay their respects at the setting up in the days before his funeral.

He didn't want to face the fact that his father had gone on to heaven.

Releasing a shudder filled with grief, Kael hunched his shoulders and rocked as his tears fell and his sadness nearly choked him. His heart—his soul—were broken.

With his eyes filled with tears, he reached for the photo of his parents and only took a little solace in the fact that at least his parents were together in the afterlife. As good as the thought of that was, he'd rather have his father here with him.

"I'm real proud of you, son. Real proud."

As his father's words that day on the ranch came back to him, another wave of grief swallowed him like a tide and he cried some more. He mourned some more.

He had been with his father when Logan Strong took his last laboring breath. His congestive heart failure had led to a heart attack that weakened his heart muscle beyond repair. During the last couple weeks after being admitted to ICU, the doctors had been clear that his days were numbered.

Still, Kael was not prepared for his father's death. Everything had happened so quickly between his illness and his death. There was no time to grieve and prepare. To recover and heal.

Knock-knock.

Moments later the door opened and Kelli stuck her head inside. "Kael, all of your friends from the hunting club and the Cattleman's Association are here," she said, her eyes just as swollen and red with tears as his own.

He nodded and set the picture on the bed before rising to follow her out of the house. He didn't bother with a coat even though the February night was still chilly. The cold actually kept him from feeling numb.

Having a wake of sorts every night up until the

funeral was a Southern tradition. And so as it had
been since the night of his father's death, the yard
was filled with people talking and reminiscing
about his father, a large can filled with burning
wood to help warm them. Many were eating of
the food their plenty of friends and family had
brought for just that reason.

"Kael, you have to eat something."

He looked down at Bea standing there holding
a plate filled with fried chicken and fried fish and
plenty of side dishes.

Kael was far from hungry. "No, thank you, Bea,"
he said politely, walking away from the woman he
still considered a big instigator in the demise of his
relationship.

He mingled with the many clusters of people,
hearing over and over again how sorry they were
for his loss and how good a man his father was.
Was. Dead and gone. Never to be again.

Needing a break, he walked to the road where
cars where lined up and down as far as his eyes
could see. He stopped when he spotted Lisha's red
Nova parked on the side of the road as well.

He was filled with surprise and anger all at once.

He turned to head back into the yard and there
she stood. His gut clenched at how beautiful she
looked. "What are you doing here?" he asked
coldly, reaching for his anger.

Lisha took a few steps closer to him. "I wanted

to let you know how sorry I am about your father's passing," she said.

He looked away at some spot he never focused on down the road. "Too little, too late," Kael said, looking at her and forcing himself not to take in that her eyes were puffy, reddened from tears and filled with sorrow.

"What do you mean?" she asked, shoving her hands into the pockets of the floor-length down coat she wore.

"Just go away, Lisha," he bit out between clenched teeth, his eyes flashing with anger.

"Kael," she gasped softly in pain and surprise.

"Go wherever you been for the last month."

"You made your choice that day and I respected your wishes," she said.

"I made a choice? What choice?" he snapped. "Between you and my sister?"

"Between the truth and a façade," she snapped back.

The air around them crackled with electricity that used to be centered on their desire and now was brimming with their anger and hurt.

"Look, I should have waited to address your sister and I apologize for letting my anger mess with what I know is right and wrong," she said, coming closer and pressing her hand on his upper arm.

"You damn right you should apologize, Lisha," he said, moving his arm from her grasp.

Lisha held her hands up. "And you have to respect why I was angry even if I expressed it at the wrong time," she stressed.

Kael closed his eyes and let his head fall back before looking down at her again. "I needed you and you were not there for me," he said bitterly, his eyes filled with tears he would not let fall as he pointed his finger at her accusingly.

"I was at that hospital every day to see your father—"

He shook his head. "*I* needed you," he stressed again, this time angrily poking his finger into her chest.

"Kael, I didn't know that," Lisha said, her face filled with sorrow as her tears fell. "I thought you didn't want me there. I called and you never called back. I left a letter in your mailbox and you never answered. That's why I waited until you and your sister were not there to visit your father. I tried, Kael."

"Well, you didn't try hard enough," he said, brushing past her.

"Kael!" Lisha called.

He ignored her and quickly maneuvered through the crowd to enter the house and slam the door shut.

Lisha turned and watched him stalk away from her, her mouth open wide in shock. She coughed when she thought she felt a tiny bug fly in and hit her tongue. She was still coughing and sputtering as she crossed the yard following his path.

"Excuse me?"

Lisha stopped as Bea suddenly stepped in front of her. She frowned and extended her arm to move her out of the way without saying a word. At the feel of a hand on her wrist, she snatched it away and turned to face Bea with a glare. "Don't put your hands on me," she said in a low voice, glad they were away from the crowd and not causing a scene.

"Acting a fool at the hospital wasn't enough for you?" Bea snapped.

Lisha closed her eyes and laughed a bit. "Am I all you and Kelli have to talk about?" she asked. "Oh, no wait, wait, wait, wait . . . . you two also plot how to trap Kael into doing something he *obviously* doesn't want to do."

"You're not wanted here," Bea stressed.

"And you're not wanted in Kael's bed, his life or his heart," she said with emphasis and a hard glint to her eyes. "Whether you and Kelli are willing to swallow that or not doesn't matter to me . . . or to him for that matter."

Lisha turned and finished her trek across the yard. She wanted to talk to Kael. To make things right with Kael. To be there for Kael.

Kelli stepped in front of her on the porch,

crossing her arms over her chest as she looked down at Lisha. She opened her mouth.

"MOVE," Lisha said in a hard voice she barely recognized as her own.

Kelli opened her mouth again.

"NOW," she said in frustration, stepping up onto the step.

Kelli jumped a bit and then stepped aside.

Lisha continued up the stairs, her emotions causing her nostrils to flare and her chest to heave as she entered the house. But at the door she stopped, amazed that she could still smell Logan's cologne. Still feel his presence. Still see his things about the house just as he left them.

Mr. Strong's dead.

She gasped deeply as a wave of pain and loss overwhelmed her. Her hand grasped the doorknob tightly as she leaned her body heavily against the door. It was hard to step into his home and know he would never walk through his own door again.

Lisha's shoulders slumped and she dropped her head as tears raced down her cheeks. "Damn," she whispered. "Damn."

Gathering her strength she quickly crossed the living room and rushed down the hall and into the bathroom. She closed the lid on the commode and sat down on it, unrolling tissue to swipe at her eyes.

Losing Logan and having Kael leave her life

was a lot to bear and her shoulders were weighed down with the burden. And so she allowed herself the type of cleansing cry that she needed to release some of the pressure of the last month.

She had missed Kael—and when he rejected her when she reached out to him to reconcile it had tore at her soul.

She missed Logan. Although she had a great relationship with her father, Mr. Logan made her feel like he genuinely liked her and was silently rooting for her and Kael to fall in love. For that she had simply adored him.

And she cried some more. She really didn't know how much time had passed until she finally swiped away the last of that bout of tears and stood. She smiled sadly as her eyes fell on Mr. Logan's bottle of Old Spice cologne.

She sniffed as she checked her reflection. Her eyes were swollen and red. Her nose felt stuffed. *A mess. A heartbroken mess.*

Opening the door she stepped into the unlit hall. "You okay?"

Turning in surprise, she held her breath at the sight of Kael leaning in the doorway of his old bedroom. She took steps towards him as she nodded.

He nodded roughly and then stepped inside his room and firmly shut the door before she could even reach it. "Kael," she said softly, moving the last few steps to lightly touch the door.

She patted the wood a few times. "You know I

love you but how can I be there for you if you won't let me?" she asked, her heart pounding.

Lisha pressed her forehead against the door. "Kael?" she called out to him. "I miss him too, Kael."

She closed her eyes and shook her head as she turned to press her back to the door. "And I miss you, Kael. I miss you," she admitted, her voice showing her torture.

"We both have to forgive," she said. "I'm willing if you are."

When nothing but the silence remained, Lisha released a short shaky breath before she pushed up off the door and walked down the hall and out of the house.

Kael had paced as much as he could inside his childhood bedroom until the anger he felt for Lisha subsided. He thought he might pace until he began to wear a hole in the floor. Seeing her again had caught him off guard and he hated that even in the midst of his anger he wanted to hold her close and kiss her. And that made him angrier.

In truth he walked away from her to keep himself from reaching her.

Lisha hurt him by causing a scene at the hospital and then retreating from him when he needed her most. But he still wanted her and loved her. The last month had done nothing to squash that.

Nothing at all.

Just last week he had been running errands in town and spotted her walking out of the Piggly Wiggly supermarket. The sight of her held him so captive that he sat in his truck and eyed her every step until she finally loaded her grocery bags into the trunk of her car and then pulled away. He felt the loss of her from his life so intensely in that moment . . . just as he had tonight.

Kael swung at the air, clenching and unclenching his fist. Needing to be free of the room that suddenly felt like a cage, he turned and snatched open the door. He had just passed the bathroom when he stopped and turned to stand by the closed door.

Someone was crying—deep heart-wrenching tears that caused an ache in him. He raised his hand to knock but pulled back, not sure he wanted the burden of comforting someone when he felt so lost and alone himself.

The person whimpered and his brows dipped. "Lisha?" he mouthed.

A deep pang hit his heart. The sound of her tears tore at him. He wanted to comfort her. He couldn't leave her completely alone.

Not the way she left him.

Stepping back from the door, he released a heavy breath as he leaned against the door frame of the bedroom. Long moments passed until the door finally opened. His gut clenched as she stepped into the hall.

"You okay?" he asked.

Lisha turned. Her face was filled with surprise at the sight of him. She took steps towards him as she nodded.

She's so damn beautiful.

As his heart betrayed his anger, Kael nodded roughly and then stepped inside his room. He shut the door, needing a physical barrier between them because the emotional one he fought so hard to maintain was failing him.

Kael dropped down on the edge of his bed and wiped his face with his hands. His anger at Lisha had subsided but the hurt he felt still remained. He wished she would just go home and leave him be . . . just as she left him during the weeks of his father's illness.

"Kael."

He looked up at the door at the sound of her voice coming through it. After a month apart, Lisha was just a couple of feet and a few inches of wood away from him.

Pat-pat-pat.

"You know I love you but how can I be there for you if you won't let me?" she asked.

Kael stood up and took the few steps to stand by the door. He started to say: "Why was a stupid argument with my sister more important than being there for me?" But he didn't. He just turned and pressed his back to the door visualizing her on the other side.

"Kael?" she called out again. "I miss him too, Kael."

He grimaced and shook his head.

"And I miss you, Kael. I miss you."

I miss you too.

"We both have to forgive," she said. "I'm willing if you are."

Kael's thoughts shifted to his father's death and he just didn't have the energy or the will to deal with Lisha. He missed his father and that was a bigger hurdle he had to cross than a relationship.

At her continued silence, he opened the door.

The hallway was empty. Lisha was gone.

"You ready?"

Lisha nodded at her reflection as she turned away from her mirror, dressed in a simple black dress with a veiled hat. She smiled at Junie, who stood in the doorway also dressed solemnly in a black pantsuit. She nodded at her cousin as she left her bedroom. Her parents stood up from the sofa and turned to eye her with concern.

"I really thank y'all for going with me," she said, before her lips quivered and tears fell.

Her mother came from around the couch and hugged her close. "We know you really cared for

Kael's father and that love doesn't go away because you and Kael . . ."

The rest of her mother's words faded and the reminder that her time with the man she loved had come to an end intensified her pain and grief. She pressed her wet face into her mother's neck and enjoyed the feel of being soothed by rocking like a child. "Aw, Mama," she wailed, her voice breaking.

Everything had just gone horribly wrong all at once.

When she left that day in the hospital, she never thought it would truly be the last time she laid eyes on Kael for nearly a month, but after trying so hard to call him and write to him, and to never get a response, she assumed she was the last person he wanted to lay eyes on. And so she made sure he didn't.

The bitter irony of finally finding a man who loved her in spite of her faults, and to love her in spite of her vow to remain a virgin, and to have that all ended over something so silly as his conniving sister. The last month of her life had been pure hell. She barely ate and she hardly stopped crying.

"We better go if we want to get a seat," her father said, coming over to rub and pat her back.

Lisha nodded and stepped back to open her purse and pull out a handkerchief. But then that reminded her of the day she found Mr. Strong sick at his house, and the grief of his death was fresh all over again. Her tears fell anew.

Her father guided her out the door and down the stairs to the Buick, helping her inside the rear before opening her mother's door and then moving to the driver's seat. Once Junie climbed in beside her, her cousin took her hand in hers and held it tightly.

She had only known Mr. Strong for a little over seven months but she missed him already and she knew Kael had to be racked with even more grief than she could even imagine.

Lisha honestly didn't know if more of her tears were for the loss of Mr. Strong or for the loss to her life of his son. Her regrets were many.

I needed you and you were not there for me.

Guilt floated over her and all of the emotions made her feel drained and weak and tired. She let her fixation of his blind trust of his sister cloud her better judgment: first by arguing with Kelli at the hospital and then by staying away from him.

As her father parked outside Holtsville Baptist Church, Lisha wiped her eyes and sniffled before she lowered the veil of her hat over her eyes.

There was already a large crowd of people outside the church waiting for the church staff to open the doors and allow them entrance. Lisha barely paid attention to where they moved as she blindly followed her father. Several people murmured and whispered as she passed. She ignored them.

She was here to say good-bye to a good man. Trying to reason with Kael wasn't even on her agenda.

Lisha looked up at the skies. They were cloudy with no sign of the sun, casting the morning in shadows. She felt like that gray sky.

The processional led by the funeral home's Cadillac hearse turned into the parking lot. The hearse pulled up near the church and the men inside it climbed out to remove the casket as the family and those in the cars following were arranged behind it. The doors to the church opened but the crowd was kept at bay with a clear path made.

Lisha rested her head on her father's shoulder as Kelli's husband climbed out before helping her. Kael exited through the other door of the family car and came around to join them, looking handsome but solemn in a black suit, tie and shirt.

As they came up behind the men holding the all-white casket, Kelli leaned on her husband for support, but Kael stood alone.

Lisha closed her eyes, unable to take the sadness she saw on his face.

I needed you and you were not there for me.

Inside the church the organist began to play "At the Cross."

The family and those who followed the family

car in the processional moved forward. Lisha
opened her eyes and they fell directly on Kael.

I needed you and you were not there for me.

His eyes stayed locked on her.

"I love you," she mouthed to him. "I'm sorry."

Kael looked away from her.

Lisha closed her eyes and pressed her face into
her father's shoulder. He brought his hand up to
pat the back of her head comfortingly. "He's griev-
ing. Give him time," her father whispered to her.

I needed you and you were not there for me.

Lisha felt a hand wrap around her wrist and pull
her. She opened her eyes and was surprised to see
Kael reaching across his sister for her. Her father
pressed a hand to the small of her back and
nudged her forward.

Lisha fought back more tears and she tightly
clasped Kael's hand and let him pull her past his
sister and brother-in-law to walk inside the church
at his side.

That night, long after the funeral-goers had enjoyed the repast and said their good-byes to Kael,
Kelli, Will, and Lisha, she lay beside him on his
bed, looking down into his face. His eyes were
closed and she assumed he was asleep.

"I knew you were coming to visit him."

Lisha was surprised by his sudden words and by
his knowledge. She pressed a hand against his

heart as he turned his head to look at her. The intensity of the brown depths held her captive. "How'd you know?" she asked.

"The nurses told me."

She nodded and said nothing, waiting for whatever else he had to say.

"I sat at that hospital damn near all day except the hour I would come home to change clothes and check on the ranch," he said, emotion filling his eyes. "That hurt even more that you were going out of your way not to see me."

"I was hurting too, Kael, and I should have put that aside, but I honestly did not think he was going to pass away," she said, her voice breaking with emotion.

"The second heart attack was too much," he said, looking away from her.

Thinking he was pulling away again, she raised her hand.

Kael covered her hand with his own and pressed it back down onto his chest. "I miss my father."

Lisha inched her body closer to his and pressed her head to his shoulder with her hand still under his over his heart. "I know you do," she said softly.

"Why did you flip like that in the hospital?" he asked.

Lisha closed her eyes and released a breath. "Kael, not now. Not today," she pleaded wearily.

"Yes. Today. Now," he stressed.

She looked down at him. "I was hurt because

you refused to see the things your sister was doing to come between us, and I decided that I didn't want to constantly have her invading in our lives. I just was fed up, Kael."

"I think you are wrong about Kelli," Kael said.

"No, I think you're wrong about Kelli," she countered. "How can you ever fix it and make it right if you stay—"

Lisha sat up and removed her hand from over his heart. "No. No," she said again, shaking her head as she rose to her feet. "Logan was your father but I loved him too. So no, I'm not doing this. Not today. Not now."

She moved to the door.

"So you're leaving me again?"

Lisha paused at the door, resting her forehead against the cool wood. She turned her head to look at him, the side of her face now pressed against the wood. "Why can't you see the truth? Why don't you believe me?" she said in a harsh whisper filled with emotion.

Kael sat up on the edge of the bed. "Why do you want to come between me and my sister?" he asked.

Lisha went absolutely weak with disappointment and regret. "Is that the kind of person you think I am? Is that what you believe about me? Then you never knew me and you can't love someone you don't know."

Kael snatched off his blazer and balled it to

throw to the floor. "Don't tell me I don't love you," he roared, jumping to his feet to stalk over to her.

Lisha pressed her back to the door and looked up at him with trepidation in her eyes.

He saw her uneasiness. Bringing his hands up, he lightly grasped her face as he bent his knees to align his face with hers. "I love you," he whispered fiercely before pressing heated kisses to her face and then her mouth.

Lisha gasped at the passion and emotion she felt, bringing her hands up to clutch at his shirt as she tilted her head up to expose the smooth length of her neck.

He lifted her by her waist as he stood up straight. He did kiss her neck and lick the hollows of her clavicle. "God, I missed you," he moaned against her caramel skin.

Lisha nodded as she shivered, unable to believe the sweet heat of being in his arms again. Kissed by him again. Touched by him again.

Loved by him again.

The issue with Kelli was far from over, but in the heated moments of their reunion it didn't matter.

Kael picked her up into his arms. She wrapped her legs around his waist as he carried her into his adjoining bathroom. "What are you about to do?"

"Wash you," he said, setting her on her feet again.

"Kael—"

"The rules have not changed," he assured her.

Lisha licked her lips as she stood there as Kael slowly undressed her until she stood before him nude. She reached up and loosened her hair from the chignon she wore, not embarrassed for his eyes to take her all in.

And he did eye her hotly as he moved away just long enough to turn on the shower, snap back the plastic curtain and rush out of his own clothing.

She pressed her thighs together to ease the throbbing of her clit as she enjoyed the hard brown contours of his muscled frame and the curving length of his dick. "We can't keep playing with fire," she said even as she let him lead her into the shower to step under the spray.

"I can't help myself," he told her, holding her around the waist before he stepped back directly under the spray, causing the water to come down on them as he kissed her.

Chapter 18

One month later

Kael looked on as the last of the boxes were placed on the back of the truck of the charity to whom they donated a lot of their father's belongings. They picked the items they wanted to cherish, gave away most of the furniture to close family and friends and donated the rest. His sister had come down from Greer for the weekend just to get the task completed. They both thought it silly for so many of his things to go to waste when they both already owned their own homes.

Plus they discovered their father had taken a second mortgage out on the home, and instead of losing the house or taking on the payments they decided to rent it out and let it pay for itself. Kael didn't mind; he preferred for it not to sit empty because it would surely rot away in time.

A house not in use is a house that dies.

Kael was still standing at the door when he spotted his sister's car turn onto the drive. He knew Bea was still with her and he was ready to be away from the woman. He still didn't appreciate how she'd invaded and violated his home and his relationship with Lisha, but she was his sister's friend and he tolerated her because he assumed his sister needed her support.

Walking out of the house, he headed to his truck.

"You leaving, Kael?" Bea called over to him. "We got Kentucky Fried Chicken."

"No, thanks," he said. "Kelli, stop by the house before you head home."

With that said, he closed the door, cranked his truck and reversed down the drive as they walked into the house. He braked at the end of the drive, remembering that he'd left behind the box of items of his father's that he wanted to keep.

Shifting gears, he drove forward and parked, leaving the truck running as he jogged up the drive and opened the door.

"I can't believe he's still with her."

Kael paused at the sound of his sister's voice.

"You would be so much better for him than her phony behind."

He frowned.

"Yeah, like when you heard her on the phone lying about being a virgin," Bea said. "Like who believes *that* shit?"

Kael's eyes widened in surprise as he stood there listening.

"If that was true, he should be good and ready for some and he would've went for it if she wasn't at his house that day."

"I know that's right," Bea said. "But don't worry, I am not done with that fine-ass brother of yours."

"You better not be," Kelli said.

Kael strolled into the kitchen and leaned against the doorframe. "You two hens done clucking over my personal life?" he asked.

They both jumped around in their seats at the table to look up at him with their mouths wide open.

Kael ignored Bea and leveled his eyes on his sister. "Good-bye Bea," he said in a hard voice as his eyes glittered with anger.

Bea stood up and stepped close to him. "Kael, I—"

"You are irrelevant," he told her, his eyes still on a guilty-looking Kelli. "You are unwelcome. You are on your way out the door on your own before I put you out."

Bea turned and picked up her purse and her keys. "I'll call you later, Kelli," she said before easing past Kael and exiting the house.

He said nothing and continued to stare at his sister.

Kelli set her plastic fork down on her paper

plate of chicken, potato salad and coleslaw. "Kael, I was looking out for you," she began.

"Wrong words," he stressed. "Try again."

"I'm not apologizing for looking out for you."

"One more shot," he said.

"And then what?" she asked. "Are you going to stop speaking to your own sister?"

Kael said nothing more and just turned to walk away from her. He was so disgusted he didn't even bother retrieving the box he came back into the house to retrieve. *I'll get it after she's gone.*

"Kael," she called out.

He stopped at the door and turned.

Kelli stood up and flailed her hands. "What's so special about her?"

"I love her and that should be enough for you," he said fiercely. "The same way your pompous, arrogant, blow-hard, tight-assed, braggart of a husband is good enough for me because you love him."

Kelli slumped down into her chair and swept her arm across the table, sending her plate of food flying against the door of the fridge. "You're wrong about her," she said.

Kale stormed back into the kitchen. "No, you are, and if you want any kind of relationship, then you better get off your position and tell me why you did this childish bullshit."

Kelli closed her eyes and pinched the bridge of her nose.

"I'm walking out this door."

"I have been there for you and Daddy since Mama died," she began, her eyes filling with tears. "And now she appears and all of a sudden neither one of you needs me. Just to hell with me. It's all about Lisha, Lisha, Lisha."

Kael sat down in the chair Bea had vacated. "You try to ruin my happiness because you're jealous of her?" he roared, slamming his hand down on the table.

Kelli swiped away her tears. "It was like Daddy wished she was his daughter and it hurt, okay?" she admitted, shifting her gaze away from him.

Kael sat back in the chair and strummed his fingers against the tabletop as he shook his head in disbelief.

I called and you never called back.

He frowned as remembered Lisha's words the night they argued at the setting up.

I left a letter in your mailbox and you never answered.

His frown deepened as he leveled his eyes on his sister. In truth, Kael had assumed all these weeks that Lisha was done with him. Had his sister orchestrated that division between them as well?

"I'm sorry," she said. "I just—"

"Lost your damn mind," he inserted.

She looked up at him with pained eyes.

"You put your own happiness ahead of mine and that hurts," he said, rising to his feet. "Our mother and father are gone. And I would never turn my back on you because we're all that we have," Kael said. "I love you and I'm going to forgive you for this, but I will marry Lisha one day. She will be the lady of our home, and if she is not ready to forgive you then I will not force her."

Kelli looked up at him.

"It is her choice if you are ever welcomed in our home. You made the bed, now lie in it," he said, turning to walk to the front door.

"Kael, you can't be serious," Kelli said, following him.

He looked out the door and never turned. "I am serious. I'll call you tonight to make sure you got home safe," he said, before walking out the door and closing it securely behind him.

Lisha pulled her car to a stop at the lone gas station in Holtsville. She smiled and waved at Cyrus as she hopped out of the car and made her way into the small store to purchase a bottle of Crush orange soda, a Snickers bar and a bag of plain potato chips. She had worked all day and barely took a break for lunch and she was starving.

She made it a habit of stopping at the store on her way home from work in Charleston. Cyrus knew everything about everybody and didn't mind sharing it. Plus, the tiny angel he whittled for her when Logan passed away had endeared the man to her. She now considered him a good friend.

"What are you working on now?" she asked, walking over to where he sat on a stool waiting for the next client who needed gas pumped.

He held up a plain band made of wood.

Lisha looked at it curiously. "What is that?"

Cyrus smiled. "A wedding band. I'm planning on asking my girl to marry me," he said.

"Your girl," she said. "I didn't know you had a girl."

Cyrus shrugged. "You never asked."

"You know what, Cyrus? You're right, I never did ask," she agreed.

"Think she'll like it?"

"I think she'll love it," she told him. "Good luck."

"Don't need it," he called back to her with a toothy grin.

Lisha climbed back into her car and headed toward the road leading to Kael's ranch. Because his sister was in town she hadn't planned on spending much time in Holtsville. He claimed to understand why she refused his suggestion that she help them pack up his father's home, but he still asked her to meet him at his house when she got off work. Even promising that his sister would not be there.

She just hoped he wasn't trying any type of sneaky moves to get them together. The issue of his sister still lingered between them and probably always would, but she wasn't willing even for him to forgive her. Not yet . . . and not without the truth of her actions and an apology.

She thought of the ring Cyrus carved for the woman he loved and wanted to marry. She wondered if the day would come when Kael would propose. She wanted nothing more than to be his wife. To love him and make love with him. To build up Strong Ranch. To have children. To create a legacy.

Maybe one day soon.

Turning down the long road leading to his house, her eyes searched the dirt-packed front yard to make sure his sister's car was not in sight, before she accelerated forward and parked. Climbing from her car she jogged up the stairs but slowed her speed at the note thumbtacked to the door.

"'Come to the cabin,'" she read aloud.

Lisha turned on the step and looked off in the distance to the path leading that way. She looked down at her uniform and sneakers, wishing she had put on jeans and boots for a trek in the woods. She came down the stairs and reached in her car for her winter coat and gloves before heading off on her journey.

It took all of fifteen minutes for her to finally see the break in the trees. Lisha was just thankful her work as a physical therapist kept her fit. Stepping off the path she walked onto the dirt-packed yard. "Kael," she called out, coming to a stop when she spotted a trail of roses leading to the front door. The wind whipped some of the roses up into the air to fall gently around.

Her heart pounded as she pushed the door open and gasped at the sight of Kael standing in the center of the flower-covered room with a ring perched between his index finger and thumb.

She barely noticed that once again he'd filled the interior of the cabin with flowers and lit candles and had a fire roaring away. Her eyes were only on him as she came to stand before him. "Kael," she said softly.

"I know you're wondering why I did this whole setup again," he began.

Lisha felt her heart melt as he looked nervous.

"I wanted to do this that night, but Bea and Kelli pulled that stupid-ass stunt and ruined every-thing."

Lisha kept the surprise from showing on her face at Kael finally acknowledging his sister's role in what Bea did.

"And then everything was weird between us after that," he explained. "And—"

"Ssssh," Lisha said, quieting him with a finger pressed to his mouth. "None of that matters now."

"It does matter because I played a role in this by not believing you about Kelli," he said, raising his free hand to lightly grasp her chin. "And I'm sorry."

"Apology accepted," she said, lifting up on her

toes to hold the back of his head as she kissed him. "And do you accept mine for the way I acted at the hospital?"

"I forgave you the moment I reached for your hand at the funeral," he told her. "Thank you for being there with me even after everything I said the night before."

"I will always be there for you. You have my word," she promised him fiercely.

"I know that and I know we haven't known each other long, but I love you. I trust you. And I want to spend the rest of my life with you."

Lisha gasped and held her breath as Kael knelt on one knee. He took her left hand in his and looked up at her with the ring poised around the tip of her finger.

"I never imagined I would love you this much," he admitted, shaking his head in wonder. "But I do, and I want to know if you would spend your life with me and continue loving me and making me a better man for you and the family we will have one day, Lisha. Will you marry me?"

Lisha dropped to her knees so that they were equals and pressed her forehead to his as she nodded with tears falling free. "Yes. Yes, I will marry you," she whispered, her voice blending with the crackle of flames in the fireplace.

Kael slid the ring onto her finger as he kissed her a dozen times. "Finally," he said, holding her close.

Lisha removed her coat, almost mistakenly

flinging it into the lit fireplace. Kael pressed kisses to her throat and above the vee of her uniform top. Needing to feel more of him, she reached down with both hands and pulled the uniform top over her head.

Kael sat back to look down at her full brown globes barely covered by white lace. It had been so long since he had been with a woman, and the fire Lisha constantly stoked in him had his mind running with wild thoughts as he lowered his head to suck one lace-covered dark nipple into his mouth.

She arched her back as she reached behind her to undo the bra and slide it over her arms.

Kael growled as he pressed his face back and forth against her soft cleavage as his hard dick nearly burst through his jeans. Quivering from wanting her so badly, he grasped both of her breasts and pushed them together to tease, suck and lick both taut nipples at the same time.

Lisha felt her panties cling to her intimacy as he made her wet from the skillful play of his tongue on her nipples. "Kael," she cried out, tugging at the hem of the sweater he wore to pull it up over his body.

Kael moved back from her long enough to jerk the sweater over his head. "Touch me," he said thickly, expanding the muscles of his chest as he stretched his arms wide and let his head fall back in surrender.

Lisha let her fingers trace the hard contours of

his chest, lightly stroking his own hard nipples before going down to the almost jagged groove of his eight-pack abdomen. She smiled and bit her bottom lip when he shivered from her touch. Feeling bold, she licked her index finger and retraced the groove before licking it again and circling his nipples.

"God, I want you," he whispered up into the heated air with his arms still open wide.

Lisha stood up and eased her uniform pants over her hips, loving the heat from the fireplace pressing against her body as she stood there in nothing but her low-slung white bikinis on her curved hips. "You like?" she asked, stretching her arms above her head.

Kael's mouth fell open at the sight of her hourglass frame and the way her nipples and aureole were much darker than the caramel complexion of her skin. "Beautiful," he moaned, unzipping his pants to free his hardness.

Lisha lay down on the thick and soft layer of petals on the floor. The embers in the fireplace reflected in her eyes as she raised her hips and removed her panties slowly.

Kael arched his hips, sending his dick against his hand as he massaged his hardness at the sight of her spreading her legs and bringing her hands up to spread the folds of her pussy.

"Make love to me, Kael," she begged him in a heated whisper.

He immediately lay down and hurriedly removed his pants and boxers. He looked down at her as the rose petals framed her body. She looked beautiful as she looked up at him, her eyes glossed over with desire and her mouth panting in anticipation. He used one strong knee to open one leg and then the other—he could feel how wet and ready she was for him to be deep inside of her.

"Kael," she gasped.

He lowered his upper body onto hers until her breasts cushioned him. Pressing sweet kisses to her cheek, he closed his eyes at the torture of being so close to being inside of her, knowing it would be sweet and wet and hot and tight. "I want to wait," he whispered into her ear, shocking himself as he refused her gift.

Kael kissed her mouth one last time and then rolled off of her, walking over to the window with his dick in his hand as he fought to stay true to his initial thought.

Lisha got to her feet and moved to him, clutching at his strong, muscled arms as she pressed her breasts against his back. "What's wrong, Kael?" she asked.

He turned and gently moved her body back from his, letting his hands stay lightly gripping her upper arms as he forced himself to look no further than her eyes. "Baby, I love you, and one of things I love about you is how you stuck to your principles—"

"But we're getting married," she explained, raising her hands to reach for him.

"But we're not married yet . . . and as badly as I want to lay on that floor and make love to you until I explode inside of you, you have come too far to give in now . . . even for me," he said.

Lisha's eyes softened with love. She started to step closer to him but covered her pendulous breasts with her upper arms before she did lean in to kiss him. "I really, really love you, Kael Strong," she said.

"And I really, really need a cold shower," he moaned against her lips.

They both broke out laughing, happy together in the midst of the strongest kind of love.

Chapter 19

One month later

"Just as beautiful as your mother."

Lisha turned away from the oval full-length cheval mirror to face her father as he stepped inside the room of the church. She smoothed her hand over the full lace skirt of her wedding dress nervously. "Think he'll like it, Daddy?" she asked, turning back to the mirror to smooth the delicate scalloped edge of the off-the-shoulder lace overlaying a sweetheart neckline.

"If he doesn't he's blind," Rev said.

"I told her she looks better in the dress than when I wore it thirty years ago," Lady said, looking quite pretty herself in a lavender tea-length dress and matching wide-brimmed hat.

Rev kissed Lisha's cheek. "I don't know about that," he said, moving to press a kiss to his wife's cheek as well.

"I got your veil," Junie said, walking into the room with the floor-length tulle floating in the air behind her.

The deep purple of Junie's maid-of-honor dress was the perfect complement to her deep brown complexion. Lisha smiled her thanks to her cousin and very best friend before turning to squat down enough for her to attach the cathedral-length lace-trimmed veil with the attached comb into Lisha's upswept hair.

Her father stepped forward to lower the front of the veil so that it covered her face. "Just beautiful," he said again, squeezing her shoulders. "It's gonna be hard to give you away at the end of that aisle and then officiate the wedding too."

Junie stepped forward with her bouquet in one hand and Lisha's in the other. "It's time," she said softly just as the organist began to play a sweet refrain.

Lisha blinked away tears and accepted the bouquet of spring flowers as her mother gave her one last hug before leaving the room to be escorted to her seat in the front row. She followed Junie and her father out of the room and down the hall leading to the front foyer of her father's church.

Two of the church's ushers dressed in all white opened the double doors that were trimmed in a beautiful mosaic stain glass. Junie stepped forward, positioned her bouquet and then disappeared into the church.

The music changed and the sounds of "Here Comes the Bride" filled the air.

Her father led her to the stand in the doorway of the open double doors.

Lisha's eyes locked on Kael as he came through a door at the rear of the church and took his spot in front of the flower-covered arch before the altar. He smiled at her, looking so handsome in his gray morning suit.

"I'm so happy," she admitted in a whisper.

"And that's all that matters," her father said, before he walked her down the petal-strewn aisle to her soon-to-be husband.

Kael smoothed the pocket flaps of his suit jacket as he stood up from the chair positioned in the center of one of the church's rooms. Dozens of other chairs suited for small children and walls covered in paper cutouts of cartoon religious figures filled the room. He reached in that pocket and pulled out one of his father's pure cotton handkerchiefs with his initials embroidered on one of the corners.

He'd wanted something—anything—of his father's to feel close to him.

Kael dug in his other pocket and removed the gold locket his sister gave him on his twenty-fifth birthday. Opening it he looked down at the black and white photo of his parents holding him and Kelli—all of them dressed to the nines—during the last Easter Sunday before their mother passed away later that year. He'd wanted something of hers close to him as well.

Sliding the locket back into his pocket, he heard the organ music begin and then after a few minutes end.

Kael took his cue and left the room to take his position at the front of the church in front of the floral arch and small table with a lit candle on it to represent the spirit of his parents.

"Here Comes the Bride" began to play and Kael looked down the long length of the flower-covered aisle to Lisha and her father taking their place in the open doorway. His heart swelled at the sight of her. He placed his hands behind his back and twisted his fingers together wishing he could run down the aisle, sweep the veil from her face and kiss her endlessly.

"Here comes *my* bride," Kael said with pride as the people filling the pews all stood and turned to watch her walk down the aisle to him.

Lisha barely heard her father's words on marriage, love and fidelity as he performed their wedding ceremony. Nothing mattered but standing before Kael with her hands in his strong grasp and her eyes locked on his eyes. She smiled as he stroked the back of fingers with his thumb.

She was just moments from him becoming her husband. *And a few hours from becoming my lover.*

The thought of that made her shiver and she bit her bottom lip lightly as she felt warmth spread across her body and her cheeks.

"Love is abiding and true and lasting. It is forgiving," her father was saying.

Kael's slanted eyes widened a bit as he studied her.

Lisha wiggled her brows at him suggestively.

His eyes darkened in understanding.

He wanted her just as badly as she wanted him. But he'd waited for her. He put his desires aside for her. And tonight they both would be blessed with a gift she wanted to share with just her husband.

Just as she would share the rest of her life with him.

Lisha felt like the luckiest woman in the world.

"I love you," she mouthed to him, easing up onto her toes in her shoes to spontaneously press a kiss to his mouth.

Her father cleared his throat. "Not yet," he said.

The wedding attendees laughed softly.

Kael licked his lips as if her kiss was sugar as he looked down at her, his heart pounding furiously in his chest. "I love you too," he mouthed back in return, his eyes taking in everything that made the beauty of her face—especially her pug little nose.

He couldn't wait until all of the fanfare was over and they could get to the most important part of him being able to call Lisha his wife. He'd never thought the whole happily ever after was in the cards for him. But here she was and they were moments from starting their life together.

And from making love together.

It's been a long time. . . .

Kael let his eyes wander down the length of her body in her gown, not caring that they were in a church and standing before her minister father. Hell, he wished they could skip the reception altogether because he very badly wanted to be buried inside his wife for the first of many, many times to come. His body was a bundle of nervous energy and pure anticipation.

He held her hands tighter and pulled her body a step closer to his.

Lisha massaged his palms with her fingertips.

Just that simple move caused his body to tense in a rush of desire for her.

It had been so long and he took pride in himself for waiting for her through every torturous moment of abstaining. It wasn't easy at all but it was what he had to do for the woman he loved.

And there was no shame in that.

* * *

"I do," they said in unison.

"Now by the power vested in me I now pronounce you husband and wife. What God has put together let no man put asunder."

As the organist began to play Barry White's "You're the First, the Last, My Everything" the wedding goers applauded.

Smiling broadly, Kael jerked Lisha forward and held her tightly around her waist as he raised her off her toes. "Hey wife," he said.

Lisha brought her hands up to clutch his face. "Hello husband," she answered softly, blinking away tears.

They blessed each other with soft pecks at first before they deepened the kiss and held each other tightly as they did.

"You have thoroughly kissed the bride, son."

Kael and Lisha shared a few more pecks in between smiles at her father's words as the church filled with laughter.

"May I be the first to introduce my daughter and my son-in-law, Mr. and Mrs. Kael Strong," Rev said.

"Welcome home, Mrs. Strong."

Lisha rested her head against Kael's broad shoulder as he carried her across the threshold of his home—*their* home. She pressed a kiss to his cheek as he lowered her to her feet and then swiftly turned her body to press her back against the wall by the closed door.

Smiling wolfishly, Kael lightly held her wrists to bring her arms high above her head on the wall. "I thought we should start right back where it all began," he said into the brief distance between them. He held both of her wrists with one hand and used the other to raise the hem of the short blue dress she'd worn to leave their reception. "Remember?"

And she did. How could she forget? Lisha gasped lightly and shivered as he lowered the rim of her lace panties to stroke her bare hip. "Think you can get me as hot as you did that day?" she asked brokenly, her half-closed eyes on him.

Kael licked his lips as he dipped his head to kiss her briefly but sweetly. "More," he promised, pulling the lace edge of her panties away from her brown flesh from one hip to the other with his index finger.

Leaning in again he kissed her deeply as he jerked her panties down. First one hip and then the other. Back and forth until the satin and lace cleared her curvy hips and thighs and finally fell down her legs to puddle around her feet.

Lisha released a guttural moan of pleasure as he stroked her tongue with his, enjoying being held in place by his strength as he used his free hand to now shift up behind her to unzip her dress. "Yes," she sighed languidly when he freed her mouth. "Yes, yes, yes."

Kael chuckled as he released her wrists and bent his legs to lower his body until he was eye level with the soft black triangular bush covering her mound. He spread her thighs and used one trembling finger to spread the lips of her pussy.

Lisha arched her back from the wall and spread her legs wider as she reached for the hem of her dress and yanked it over her head roughly to fling away without a care.

Still fully dressed in his navy blue shirt and slacks, Kael reached for one of her legs and brought it up to rest on one of his shoulders. He turned his head to press a warm and moist kiss to her inner thigh before following with a soft bite.

Lisha bit her bottom lip as her toes flexed. "Kael," she whispered hotly into the air.

A dozen different bites up her thigh led to Kael blowing a cool stream of air against her clit before he stroked the pulsing pink bud with the tip of his tongue.

Lisha arched her back again with a sharp gasp as she moved her hands to hold the back of his head.

Kael pursed his lips to pull and suck her bud, loving the slick feel of her flesh. "Uhm, tastes good," he moaned in between intimate kisses, his dick thickening and tightening as he pleasured her.

She opened her eyes and looked down at his

head buried between her thighs. "Feels good," she whispered hotly, the electricity they generated pressing against her body. "Damn good."

Kael moaned as he tasted her sweetness, bringing his hands up to massage her buttocks and lift her hips to bring her core forward. He eyed her femininity splayed before him, enjoying the womanly scent of her, and then dipped his head again to taste of her moistness.

Lisha lightly pounded the back of her head against the wall as white hot shots of electricity filled her body. She cried out. It was a wild mix of pleasure and somehow torture as she felt pushed to the edge. She knew in those electrifying moments of him pleasing her that too much of a good thing could make her straddle the line of sanity. "No, no, no, no," she begged, blindly pushing her hands against his face to free her clit from his mouth.

Kael sucked harder and deeper, soaring high off the feel of her body quivering, her moans escalating, and her clit swelling in his mouth until soon he tasted her release on his tongue.

Lisha whimpered and shivered, feeling the strength leave her body as her climax shook her emotionally and physically. "Damn," she swore softly, her heart pounding.

Kael stood to his full height and gathered her into his arms. "Now you're ready," he told her thickly, turning to carry her up the stairs.

"There's more?" Lisha asked, her voice barely above a whisper.

Kael chuckled as he reached the top step. "Much more," he promised.

She pressed a kiss to his neck just as Kael entered their master bedroom and crossed the room in three long strides to press her body down onto the bed. He kissed her lips and she tasted her intimacy when she licked away the dryness of her lips caused by their heat.

Rising, he stepped back to reveal the hard contours of his body to her with the removal of each piece of his clothing. Bit by bit. Soon he stood before her naked, the hard and curving length of his dick standing off from his body as his roaring blood caused it to throb.

Lisha sat up on her elbows, her eyes widening as she took in the length and thickness of him with a hard swallow over a sudden lump in her throat. She felt apprehension at him filling her with his inches. At him being her first and the pain she might feel. *And for how long?* she wondered, her thighs inadvertently closing.

Kael lay on the bed beside her and pulled her body against his as he stroked her back. "Don't be afraid," he assured her, having seen the trepidation on her face.

Biting her bottom lip, she reached out to take his hard heat into her hand. "You're so . . ."

He chuckled lightly. "Would you rather I wasn't?" he asked.

Lisha tilted her head up on his chest to look at his handsome face. "In the future? No. Tonight? Tonight I'm not so sure," she admitted.

Kael smiled as he pulled her entire body atop his and hoisted her up a bit so that her face was directly above his. "Kiss me," he ordered her, his words caressing her lips.

Lisha brought her hands up to press against his cheeks as she tilted her head. Licking her lips she lowered her head to outline his mouth with her tongue. When he opened his mouth a bit for her she enjoyed the feel of her tongue tangling with his. Slowly. Hotly.

They both moaned.

Kael eased his hands over the smooth expanse of her brown back and then down to enjoy the softness of her buttocks and the slight firmness of the top of her thighs.

Lisha spread her legs atop his and Kael immediately dipped his hands down to play in her slick wet folds from behind. Gasping hotly into his mouth, she tilted her head back and clutched at the covers on their bed with her fingers. "Hmmmmm," she moaned with a lick of her lips.

Kael pressed his head back into the plush pillow to peer up at Lisha's face as he filled her slowly with two of his fingers. He felt a surge of power when she writhed against him and bit her lip as she pressed her eyes closed. Lisha was a virgin but he loved the way she gave in to her instincts on the pleasure he gave her. Her face held nothing back and he knew she was just as eager to learn how to please him. He planned to spend an entire lifetime teaching her.

She sat up, pressing her hands into the mattress to steady her body as she dangled her full breasts above his face.

Kael wasted not a second raising his head to capture one taut brown nipple into his mouth. With his fingers inside of her, he felt her walls tighten and then release. He circled her nipples with his tongue, released a cool stream of air onto it and then sucked it deeply.

"Yes," she sighed in pleasure, moving her hips against his hand.

Kael's gut clenched. *She's a natural.*

Freeing his hand and then wrapping one strong arm around her waist, he quickly turned her over onto her back, pressing her body down into the softness beneath him. Gently grasping her chin, he kissed her deeply and passionately as he settled himself between her open thighs. Her hands were splayed on his back and he felt her fingertips dig deeper into him as his throbbing thick tip pressed against her moist core.

Lisha's eyes opened. Her heart pounded. Her body tensed. Her nails dug into the muscled flesh of his strong back. Her fear was fighting her desire . . . and winning.

Kael felt her resistance and pressed a dozen heated kisses against her mouth as he slid his hand under her buttocks. He was bursting with a need to be in her but he put her first and knew he had to take things slowly. Ease her worries.

She moaned in the back of her throat in pleasure, her fingers easing up from the tiny dents they made in his back. "Kael," she gasped into the heated air, her clit hot and aching from wanting him.

His kisses moved down to her earlobe and then the base of her neck as he fought to maintain control of how badly he wanted to plant himself within her. He could feel the heat of her flesh and the wetness of her earlier climax against his dick. Kael trembled with restraint as he slightly arched his hip and flexed his square buttocks to give her just the tip.

Lisha's ankles locked around his calves but she was lost in a madness created by the feel of his lips and his tongue on the pulse in her throat. She shivered. She was lost to time and place. She felt high on the purest drug.

Kael kissed a trail back up to her mouth, tracing her lips before drawing her tongue out to suckle gently in a sweet one-two motion that caused the walls now pressed around his tip to throb in a similar motion. Holding her tightly against him he opened his eyes to peer down at her as he kissed her deeply and then raised her buttocks higher off the bed as he arched his hips and entered her tightness with one swift thrust.

Lisha's eyes opened and for a second the pleasure that filled her brown depths was replaced with pain.

Kael swallowed her gasp and continued to kiss her as his strong muscled body went deathly still as he fought not to fill her with a rushed, explosive nut. He moaned as his dick throbbed inside her. She was tight. Very tight. And hot. Very hot.

Lisha's eyes locked with his even as they kissed and she smoothed her hands over the wide breadth of his back. "What's wrong?" she whispered between fevered kisses.

He raised his head and there was just millimeters between them as his eyes searched hers. He saw passion. Desire. Need. Want. "Not a damn thing," he said fiercely.

Lisha sucked his bottom lip into her mouth.

"I have dreamed of this right here, Lisha," he whispered down to her even as he began to glide his hips back and forth as he slowly made love to her for the very first time.

Lisha eased her hands down his back to fill them with his buttocks. She enjoyed the tensing and relaxing of his flesh as she got adjusted to the feel of his hardness inside her. Filling her. Spreading her. Pleasing her. "Yes," she sighed, following an instinct as she began to move her own hips in countermotion to his.

Back and forth. And back and forth again. And again. And again.

She arched her back and released a guttural cry that only hinted at the wildness he unleashed.

"Shit," Kael swore at the feel of her hands, the motion of her hips, the shiver of her body, and the glide of her walls up and down his length.

It was beyond physical. That was easy. That was common.

What they evoked for one another was pure passion. Chemistry. Heat.

They made love and nothing outside of their bedroom—their union—even mattered. Nothing at all. They were floating on intimacy fueled by love and a belief that they were meant for each other.

Lisha cried out and held Kael close as she felt her climax brewing with more intensity than a Southern summer thunderstorm.

"I'm coming with you, baby," he told her thickly, looking down into her glazed eyes as he felt his dick harden with the first rush of his come.

They held on to one another as both of their movements quickened as they rode each other to fiery white-hot spasms of release that left them both sweaty and spent. They seemed to topple off the edge together as their climaxes seemed to go on endlessly. They both enjoyed the fall with guttural cries and shivers until their bodies went slack and they both were damp with sweat.

"I . . . love . . . you," she said in between deep gasps that made her throat dry.

Kael kissed her before dropping his head onto her shoulder as his heart pounded furiously. His chest heaved with the exertion of even breathing properly. His heart pounded wildly and quickly. "I . . . I—"

Lisha rubbed the back of his calves with her feet. "Speechless?" she teased, as she wiped the sweat from her face with her hand.

His body shook with his chuckle. "I thought I would never stop coming," he said.

"Me either," she said with a soft smile.

"Hey, I'm a little backed up," he said in between kisses to her collar bone.

"Worth the wait?" she asked, bringing her hands up to massage his shoulders.

Kael raised his head and looked down at her as he nodded. "Worth the wait," he answered without a doubt before climbing off her and rising to his feet to scoop her up into his arms.

"Where are we going?" she asked, already feeling the need for a sex nap.

"Shower time," Kael said, his limp dick now hanging.

"And then?" she asked, pressing a kiss to his neck.

"And then we do it all over again," he promised. "And again. And again."

"Sounds good to me, Mr. Strong," Lisha said, her heart filling with love for him.

"Sounds even better to me, Mrs. Strong," he said, kissing her forehead before he entered the bathroom and kicked the door closed with his foot.

Epilogue

Present Day

"And that's the story of how we fell in love," Lisha said, reaching over to stroke Kael's face as she looked over at him with as much passion, love, respect and dedication as she had for him over forty years ago.

He turned his face into her hand and pressed a warm kiss to her palm.

Sometimes actions spoke much louder and clearer than just words.

"And everything we dreamed about—including having our five beautiful children—came to fruition," Lisha said, shaking her head in wonder. "So thankful, so blessed, so loved."

"Amen," Kael said, taking her hand in his to caress her wrist with his thumb.

Brian McKnight's version of the classic Christmas carol "I'll Be Home For Christmas" was the perfect tune for that moment as each of their children looked to the loves of their own lives and smiled with hopes and wishes and dreams of their own that they prayed came true as well. Especially the wish to live with their mate for the rest of their lives. A lasting love.

"So that's why you never went with us with Dad to visit Aunt Kelli?" Kade, the oldest of their children asked, filling the silence.

Lisha smiled sadly. "We just never got our relationship back on track but I never wanted to keep you all from your aunt. She's your family," she said, reaching over to squeeze her husband's hand because she knew that even after these years he wanted so much unity in the family.

But he kept his word and never pressed her to forgive Kelli or to welcome her into their home. As the years went by it had just become easier for them to never cross paths.

"That turkey should be ready, so let's all go to the dining room and have dinner," Lisha said, rising to her feet.

"I'll get the kids," Kaitlyn said, leaving the living room as everyone made their way into the dining room.

There was a tree in the corner and the table was set with festive green and red décor with a miniature lit tree as the centerpiece. The men took their seats while the ladies followed Lisha into the kitchen to retrieve the food.

"So Mama Lisha, may I ask you a question?" Zaria said as she accepted the massive bowl of potato salad her mother-in-law pulled from the under the counter Sub-Zero fridge.

"Sure," Lisha said, handing Jade the pan of macaroni and cheese and Bianca the pot of collard greens.

"Was *it* worth the wait?" she asked, her voice conspiratorial.

All of the ladies paused in their tracks in front of the swinging door leading into the dining room. It was clear everyone knew what "it" was.

Lisha looked at them over her shoulder. "Yes, it was and yes, it still is," she assured them before she grabbed the counter and dropped down and brought it back up with ease. "I don't call him Daddy because he has five kids."

The ladies all roared in surprise.

"A'ight now," Zaria said. "That's what I'm talking about."

They were still laughing as they all made a few trips from the kitchen to the dining room until the long length of the table was filled with food. "Where's Kat?" Lisha asked, moving to the opposite end of the table to take her seat. "And Quint?"

Kade chuckled. "She needed help bringing the rest of the babies down because Kadina and

Lei were asleep," he said. "Sneaking around the house all morning must have tuckered their behinds out."

"You caught 'em too?" Kaeden asked, rubbing the top of KJ's head where he sat in between him and his father Kahron.

Kade nodded.

"So did I," Bianca said.

"We did too," Kaleb said with a grin.

"No wonder they're tired," Kael said, shaking his head.

Kaitlyn entered carrying Kasi Dean in one arm and Quint followed with Karlos in his arms.

"They're still asleep?" Lisha asked.

Before anyone could answer both teenagers entered the room and sheepishly took their seats at the table.

"Let us pray," Kael said, holding his hands out to his sons flanking him on either side.

The family held hands and bowed their heads.

"Here's to the goodness of being surrounded by lots of family on this holiday. May those who are not as lucky one day be blessed."

"Amen," they all said in unison.

The next hour was spent with plenty of food and plenty of funny tales being passed around the table. Lisha and Kael shared many long looks across the table as they enjoyed their boisterous family.

Ding-dong.

"I'll get it," Kaleb said, rising to leave the dining room.

"Thank God you fixed that bell back then," Kade joked as he took a big bite of a slice of ham.

Everyone laughed.

"Thank God we fixed everything," Kael said. "This house looks nothing like it did back then."

"I remember if nobody else," Kade said.

"Merry Christmas, Kael."

Everyone at the table slowly became silent as they all looked to their Aunt Kelli and her family standing in the entrance of the dining room. The adults' eyes shifted from their mother and then to their father. The silence was awkward.

Lisha stood and turned to face them. "Merry Christmas, Kelli. Welcome to our home," she said, stepping forward to embrace the tall woman, her husband and their two sons Will, Jr. and Jared.

Kael stood, the napkin in his lap falling to the floor as he came around the table to hug his sister close and press a kiss to her cheek. "Merry Christmas, Smelly Kelli," he said.

She smiled and playfully pinched him. "Merry Christmas."

Lisha stepped back and looked on as her children all stood up to greet their aunt, uncle and cousins. She looked at Kael and his happiness made it worthwhile for her to finally set aside her grudge. As they told the story of them falling in love, she discovered that the anger she had for her sister-in-law had faded. She knew it was time to put their hard feelings aside for Kael, so she snuck into the kitchen hours earlier to call Kelli and invite them down to spend Christmas.

She quietly moved into the kitchen as everyone made room at the table and retrieved chairs from around the house for the rest of the family to take a seat. She was lining up the desserts on the island and making sure there were a stack of utensils, saucers and napkins for her family to use.

"You and Kael are still doing dessert buffet style, I see."

Lisha glanced over her shoulder at Kelli as she pulled the bowl of fresh whipped cream from the fridge. "Yes we are," she said lightly, hoping she hadn't made a mistake.

Kelli smoothed the edges of her soft silver hair with a wrinkled hand. "Thank you for inviting my family and . . . please forgive me for how foolish I was back then," she said.

Lisha set the bowl on the island and looked up at her. The look in her eyes seemed sincere. "It's all in the past," she said.

"The house looks so different, especially with all the brick," she said.

"Trust me, Kael will take you on a tour," Lisha

assured her as they moved back into the dining room.

Kael immediately came over to wrap his arms around her waist and pulled her body close to his. "After forty years you still show me every single day that I made the right choice to propose to you, Ms. Strong," he whispered against her ear.

"And just you remember I will always love you, Mr. Strong," she answered, looking into those same sexy eyes as she kissed him.

"Merry Christmas," they said together in unison.

Dear Readers,

I have been writing about the Strong Family romance since 2006 and now, seven years later, I feel I could still continue on with them, but this is the last book in the series . . . for now. As with each of the titles in the series, their love has been filled with fiery passion and I hope it has inspired many of you to believe in love because there is such a thing as happily ever after for us all.

For those that are new to the series I highlighted the romance of each of the Strong Family siblings before ending with this book—the story of how their parents met and fell in love. I definitely recommend going back and enjoying the stories of Kahron and Bianca in *Heated*, Kade and Garcelle in *Hot Like Fire*, Kaeden and Jade in *Give Me Fever*, Kaleb and Zaria in *The Hot Spot* and Kaitlyn and Quint in *Red Hot*. And you may be introduced to some other family members who may get their own book . . . one day.

I hope you have enjoyed this journey with the Strongs as much as I have, but I also hope you continue on this romance writing journey with me as I introduce all new characters in my upcoming new series. Stay tuned for more details via my Web site (*www.niobiabryant.com*), my Twitter (*www.twitter.com/INFINITEink*), my Facebook Fan Page (search for: Niobia Bryant) or my all-new Pinterest (*http://pinterest.com/infiniteink*).

My very best wishes to all of you, and remember . . .

> "Love 2 Live & Live 2 Love."
> N.

Don't miss any of the Strong Family novels

HEATED

Bianca King is living the golden life—until her
somewhat estranged father asks for her help in
keeping the family ranch afloat. When Bianca
returns to Holtsville, she meets the latest threat,
neighboring rancher Kahron Strong, a man with
knowing eyes and the body of a gladiator. But this
competition may just do Bianca some good . . .

HOT LIKE FIRE

Sexy widower Kade Strong has just moved
back into the house he once shared with
his wife, hoping to bring some stability into
his daughter's life. He certainly isn't looking for
a relationship, but the women of Holtsville
have a different idea. Only Garcelle Santos
respects Kade's grief. Although he isn't ready
to let anyone into his life, Kade can't help being
irresistibly drawn to Garcelle . . .

GIVE ME FEVER

Kaeden Strong is a workaholic who's allergic to
the outdoors. Jade Prince is an adventuress with
a vixen's body and a tomboy heart. He's wanted
Jade from the moment he saw her, but so do
a long line of men—including her business
partner, Darren. On paper, Kaeden is all wrong
for Jade—but can he prove he's right in
all the ways that really matter?

THE HOT SPOT

Zaria Ali is looking to make up for lost time.
Who says she can't be living *la vida loca*
in her forties? And who says she can't date
hot twenty-six-year-old Kaleb Strong? Zaria
lightens up his serious side—and turns him on
like no one ever has. But is there more
between them than just explosive chemistry?

RED HOT

For Kaitlyn Strong, life has been a fun-filled free
ride, all expenses paid by her wealthy father.
But when her father cuts her off, a shocked
Kaitlyn gets a job and an affordable apartment
to go with it—where she meets hardworking
single father Quinton "Quint" Wells. He's
never met a demanding diva like Kaitlyn.
Yet despite their verbal clashes, there's
a sizzling attraction between them . . .